SHADOW ORDER

Rebecca F. John was born in 1986, and grew up in Pwll, a small village on the south Wales coast. She holds a BA in English with Creative Writing and an MA in Creative Writing from Swansea University, as well as a PGCE PCET from the University of Wales Trinity Saint David.

She is the author of four books for adults and her short stories have been broadcast on BBC Radio 4 and BBC Radio 4Extra. Her short story 'The Glove Maker's Numbers' was shortlisted for the *Sunday Times* EFG Short Story Award. She was the winner of the PEN International New Voices Award 2015, and the British participant in the 2016 Scritture Giovani project. In 2017, she was named on Hay Festival's 'The Hay 30' list. Her first novel, *The Haunting of Henry Twist,* was shortlisted for the Costa First Novel Award.

The Shadow Order is her first book for children.

Rebecca lives in Swansea with her partner, her son, and their dogs.

The Shadow Order

Rebecca F. John

First published in 2022
by Firefly Press
25 Gabalfa Road, Llandaff North, Cardiff, CF14 2JJ
www.fireflypress.co.uk

A CIP catalogue record of this book is available from the British Library.

1 3 5 7 9 8 6 4 2
ISBN 978-1-913102-95-1
ebook ISBN 978-1-913102-96-8

This book has been published with the support of the Books Council Wales.

Typeset by Elaine Sharples

Printed by CPI Group (UK) Ltd, Croydon, Surrey, CRO 4YY

To Betsy, Teddy, and Effie – my companions – every bit as brave and good as the characters they inspired.

CHAPTER ONE

Shadows

The city is prattling as the moon brightens and Teddy James lopes towards his shift on the river, his slim shoulders hunched against the cold and his hands stuffed into his pockets. He keeps his eyes low and slows only to skirt carefully around the dim umbrellas of light cast by the gas lamps. He does not want to be late. Factory workers boot-thump past parlour windows, and chimney sweeps gather on the pavement outside the townhouses on The Crescent. Sellers of fruits, ceramics, pies, flowers and clockwork toys set up their stalls on the square near the cathedral, clouding the bitter air with their greetings and laughter. Though he would like to pause to buy an apple and a hot steak pie, Teddy does not lift his chin from inside his green wool scarf to speak to anyone. The sooner he starts and finishes his shift, the quicker he can get to Betsy's.

They have agreed to meet at six o'clock, which will give them an hour before sunrise.

Teddy does not think an hour will be enough, but Betsy had insisted. 'I'll never get away from Mrs S any earlier,' she'd said. 'You know I won't.' And she was probably right. Henrietta Saltsburg allows Betsy to rent her attic room in exchange for six twelve-hour shifts a week in the laundry. Saltsburg's Laundry is the busiest in Copperwell and every time Teddy calls there for her, Betsy is tearing off her white pinafore, throwing it aside, and brushing damp strands of hair back off her forehead, having already worked on.

'It's a perfect misery,' she says about her job bending over the enormous wooden barrels, dropping the clothes into the steaming water, scrubbing and scrubbing until her hands throb and her pitch-black curls cling around her neck and ears. But Teddy knows that, despite Betsy's protestations, the work is good for her. It helps to expend a fragment of the energy that bounces around inside her. If Mrs S made her work seven shifts a week instead of six, she might never have come up with her plan.

'It's been a year, Teddy,' she'd insisted. 'A whole year. I have to see it again. Don't you want to?'

He did. She knew that. But so does everyone else, and Teddy cannot imagine what makes him and Betsy and Effie so special that they might get away with it. Teddy James, Betsy Blue and Effie Hart have mischiefed around the city together since they were eight or nine years old. It started when Effie, walking along Cathedral Row with her father, had spotted Betsy pilfering a bag of peaches from a costermonger's cart and distracted her father, Jeremiah Hart, so that he would not notice the theft. Betsy, seeing what Effie had done, had insisted that she and Teddy follow the girl home. It was Betsy and Teddy's first time on Berliner's Square, and they'd waited outside behind the hedges. They'd eaten the peaches until it was dark, then thrown peach stones at the window through which they'd seen Effie draw her curtains. They didn't know her as Effie then, of course, but they had persuaded her to clamber down the drainpipes and disappear into the night with them all the same. Being posh and ladylike, she'd likely never done such a thing before, but Effie had been willing to follow Betsy's lead as they explored the city rooftops and climbed trees in the Elm Gardens, and Betsy had decided that she must be both brave and worth knowing.

Though Betsy had intended to say 'thank you' just that one time, they were soon calling for Effie three or four nights a week. Always, they found her ready for adventure.

But everything is different now, since the shadows shifted.

What Betsy has planned would be more than mischief. It would mean breaking the law.

Teddy turns off Inca Street and on to Holloway Road, strides past the Duke's Theatre, and continues down through narrowing streets towards the water. The cold is biting, though there is not a wheeze of wind tonight. Even the clouds, ragged ropes of mauve and indigo, do not scud across the shivering sky. Teddy wishes he possessed a fine pair of gloves, but he has only those he must use on the river, to lift the heavy crates off the barges and stack them onto the waiting cart, ready to be transported to cellar doors and servants' entrances and backyards across

Copperwell. Made from undyed leather and held together with thick black stitching, the gloves reveal him to anyone who cares to look as a canal worker, and Teddy does not want to be a canal worker forever. He wants to be… He is too embarrassed to utter it, even to Betsy, who would well understand, but what he wants most is to find the bravery to become an explorer: to hike and sail and fly and swim through all the world's wildest places; to spark fires on clifftops and sleep under the stars; to climb trees and balance in branches higher than Copperwell's tallest buildings. In his every imagining, he sees himself beneath the marbled, silver-blue gleam of the moon. He is surprised by how completely living in darkness has transformed the landscape of his dreams.

He leaves behind that part of the city where table lamps light the windows of gentleman's clubs and gambling dens, and enters those streets where naked flames gutter inside soup kitchens and soap works. Wealth enters the city by the canal, but it does not linger there. While the rest of Copperwell is overwhelmed by the snug scent of burning wood or coal rising out of chimney stacks, the air along the canal smells dank and stagnant and claggy. Stinking green algae slimes the planks of the jetties the fishermen have built over the water. The cart horses leave piles of dung on the towpath to be kicked into the water, or trodden flat, or stepped around until they stale to crust and crumble away. Still, Teddy loves the horses: the warm, white plumes of their snorts; their soft bristled noses; their big, calm eyes. Often, he puts his hands to the smooth heat of their necks and breathes in their grassy spoor. When Teddy was a little lad, his father had driven cabs, and Teddy remembers the slumberous weight of the horses as he helped stable them each night, his father's tuneless whistling as he set about brushing them down, that quiet time spent together in the candlelit dark.

He remembers, too, his father's dream of going off in search of the Aur – the fabled golden horse which had once roamed all the wild parts of the world, galloping over Russian plains and wandering the Peruvian mountains, until people saw its gleaming coat and coveted it, and the Aur was forced to turn and flee. Before blowing out his candle each night, Edward would sit at the foot of his son's bed and recount the latest rumoured sightings of the horse: cantering along a pure white beach in Constantinople; stepping off a crag of the Cymru coast into the spumy sea; climbing into the hills above Algiers. And Teddy would carefully memorise the words, determined that one day he would help his father find the beast.

'What will you do with the Aur?' he had asked, early on, after perhaps the second or third of his father's stories. 'If you find one?'

'I will look at it,' Edward had replied, quietly. 'And I will see it. And then I will return home and never tell a single soul about it.'

It had taken Teddy a long time to understand his father's words. Since The Shadow Order was passed, however, he feels that perhaps he is beginning to.

Tonight, in his eagerness, he reaches the canal before the cart horses, the other canal workers, or the first barge. Mist slinks over the water; jigsaw-pieces of frost float on its silvered surface. Gooseflesh shudders around Teddy's neck and down his spine. He takes his gloves from inside his heavy sheepskin coat, and forces them over his stiffened knuckles, then stomps his boots against the frosted ground in an attempt to fend off the cold. His footfalls echo like hammer blows. A year, he thinks. How can it have been a year? When The Order had first been issued, no one had believed it would last for more than a week. A long, dark year later and it is still only the Constabulary who are permitted to move outside in daylight, trotting their enormous black horses noisily over the cobbles as they patrol for rule-breakers. It is said that life sentences are issued to anyone found to be flouting The Order. People have stepped out into the day and never been seen again.

In a way, Teddy is glad that his father died before all of this. Edward James, with his big-knuckled hands and his flick of thick brown hair and his wide, wind-burnt cheeks, could not have withstood being locked indoors through twelve hours of light – more in the summer – to wait for the drop of darkness. He'd been angry enough when the Unified Government passed the decree stating that any person who allowed their building's weather pipes to deteriorate so far that the music they made stopped would be fined. He'd been angrier still when they issued another decree preventing any man or woman from changing their job or being promoted. *Basic human rights*, Teddy would hear him muttering to himself, though he didn't think much then about what that meant.

The other canal workers arrive on hushed feet, nodding their newsboy caps in greeting, then glancing up the canal for first sight of a barge, nosing its way deeper into the city. The horses clomp down the towpath and are reined to a disgruntled halt. Within minutes the mists stir and the barge pushes into view. Teddy can see no one aboard. All along the canal, small yellow lights have been strung from bridge to bridge, to guide the barges in, and in the darkness the wire linking them becomes invisible so that they seem a line of floating orbs. The barge workers have learnt to stand pinned to the edges of the vessels, hoping the lights won't throw their shadows over the water. Even those who have nothing to fear from the shape of their shadows have learnt to conceal them. It's incredible, Teddy thinks, that simply being told often enough to be ashamed of something can persuade people that they are.

As the barge nears, the canal workers crowd closer to the water's edge, jostling for position. The barge will stop here for mere minutes, during which the waiting men and women will lift as many crates as possible off the barge and stack them into individual piles. They are paid by the crate. Some of the canal workers have taken to wearing waders, so that they can stride into the water and be the first to start unloading, but Teddy has not adopted this approach. It is more tiring to lug the cargo out of the canal, your boots being sucked at by its silty bottom, and those workers slow sooner than Teddy, who keeps an even, rhythmic pace, and often boasts the largest stack of all by night's end. Though he remains spare for his height – his limbs are slender; his hands and feet a tad too large – his chest and back have strengthened from so much lifting and carrying, and he feels more optimistic lately that he will soon grow into the body he requires to set off on his explorations.

The barge bumps against the bank with a slow thunk, and they set to work. Nearest to Teddy are Octavia Bennett, Briny Erwin, Old Man Hatch and Trudy Birdwhistle. There are others, waiting along the length of the barge, who Teddy knows less well or not at all – and nor does he want to acquaint himself with their rough, scrabbling ways. Teddy and his workmates are respectful of one another. They never shove or argue or take more than their share. Old Man Hatch – silver haired and bowed over his belly now – is particularly appreciative of the arrangement they have come to over the last year. Teddy wonders how he would eat if Briny Erwin – a bear of a man, with a wild beard and a barrelled chest – didn't slip the odd crate into the older man's stack. Teddy has taken to doing the same for Octavia, who was sprightly and energetic last summer, but who has been steadily paling and sickening since. Some nights, she spends more time coughing into her hand than reaching for the crates of dandelion tea, spices, whale ivories, elk antlers, bamboo bee nests, jarred honeys, or skins which are transported all the way from the Chinese Empire, India, Siberia, the Amerikks, to the heart of Copperwell. Her fascination for those exotic packages – Teddy cannot help but sniff at the crates, seeking the scents of his possible futures – has withered. Teddy and Trudy have exchanged worried looks about her as they have passed in the darkness, but what can they do? They, too, are struggling. It is only the city's rich, now, who are not working on empty stomachs to pay for their next meal.

Tonight the first barge carries a scant load and, in less than five minutes, it is gliding away again, empty, into the mists. The sound of thin ice breaking against its hull lingers behind it long after it disappears from sight. The canal workers take a moment to rest, sprawling on the bank and sipping from steaming flasks of tea or cocoa, but after twelve months of living by night they have developed the hearing of bats and they are soon rising to the approaching thrum of the next barge, relieving it of its load, counting their crates, stepping back towards the water's edge, anticipating the barge that will follow… At intervals, they crane their necks to consider the startling wolf moon. Teddy knows it has a name because Betsy has taught him the difference between a wolf moon and a snow moon, a hunter's moon and a beaver moon. Betsy studies the heavens. But here, Teddy's sole reason to look to the sky is the same as everyone else's. They need to know: is it starting to dim yet? Is there a hint of ripe-peach dawn rising over Copperwell's chimney tops? However desperate they are to stack one more crate, they must leave themselves enough time to return home before first light.

The seventh barge arrives at half past five. Teddy is keenly aware of the time. He will have to hurry to reach Betsy by six. Some of the canal workers have already retired, exhausted and hungry and having calculated that their stacks are valuable enough to make the shift worthwhile. This is a blessing. Teddy is able to move quickly around the last barge of the night, distributing the crates evenly between his own stacks and Octavia's; only Briny Erwin and Trudy cross his path. With the last crate set down and counted, he calls out a breathless, 'See you tomorrow,' and, waving, takes off at a run. The barge follows in his wake, chugging determinedly through the night. It is no match for Teddy, who races along the bank, leaps cleanly over a small gate, and hurtles up towards the sprawl of enormous university buildings, through the Elm Gardens, past the Observatory, and downhill towards that part of Copperwell, tucked beneath the railway station and its elevated tracks, where Betsy will be waiting for him.

He is less than three streets away when he is forced to stop, panting, and retrace his steps. He thinks he has just seen… Yes… Standing directly under the glow of a gas lamp is Old Man Hatch. Why hasn't he gone home yet? He left the canal over an hour ago. Teddy vacillates, shifting his weight from one foot to the other, then, dragging his father's old pocket watch from inside his coat to confirm that he is very definitely late, he takes a few measured steps towards Hatch. In the moonlight his silver hair shines like a coin. The hump on his back looks like a mound of crumpled laundry.

'Hatch?' Teddy says quietly. He does not want to startle the old man.

Slowly, Hatch turns blank eyes on Teddy.

'Come out of the light,' Teddy whispers, beckoning with his hands. 'Before anyone sees.'

'I've nothing to hide,' Hatch returns. 'Come, lad. Look for yourself.'

When Teddy does not move, Hatch begins the excruciating process of pivoting about to face his young friend. On bad nights his bent-stick legs can hardly propel him forwards, and the manoeuvre is complicated and painful. Teddy waits through each shuffled step. The ticking of his pocket watch thunders in his mind. Betsy is going to be furious.

'Look at it, Master James,' Hatch insists. 'Or I shall stand here all the day through.'

Snatching a deep breath, Teddy moves closer. He does not want to gaze down at Old Man Hatch's shadow, but if it will persuade him to go home before he finds himself reported to the Constabulary…

Teddy shows Hatch his opened palms, as though he is likely to spook, and nods. 'All right.'

Satisfied, Hatch returns his attention to the ground, where his shadow waits. Heart thudding, Teddy creeps closer until he is able to peer over Hatch's shoulder. He squints into the spray of light and there appears the shadow of a man twice Hatch's height. He is straight in the back and firm in the leg. He sports a heavy thatch of hair and an elegant neck, and … he is dancing: one arm is held stiffly out in a hoop, as though the palm is resting on a partner's back, and the other is pressed to his chest so that his elbows make two perfectly level points. The shadow thins and thickens as it revolves around and around in a waltz.

'It's me!' Old Man Hatch laughs. 'Would you have recognised me, Master James?'

Teddy shakes his head. 'I can't say I would have, Hatch,' he murmurs.

'And yet…' Hatch says. His voice is snatched by sadness.

'What?'

'And yet, that's *me*. That's who I am.' The gas lamp hisses and flares, and the shadow trembles in response. Hatch gives a sigh and turns to walk away on his stiff, uncooperative legs. 'I was there,' he mutters, more to himself than to Teddy, 'for a moment or two. That was me.'

Teddy inches along beside him. Hatch seems to miss his shadow – or, rather, the person it shows him. When The Shift first happened, Teddy, like so many other people, had been frightened. He had never studied his shadow. There had been no need to: it had always followed him, silently, unobtrusively, into any situation. He had never wondered, before, what it might or might not want.

But, he'd thought afterwards, if his shadow had chosen no longer to mirror him, it might be liable to decide to do anything at all. And the horror of that realisation had persuaded him not to go looking for it in the year since Prime Minister Bythesea and the Unified Government had declared that no one was permitted to go outdoors during the day, when the sun might reveal what they had eventually realised those new, changeable shadows were revealing – people's truest selves.

They have existed since then in darkness, moving around the glow of guttering gaslight as though humans are nocturnal creatures: owl people; fox folk. They wait now for moonrise instead of the sun.

'Promise me you'll go straight home,' Teddy says, putting a hand to Old Man Hatch's wilted spine to hurry him on a little. 'It's almost dawn.'

Hatch nods, and Teddy wishes he had time to watch him scuttling away, to make sure, but already – he fumbles again for his pocket watch and tears it free – it is six minutes past the hour, and Betsy will be waiting for him. If he doesn't hurry her plan will be ruined. With a grunt, he thrusts the scuffed bronze watch back inside his coat and lurches into a run.

CHAPTER TWO

The Observatory

'And what time d'you call this, then?' Betsy hisses as Teddy approaches. She is waiting for him outside Saltsburg's Laundry, her arms held tight across her chest – in fury rather than against the cold. Betsy never seems to feel the cold. She stands in the shelter of the low doorway, tapping her foot. Her dark grey eyes are shards of slate as she watches him slow to a stop and hang gasping over his own knees, attempting to recover his breath. She has on a thin pair of tan trousers, over the bottoms of which she has pulled a pair of cream woollen socks. Laced around the socks are the worn cuffs of brown leather walking boots. Her long coat is buff coloured, with an overly large collar. On to the black spring of her hair she has pressed a small-brimmed hat. She looks as though she is embarking on an odyssey. Then again, she usually does. It is more, Teddy supposes, to do with her stance than her attire: she holds herself straighter than a pin.

'It was Hatch,' Teddy pants. 'He was just standing under one of the lamps … showing everyone his shadow… I had to persuade him home.'

Betsy cocks one eyebrow and huffs. 'All right. Well…'

She glances down the street as a steam locomotive huffs overhead, its deep-green front carriage glinting in the moonlight. White clouds billow permanently over Hangman's Alley, dampening the workings of the weather through the system of copper pipes, cogs, wheels and whistles which adorn the front of every building in the city. The invention – designed to make music from the elements while channelling fresh water into chambers buried beneath the pavements – gave Copperwell its name so long ago that now only the dustiest inhabitants remember it being called anything else. Everyone knows as intimately as their own voices the rhythmic patter of the rain music, the high-pitched whisper of the wind music, the gentle clang-and-creak of the sun music as the copper expands in the heat, and the sharper chime of the snow music as the copper contracts again in colder temperatures. Copperwell is never quiet, but here, under the clouds, it is muted – which is just one of the reasons Teddy loves Hangman's Alley.

Betsy huffs whenever she sees him looking admiringly around the alley. 'It just means you can hear more of the other noises,' she warns. 'The ugly noises.'

Betsy spends a lot of time huffing at Teddy, but Teddy doesn't mind. He knows that, deep down, she is being caring not cruel. She doesn't want him to be disappointed in anything.

'Do you think you can hurry up now?' she asks, flicking at the helix of his ear with a quick forefinger.

'Ow!' He springs upright to find her grinning at him. He grins back. 'Yes, I can hurry,' he says, pressing a hand over his throbbing ear and nodding slowly. 'I am hurrying.'

'Doesn't look much like it to me,' Betsy quips. 'Come on.'

She starts up a purposeful stride, and – though she is small and sparrow-light, and Teddy is twice her height – he is forced to lope after her so that they can walk side by side. He does not want to rush out of Hangman's Alley without pausing to watch the locomotive grind and puff back out of the station, or to inhale the sticky-sweet scent that seeps out of the coffee and bun shop next door to the laundry, or to stand under the shelter at the alley's dead end and put his hands to the open fire which burns there. The shelter's roof and walls have been constructed from irregular triangles, set at difficult degrees, so that the shadows cast by the flames can find no flat surface to fall on. Similar shelters have been built all around the city since The Order was passed, but the one beneath Betsy's attic window, where he and Betsy and Effie have sat talking and melting chocolate to drinking cocoa in metal tankards at the ends of so many nights, is surely the best.

'Effie said she'd meet us on the corner of Broken Sparrow, since she'd have to make certain her parents saw her go up to bed first. But now that we're *late*...' She sneaks a look at him and pops her eyes to emphasise that last word. 'We shouldn't have to wait long for her.'

Teddy readies a finger to flick her ear and return the

smarting pain of it, but Betsy sees his intention the instant he lifts his arm and ducks easily out of his reach.

'You're going to have to do better than that!' she laughs, and, tugging the end of his scarf so that it throttles him just a little, she persuades him to resume a run.

They are both breathless as they turn onto Broken Sparrow Road and spot Effie leaning against the railings of a teetering townhouse which has ivy clambering between the stonework and the weather pipes. Effie is recognisable by her short, curved outline and her strong legs. She is wearing an olive-green skirt which stops just below her knees and a pair of flat leather shoes. She has her long brown hair tied into a silky plait. She appears, as always, as though she is attending a posh luncheon. Teddy and Betsy slow to a walk as they approach her, and she spins around to show them her worried face.

'Are you certain about this?' she whispers. 'Bets? Have you really thought it through?'

'I've recced the route and everything,' Betsy replies, patting Effie's arm.

'And if we get found out? Arrested?'

Teddy stays quiet. Effie is voicing the questions he has wanted to ask since Betsy first told him what she intended.

'Do you really think the Constabulary are going to bother with three kids on a rooftop? We'll be silent as cats, Ef: a tom and two queens.' She pokes her tongue out at Teddy – the plain old tom amongst royalty. 'We'll pad about like Madam Bee.'

Madam Bee, or Beatrice, is the Saltsburg Laundry cat – employed to keep out the mice, but more likely to be found licking a delicate black paw on top of a pile of freshly folded clothes than hunting. Betsy admires that quiet impudence in her. It is why she took to calling her Madam Bee. That, and because the shared initial serves to persuade Betsy that if a simple cat could elevate herself so far above her intended position, so might she.

'Besides,' she continues, noticing that the crease of worry between Effie's eyebrows has not yet smoothed out, 'we'll hardly be on the grounds. There's a tree in the Elm Gardens big enough that we can climb it to the top of the railings. From there we can reach over to the ladder on the back of the building, get up onto the flat roof, slip around the dome, and we're there.'

All three of them know the design of Copperwell's Observatory well enough. It is built like a small castle, with towers and nooks and cream-coloured crenellations on top of red bricks. It has five or six different small roofs, some pitched, some rounded, and, supporting the enormous main dome, there is the flat section where staff go up to check on the equipment. This flat section extends around the sides of the dome by a narrow couple of inches. They will have to cling to the white steel to edge around it.

Betsy cannot conceal her grin. She hasn't told Teddy and Effie that she has not just plotted the route to the Observatory, she has actually done it. She has clambered onto the roof and sat with her back against the dome while the sun blushed on the horizon. She wasn't about to leave today's adventure entirely up to chance and risk getting Teddy and Effie arrested. If Betsy were going to be thrown into gaol, she would face it alone.

Following Betsy's lead, they creep through the Elm Gardens, flinching now and then beneath the sway and whisper of black branches. They are not scared of the dark – they have lived in it for long enough now – but they are anxious not to be seen. If they are reported, the last thing they will need is some eyewitness with a good description coming forward. When they reach the elm tree Betsy has specified, they clasp hands and hold tight for a second. It's their way of promising that they will always stick together.

Teddy, being the tallest, hoists the girls up onto the lowest branch then scrabbles up after them. When Betsy had come alone it had taken numerous attempts and quite a commotion to clamber onto this first branch, and she considers that being helped up this time is less conspicuous. They begin to grunt and heave from branch to branch. Upwards. Upwards. Their fingers cramping and their feet slipping. Until they are shuffling amongst the outstretched, scratchy arms of the highest twigs. This deep into the winter, the tree is bare. It smells, Betsy thinks, like the fur of a wet dog. She crunches her nose against the stink.

'Ready?' she says when they reach the point from which they will be able to grab for the top of the railings and swing themselves out of the Elm Gardens and into the private land belonging to the Observatory.

Panting, Teddy and Effie nod their heads. They line themselves up, wrap their palms around the railings, and drop as one. The clang of the iron is cacophonous, and they hang there a moment, holding their breaths and hoping that the chatter of the street sellers and the hiss of griddled meat and the snow music working through the city's copper pipes will be enough to disguise it. A minute passes and no one comes running, so they slide their feet up to the next bar in the railings and climb to the top.

The ladder demands another act of trust, as they must once again stretch out, grab lengths of noisy iron in their hands, and swing themselves towards the building. Since the ladder is thin, they go one at a time now, and the *clang, clang, clang* of it convinces Teddy that they will soon be discovered. But after each sharp bang they stop and hold their breaths, and nothing happens. No shouts issue; no lamps lurch at them in the dark; no rattling alarm bell sounds; no Constabulary whistles shriek.

'Nothing?' he enquires.

'Nothing,' Betsy confirms, grinning.

They scale the ladder and drag themselves up onto the flat roof. Here, the must of the trees is replaced by the cold whoosh of clean air in their noses. With Betsy again at their helm, they put their arms out to embrace the steel curve of the dome and, leaning against it, slide their boots inch by inch around its circumference until, finally, they are able to stand upright on the flat roof on the other side and grin and clasp hands again, congratulating each other.

Teddy thinks it must have been hours since they met on the corner of Broken Sparrow Road, and yet it is still dark. Just.

'Sit,' Betsy says, ushering them to the spot at the front of the dome, where the steel opens to allow the telescope its sight. Beneath the opening there is a shallow sill, which they can slot under. Instinctively, they tuck their knees in close to their chins and speak in a wisper.

'I can hardly remember what the day feels like,' Effie says.

'Do you miss it?' Betsy asks.

'Of course.'

Betsy hadn't imagined Effie would, particularly, given how much time she has always spent indoors waiting for night to fall. Effie's life revolves around playing her double bass: she goes to school to learn the notes and ornamentations, how best to manipulate the strings, the most intricate scales and arpeggios; then she sneaks from her parents' fancy townhouse to go down to the jazz clubs in the Factory Quarter and learn how to really play. She could never tell her parents – jazz being considered lowly and base amongst the upper classes – but she makes up one fourth of a quartet known as The Quartet, which refuses to book a performance in advance and so, naturally, is the most sought-after band in the city. To protect their privacy they wear masquerade masks. Effie's is cream with sapphire detailing and a single peacock feather protruding from one side.

Initially, when Betsy and Teddy had gone to watch her perform, Betsy had laughed at the masks. But her laughter had stopped as soon as Effie rested the instrument's neck against her shoulder and started to pluck sorrow from its strings. Onstage, Effie is more confident than ever; she stands straighter; she holds her head higher. When she plays, she is magical. It is as though she is two different people.

Betsy sometimes wonders if there are two different people inside her, too. She wonders what it would take to find out.

'I even miss early mornings on the canal,' Teddy says. 'I used to think I hated waking up while it was still dark and watching the day start while I was unloading, but I didn't really. It was the best time, when I think about it now.'

The girls hum their agreement and the three sit in silence to await the arrival of the light. They are soon rewarded. Far over Copperwell's icy roof tiles and bony winter trees, there comes a blush of rose gold.

'Look!' Effie gasps, pointing.

'Brilliant,' Teddy mutters.

Their breath gathers on the air around them in writhing mist-white shapes as the sun fans out over the roofs of the grain and soap factories which line the canal, the elevated steam locomotive tracks, the labyrinth of alleyways which lead to the centre of the city, where the University, the Cathedral, the Observatory and the Unified Government buildings are clustered together to look down over the rest. Copperwell is vast, with so many hidden lanes and alleys, underground apartments and towering office chambers, canal ways and tunnels and stilted tracks and walkways, that even Betsy, Teddy, and Effie would not be able to explore every nook of it. But it is just a clearing in the forests that surround the city, spreading so far east, south and west that the looming spruce and pine trees don't stop until the land drops away into crashing waves or sandy beaches. All the other cities in the Britannic Isles are to the north of Copperwell. They can be reached only by air-train – great carriages tethered to hot-air balloons and carried through the clouds.

'I'm so glad you made us come, Bets,' Effie says. And in the quiet of the stilled city, even her whisper is loud.

When the first blossom falls onto the Observatory roof, just in front of them, they hardly notice it. After all, it is the same delicate pink colour as the sky. But the first is soon followed by three more, and then five, and before long the flowers are raining down over Betsy, Teddy, and Effie. They spiral and eddy and float, their petals twitching though there is not a hint of wind here, in the shelter of the dome. Betsy leans forwards and lifts one from where it has settled on the cuff of her boot.

'There shouldn't be...'

She was going to say, *any flowers blooming in the middle of winter*, but the words stall when she realises that the blossom has legs, six of them, four of which it stands on and two thicker ones which it holds up before its body like weapons. She peers closer. It has a pair of whisker-thin antennae, too. And – it becomes apparent as she lifts it right up in front of her nose – a small, triangular face. The tiny creature is looking straight back at her, head tilted in confusion.

'It's alive,' she says.

'What?' Teddy scoops one up off his bent knee and lets it rest in his cupped palms. 'How can it…'

'Mantises!' Effie explains, laughing as one alights on top of her head. 'It's called an orchid mantis. They're insects, dressed up to look like flowers for camouflage. Although…' Her smile falls into a frown. 'I don't know what they're doing here. They belong in the tropical forests, in the East.'

Having never left the Britannic Isles – having never left Copperwell – neither Effie, Betsy, nor Teddy have any true idea of what East Eurasia looks like, but they know as well as the next grammar school student that the world consists of four continents: Eurasia, which the Britannic Isles, and therefore Copperwell, sits on the west of; Amerikk, which is further west again; Africa, which sits close below Eurasia; and The Antart, which is far south and extremely cold. The tropical forests of East Eurasia might just as well be on the moon. How, then, have these flimsy little mantises managed to fly all the way to Copperwell?

The creature sitting in Betsy's hand gives a last feeble tremble of an antennae, and then stops. She shakes her hand lightly but gets no response.

‘Do you think they might all freeze to death?’ she asks quietly.

Effie holds out her arm, in the manner of a falconer awaiting the return of their hunting bird, and a twinned pair of mantises land on her wrist.

‘I imagine they will,’ Effie replies sadly. ‘They need heat, humidity.’ She shrugs, knowing that they cannot offer the insects sanctuary.

‘Is that why they’re falling?’ Teddy enquires.

‘I think so,’ Effie confirms.

‘How do you know all this?’

‘I listened in sciences.’

In response, Betsy gives a weak smile. She does not want the mantises to die: they are so gentle and dulcifying. And she does not want to watch the sun rise from an insect’s graveyard. She sets the dead one down beside her and opens her hands to catch one of its descending fellows. She inspects the inquisitive, pointed face.

‘Let’s try something,’ she murmurs and, lifting her hat briefly, she slips the petalled creature into the vaulted space between the fabric and the crest of her skull. She cannot offer it a tropical forest, but her body heat, a nest of hair and a chance, she can. Betsy has always brimmed with hope. She has had to. Not only did it keep her alive when she was cold and starving, it is also the one thing she’s ever owned that has not eventually been taken away from her.

They watch the scattered bouquet of orchid mantises

drift and drop until they have all reached the ground. And they watch the cold pink sky fade to white. And they wonder if it will snow properly.

Effie hopes that it will. She loves it when Copperwell glints under falling snow: the gleaming pipework singing a bright F sharp and the paled streets punctuated with footprints. It makes her feel as though she might be somewhere else entirely. It convinces her, momentarily, that there is no perfect townhouse, no Chief Justice Hart, no rules, and that she can finally be the musician she ought to be. The thought leaves her heavy with guilt: her parents love her, and she them. She would not dream of complaining, as Betsy would. She is not brave enough to tell them that their expectation is too much. She wishes they could recognise that she is not the Effie they work so hard to pay a private tutor for, nor the Effie who wants to be introduced to their friends in the Imperial Orchestra, nor the Effie who adores the sight of stave music undulating across a page of manuscript like a line of little black bees. That Effie has never existed. The real Effie Hart, the one behind the peacock-feather mask, does not need to read music: she can feel it throbbing through her blood.

'Listen!' Betsy hisses, and Effie glances around, trying to locate the sound Betsy has heard. There is a moment of silence and then, as if from a dream, the unmistakeable *thud, thud, thud* of feet pounding the cobbles below. They are chased by the repeated *clomp-clomp* of horses' hooves.

'The Constabulary,' Teddy mouths. Instinctively, he

reaches out to grip Betsy's wrist, knowing that she will stand up to look. The moment she steps out from the shade of this sill, her shadow will be on display and she will have broken the law twice over. She tenses against the restraint but does not struggle.

'There,' Effie says, pointing towards the edge of the rooftop. Teddy and Betsy understand her meaning; they can slither across to the crenellations on their stomachs and look out from the series of dips in the stones, like archers with arrows poised. Yes. That will work. Slowly, they fold themselves down and tuck their feet up beneath them.

The frantic footsteps cease abruptly, and they pause.

'The shadows!' a woman's voice bawls. 'I know what happened to the shadows.'

Betsy turns cold; her scalp seems to tighten around her skull. She stays very still and does not look at Effie or Teddy. Nobody knows what happened to the shadows. Not really. They know that when The Shift happened they altered overnight and without warning, that all of a sudden they started to show the contours of a person's deepest secrets instead of their physical form, that it is a crime under the Unified Government to let them be seen. Everyone in Copperwell knows those things. There are posters pinned to lampposts and stuck in shop windows to remind them. If you are morbid, you can watch the day's offenders marched through the city to gaol every midnight. But nobody knows *why* The Shift occurred.

Nobody knows *how. What happened?* is the question the whole of Copperwell has learnt to stop asking.

'Come on,' Effie purrs, and they crawl towards the edge of the roof together, until they reach the crenellations and can rest their chins on the stone and look down onto the long stretch of Wild Goose Way. It is named, Effie presumes, for the alliteration, because it is in fact an avenue, guarded by the gnarled skeletons of enormous oak trees. Their shadows are etched over the pavements by the flimsy sunlight, the perfect copy of the trees themselves: it is only people who are duplicitous enough to have more than one self to show to the world. In the middle of the road stands a woman with a small, neat body, and dishevelled clothes. Thick locks of her long black hair have worked free of her bun and hang about her shoulders. One side of her blouse is untucked. The laces of one of her brogues have come loose and trickle down onto the cobbles like water. She is not dressed for a winter's day. She must be chilled to the bone, but she does not show it.

Throwing out her arms and tossing back her head, she shouts again. 'I know what happened! If anyone can hear me, listen carefully. It's a game. It's the Unified Government's game. They're playing with our lives. *They* shifted the shadows. I can prove it. I can prove it and they'll kill me for it. Listen!' Her voice catches as she strains to bellow as loudly as possible. Effie feels an ache in her own throat, imagining the woman's vocal chords stretching and snapping. 'LISTEN! Find the orrery!'

As she hurls these last words into the sky, Effie finally plucks up the courage to look at the woman's shadow. Her shadow will reveal whether or not she ought to be trusted. And the moment Effie lays eyes on it, she is glad that she chose to look. The woman's shadow is shaped just like she is, except that her hair and her clothes are not thrown about. In fact, she is not even wearing the same clothes. In shadow, her attire is as neat as her body, and it consists of a large cloak of some kind, fur perhaps, and trousers in place of a skirt, and boots with high cuffs instead of brogues. In shadow, she is three times the size. She is powerful, imposing, beautiful. While the woman fidgets from foot to foot, the shadow stands stock still, facing down the Constabulary without so much as a flinch of fear. Honesty – that's what Effie sees, silhouetted on the ground behind the poor woman. Honesty and bravery.

'She's telling the truth,' she murmurs.

Beside her, Effie feels Betsy nodding. 'No one could fake a shadow like that. Look at it. It's incredible.'

'Incredible,' Teddy echoes.

And perhaps it is because his voice has plummeted into a gravelling baritone over the last year and therefore carries more readily than do Effie's or Betsy's, or perhaps it is because one of them shifts their weight slightly… Whatever the cause, something entices the woman to glance up towards the Observatory crenellations and to halt, momentarily, when she spots three distant faces staring down at her.

Her front teeth are pressed into her bottom lip, preparing for her next shout, but she stutters over it, her concentration thrown by this strange and unexpected sight.

Don't give us away, Betsy begs, in the privacy of her own mind. Her heart is hammering so loudly she fears the Constabulary will hear it. *Please don't give us away.* And for reasons none of them can fathom, the woman does not. She gives the tiniest of nods, and then she turns her eyes back to the Constabulary as they urge their snorting, black, nineteen-hand horses closer, their strong chests barrelled, their hooves held high with each forward pace, their ears flicked backwards and their tails swinging with barely-contained strength. Their metal shoes ring over the cobbles. Heat rises off them as steam. Close up, they must be terrifying.

But the woman's shadow does not falter. It waits, unmoving, as the constables dismount their horses and flank her. Then it grows a couple of yards more as the woman flings her head back again and screams, 'FIND THE ORRERY! FIND—'

Before she is able to shout her appeal again, one of the constables lifts his truncheon and swings it hard against the woman's temple. She falls silent with the sickening wallop and crumples downwards. The constables catch her under her arms and, hauling her upwards, throw her over the back of one of the horses, mount, and trot away.

'Do you think they'll kill her?' Effie says.

'Yes,' says Betsy, at the very same time as Teddy says, 'No.'

Teddy is not sure why he even said it when, in truth, he too suspects that the woman will be killed. He would not be surprised if she is already dead, given how hard the masked constable hit her.

'She must have found out something important to risk screaming about it in the street,' Teddy continues.

'And during the daytime, too,' Effie adds. 'Why not at night?'

'Perhaps she'd been imprisoned somewhere,' Betsy suggests. 'And this was her one chance at escape.'

They are quiet for a moment, listening to the retreating *clop-clop* of the horses' hooves. The only other sound is that of the birds: a sudden murder of crows, swirling and diving between the empty branches of the oak trees and screeching as though in terror.

Finally, Effie speaks again.

'What's an orrery?'

Betsy shuffles onto her side so that she can look into Teddy and Effie's faces. 'I can show you,' she says.

CHAPTER THREE

Hangman's Alley

They clamber all the way to Hangman's Alley across Copperwell's rooftops. They slide over frosted slates and cling to chimney breasts; they hang from gutters and edge along window ledges. They move in silence, their occasional slips and gasps lost amongst the chimes of the snow music. Sunlight spreads across their backs, warming their necks. The skin of their cheeks and ears, paled by so many months in the dark, tingles and reddens. That they will make it across the city unseen is an impossibility, but by refusing to speak the fact out loud, Betsy, Teddy and Effie are giving themselves a chance.

And somehow, three hours and several bruises later, they find themselves crawling up the steeply pitched roof of Saltsburg's Laundry towards Betsy's attic window and prising it open with numb fingers.

Teddy drops inside first.

'I can't believe we made it!' he whispers frantically as he helps Effie and then Betsy down. 'I was sure, *sure*, we'd be caught.' He clasps Effie in a tight hug and claps Betsy's back as he laughs his wide-open laugh. Betsy has never known anyone to laugh as sincerely as Teddy. 'I feel like we've survived an expedition to The Antart!'

Betsy and Effie laugh with him, all of them breathless, all of them desperately tired from gripping and climbing and being afraid. They fall onto Betsy's narrow bed.

'I want to do it again,' Effie says.

'You do not!' Betsy replies. 'I don't.'

'All right. Maybe not. But, the gods, it was exciting! I want to feel that excited again.'

'Then perhaps we should find the orrery – like the woman said.'

'You haven't even told us what it is yet,' Teddy says, springing up to pace around the room. He is fizzy, unable to calm down. Given his height, the angle of the rafters, and the fact that the room is just six yards in length, he spends more time spinning about than he does actually pacing. He looks as though he is choreographing some stuffy formal dance and the girls smirk at him.

'I said I'd *show* you,' Betsy replies. 'Not tell you.'

'So, show us.'

With the smallest movement of her head, she nods towards the single table pushed up against the wall. One side of it is taken up with a scratched and misted vanity mirror, which shows Betsy to herself as a vague distortion: she doesn't bother with it much. On the other side sits a clockwork model which, in the past, Teddy has flicked at impatiently while waiting for Betsy to finish her shift. He has never looked at it properly and now, considering it in the slant of sunlight falling through the attic window, he sees that it is a small but magnificent thing.

'Where did you even get this?' Teddy asks.

'Stole it,' Betsy replies.

'You did not.'

'Maybe not,' she concedes with a shrug. 'It was here before I was. Mrs S didn't know what it was. She said I could keep it for as long as I kept the room clean and tidy. I didn't know what it was then either, but I found out.'

The model has a disc-shaped bronze base, into which are set a series of shining cogs. From the middle of the base rises a sort of rod, again of bronze, which supports a gleaming golden ball. This, Teddy knows, is the sun. From the rod protrude eight arms, which extend to hold out marble-like representations of the eight planets of the solar system. They are of varying sizes. Mercury is a small, dulled-silver orb. Venus is swirled with lines of every shade of brown, cream, and gold. Earth is mostly a shimmering blue, with Eurasia, Amerikk, and Africa described in vivid green; The Antart, he finds when he ducks his head to check, is white. Next is Mars, neat and red as a ruby. Then Jupiter, the largest of the planets, which is the mottled yellow-orange of a piece of excavated amber. Saturn is made up of layers of sand and white and stone, with a glowing yellow ring belted around its middle. Uranus is a green splash, circled by a bright emerald ring, thinner than Saturn's. And finally, there is Neptune, a smooth blue sphere pinned with tiny silver dots. Each planet represented on the orrery shines. It is a beautiful object, but it does not do anything. It cannot be so important. It cannot be what the woman on Wild Goose Way was screaming about.

'What does it do?' Teddy asks.

Betsy grips a small gold key, which is pushed into the base, between her thumb and forefinger and rotates it through ten clicks, fifteen, more. 'Shows the motions of the planets,' she says. And eventually the shining planets begin to spin and shift around the sun which sits proud at their centre. As they move, they emit a gentle clicking sound.

Betsy stopped attending school two or three years ago now, and she never listened in sciences even before that, but Teddy knows that she could answer any question he might ask about the skies. Under her bed are stashed books and cyclopaedias about the moons, the solar system, the stars: she has spent years rescuing them from boxes left out for rubbish collectors or bargaining for them with Mrs S's kinder customers.

'Why?' Teddy asks.

Betsy shrugs. 'To prove stuff.'

'What stuff?'

'Gravity, for one.'

'How would a bunch of spinning marbles prove gravity?'

'It's about what they represent,' Effie says, moving closer so that they are all leaning over the moving model.

The sunlight above them is pale and the silhouettes of their heads are hardly discernible against the glint of the clockwork orrery.

'Aristotle thought that Earth was the centre of the universe,' Betsy begins, her voice more cautious than usual. 'Because he couldn't feel Earth moving, he was convinced it must be stationary, and that everything else in the universe revolved around it.' As she speaks, they watch the arms of the orrery sweep, casting their own simple shadows. 'His theory was '*geo*centric'. But then this other chap, Copernicus, came along with a '*helio*centric' theory – meaning that the sun was at the centre of it. *He*...' She drops her forefinger carefully onto the crest of the model sun. 'Copernicus... What was his first name, Ef?'

'Nicolaus,' Effie replies without hesitation. She knows the names, the dates, the facts – she is a good student. But she does not possess the working knowledge Betsy does. She has never attempted to apply those facts to anything.

'Nicolaus Copernicus said that it was the sun the planets revolved around, not Earth. Then a load of other people proved it, with a stupid amount of calculations, and when it came to name the force that kept the planets on their same orbit, they called it gravity.' She rushes the last of her explanation; she's less sure of that part of things.

'And that's all an orrery does?' Teddy says. 'Just shows the orbits of the planets around the sun?'

Betsy nods.

'Then what's that got to do with the shadows?'

The girls glance at each other, checking whether either of them has a suggestion. Effie twists her mouth and Betsy huffs.

'I have no idea,' Betsy admits. 'But there's an ancient one kept in the Observatory. I've read about it. I think we need to see it.'

'They'll never let us inside,' Effie replies. 'Only University scholars ever go inside the Observatory.'

'You could be a scholar, Ef,' says Betsy.

Effie does not have chance to protest before Betsy remembers what she slipped beneath her hat hours before and lets out an 'Oh!' She flips off the hat and tosses it onto her bed. The forgotten orchid mantis tests its wings, pauses, tries another flutter, then frees itself from the dense curls of Betsy's hair and rises towards the rafters.

'Do you think you could, Effie?' Teddy asks.

They watch the little creature's frail pink flight across the attic room, each plotting how they might get into the Observatory unnoticed, and each knowing that it ought to be impossible. Then again, watching the sun rise in the open air had been impossible too, until this morning.

'It won't be easy,' Effie replies. 'But that woman risked her life, shouting in the street like that, so it must be important. I think we should at least try.'

'Me too,' Teddy agrees.

'What if we can't persuade them to let us in, though?'

'Then we'll have to break in,' Betsy says, and when the other two throw narrow-eyed glances at her, she smiles. She could never have guessed today would prove to be so exciting.

CHAPTER FOUR

Plots and Problems

For a full week they plot how they might get inside the Observatory and search out the orrery. But every time they think they have found a reasonable idea it is immediately chased by an obvious flaw. They begin by planning to have Effie disguise herself as a University scholar, in shirtsleeves and a tweed skirt and floor-length robes, and claim that she has misplaced her identity card at the entranceway: supposing she is permitted entry, though, she would soon show her ignorance by not knowing her way around. They think then about breaking in, as Betsy had suggested, but there is a reason criminals so often acted under cover of night before The Order, and they decide that climbing the roof is one thing but that getting into the building during daylight hours is quite another. And even if they did manage to get inside, they wouldn't know what they were looking for. Finding the orrery might be simple enough, but what then? They wouldn't be able to touch it, study its workings. They would only be able to look at it and speculate as to what the shouting woman had meant them to do next.

By the Friday following their escapade onto the

Observatory roof, it all seems entirely futile. They are downhearted as they sit in a shrouded corner of The Blackened Lantern, sipping pints of apple ale and adding their whispers to the pipe smoke and the laughter and the fragrance of charred and skewered whelks. The pub is crowded – too busy for anyone to wonder whether Betsy, Teddy, and Effie are yet the full fourteen years of age they ought to be in order to visit a pub without a chaperone. Besides, they have not attempted to order anything intoxicating.

'Find the orrery,' Betsy says, for the hundredth time. 'But … then what? What are we supposed to do with it?'

'Maybe that will become clear later,' Effie suggests.

'But if we can't even see it working…'

'We'll have to see it working, won't we?'

'I think so.'

'Then it's not enough to just break into the Observatory. We're going to have to get the orrery out.'

Teddy shakes his head. 'That'll never work. Do we even know how big it is? How heavy? We'd need…'

He stops when he notices the sudden glint in Betsy's eye.

'A horse and cart,' she finishes.

Teddy sits back, breaking their huddle around the table. He can feel his face paling, despite himself. 'I'd never manage it. How would I…?'

'You've worked on the canals for three years, Ted. I'm sure somebody owes you a favour by now.'

Teddy shakes his head – *no* – and crosses his arms over his chest. 'It's mad, Betsy. The Constabulary would be on to us in minutes.'

'Would they?' she pushes. 'Are you telling me the Observatory has never taken a delivery that comes off the canal? Course they have! They need fuel the same as anyone else, especially in winter…'

'She's right,' Effie interjects. 'I might not be able to persuade them I'm a scholar, but you could easily be a delivery boy. And you know horses well enough, how to calm them. You could do it, Teddy.'

'And supposing we got it out,' he replies. 'Where would we stow it?'

'Berliner's Square,' Effie suggests, and Teddy sees the perfect townhouse, the immaculate square, the carefully sculptured hedges, the brushed white stone steps which lead to every freshly painted front door. Most of the homes on Berliner's Square are kept by a flock of neat, stern-faced staff. Chief Justice Hart might not notice the arrival of an ancient orrery at his back door, but surely the staff would. Effie reads his mind.

'I'll say it's a surprise for mother and father,' she says. 'That it's a gift, from me, for their wedding anniversary, and that it must be kept secret. It won't be forever. They wouldn't breathe a word. We can keep it in the music room – my parents never go in there.'

'Then it's settled,' Betsy declares, slamming her fist down on the table so that the apple ale spits from their glasses. Such is the noise inside the pub that nobody reacts to the thump; it disappears amongst the excited voices and the chinked glasses. The atmosphere is jubilant. Rumour has it that The Quartet will play The Blackened Lantern tonight. Naturally, Betsy, Teddy and Effie all know this rumour to be true; it is how they have come to be sitting here.

'Listen. I have to go and get ready,' Effie says. And they understand that she means she must take her double bass from its case and tune it, meet Celeste, Poppy, and Ness at some unknown entrance, put on her peacock feather mask, and sneak in through the staff corridors to shock their waiting audience. Betsy and Teddy will stay and watch. They are proud of Effie. She could already be playing in the Imperial Orchestra or studying at the Royal Academy – it would take nothing more than a nod of her father's head – but she chooses this instead. Honest audiences. Remaining unknown. Being appreciated purely for her talent.

Betsy feels certain she would have chosen the Royal Academy if she were in Effie's shoes. She has never seen the building itself, hidden as it is inside acres of private land on the southernmost edge of Copperwell. But she has seen the entrance gates – fifteen feet high and cast in iron, with the words His Majesty's Royal Academy of Musical Arts set in enormous gilt lettering above – and they have persuaded her of the grandeur which must lie within. Betsy is not entirely sure she would suit grandeur, but she considers she's a pretty adaptable person. After all, she's managed all this time without a mother or a father. She has a job, and a roof over her head, and a bed of her own. She could cope with just about anything. Grandeur certainly wouldn't take long to adjust to. She'd asked Effie once why she didn't want to attend the Academy, and Effie explained that something she had not earned for herself held no worth in her eyes. Betsy considered that Effie had earned the opportunity to audition, at the very least, because she played so often and practised so thoroughly, but she didn't say that. She liked Effie's answer. She didn't want to bury it under her own words, which are so often too loud, too quick, too far away from what she actually means. Sharp words, she learnt when she was living on the streets, were a form of self-defence.

When Effie, Celeste, Poppy, and Ness stride out from behind the bar, fall into their usual places, and immediately put their horsehair bows or their lips to their instruments, The Blackened Lantern erupts, but no one cheers louder than Betsy or Teddy. With each song, the crowd inside the pub grows closer, wilder and, before an hour has passed, the girls are penned between four sweating walls of over-excited, jigging people. They play faster. Poppy dips and swings, her fingers blurring over the neck of her violin. Ness blows into the mouthpiece of her trumpet until her eyes bulge. Celeste sings so passionately her voice starts to crackle. This is why The Quartet has grown famous across Copperwell: they give everything to their performances;

they are truthful. Betsy notices Effie setting down her bow to rotate her aching wrist in the diminishing pauses between one piece and the next. And so lost are they all in the swoop and scatter of the music that no one realises that, outside the window, snow has started to fall.

They do not realise, either, that it is falling so much quicker than it ordinarily would; that it is already heaping into mounds, whitening the pavements and the cabs and the roofs and the trees; that soon they will all be trapped inside the building by its gathering weight. If, come daybreak, they are found here rather than in their own homes, the Constabulary will come down hard on every one of them, but no one has yet noticed that they ought to be growing fearful.

'Look!' the barman, a long-limbed, small-eyed man, cries finally in a rare beat of quiet. 'By the four gods, would you look at that?' He tosses his grubby dishcloth over his shoulder and, rushing around the bar, shoves his way through the swell of customers in the direction of the door. It takes some time, though he yells and grabs and claws. His dishcloth is dragged off him and trampled underfoot. His necktie is sent askew.

Betsy, seeing this, nudges Teddy with her elbow and they watch the barman's difficult progress. They follow his fixed stare. And they realise, at the same time, that the snow is three feet deep at least, though it can't have been falling for more than twenty minutes. Teddy's brown eyes darken further under a frown.

‘That’s not right,’ he says.

‘Not at all,’ Betsy agrees.

They have lived in Copperwell their whole lives, and they know that even the heaviest snowfall rarely reaches to the cuff of an ankle boot, let alone to the stone of a windowsill. And for it to have gathered so swiftly! It’s unnatural. The Quartet still their strings mid-song as more and more people turn towards the barman, who is now frantically shunting the heavy oak door open to create a wedge they might all pass through into the night. Beyond the window, the flurries whirl and thicken until nothing is visible but the dancing descent of heavy snow. With the music inside the pub stopped, there is no sound but the rhythmic thud of the barman battering at the door and the weather pipes, singing their cold, sharp, snow music. Betsy wonders then, for the first time, what sound the pipes might be singing to disguise.

The barman succeeds in creating a narrow opening through which the frozen wind and snow push immediately, but, for all his straining, he can move it no further. He turns back into the room, his shirt already sticking to his chest in his exertion, and calls, ‘Is there anyone small enough to fit through?’

Betsy is already stealing towards the door. She understands what is required. She stops with a little bob before the panting barman and, lifting a foot in a wiggle, shows him the brown leather walking boots she has worn almost permanently since she acquired them. They are, she thinks, perfect for walking, running, climbing, and kicking, and she has no intention of ever taking them off.

'You'll do,' the barman says, putting two bony hands to the door's edge and pushing with all his might to give her an extra inch or two. 'You'll need to kick the snow out from the other side.'

'I know.'

Betsy lowers a shoulder and sidles through the gap. Her left shoulder blade thunks against the door knocker, but she does not yelp. She is braver than a little bruise. She straightens up and begins pounding her solid boots into the snowdrift. Surprisingly, it hurts. The white bank is already tightly packed and stone hard. But she kicks and kicks, grunting with the effort, until the snow starts to burst free like fireworks made from dust instead of light, and soon she weakens it enough to allow the patrons of The Blackened Lantern to spill out into the night.

They do so breathlessly, their mouths gaping, as if they had been on the verge of suffocation. Their reaction might be attributed to the sudden transition from the fire-stoked warmth of the pub to the frost-bitten street outside, but everyone in the dispersing crowd seems to know that it is more than that. That something unusual is happening. They huddle into their coats and scurry away without a backward glance, glad to be free of the cosy building, their tongues tasting the air as though they have been denied it for years. They gabble about what has happened. Betsy hears the word 'trap' bouncing off the frosted ground. 'A trap… It must have been… The snow was too thick… It blocked the door so fast… The Constabulary…'

The pub door is flung wide now, and the burning fire within casts a rectangle of gold light onto the fallen snow. After a pause, Teddy steps through it. Though he was near the front of the crowd, he has stayed until the last to make sure Effie gets out safely.

'What *was* that?' Betsy blurts the instant she spots her friends.

'Isn't it weird?'

Effie tilts back her head and spins through a full circle, studying the sagging grey clouds.

'The snow music always plays an F sharp,' she says slowly. 'It's a different note now.'

'Which note?' Teddy asks.

'Does it matter?' Betsy snips.

Effie has perfect pitch. She doesn't need to concentrate on the sound to know that the snow music has shifted up one full tone: 'G sharp.'

'It might matter,' Teddy protests. 'Don't you think…'

'What?'

Teddy huffs as he thinks through what he wants to say. 'Effie said that the mantises belonged in the East Eurasian forests. And it seems as though this much snow would only belong in The Antart. So why have they both appeared in Copperwell now?'

'It's strange, now you say it,' Betsy concedes. 'Something unexpected from the East; something sudden and wrong from The Antart. Maybe we ought to keep a look out for something from Amerikk or Africa. Maybe that would be a clue.'

Effie hums. 'But a clue to what?'

Betsy shrugs and digs a canine tooth into her lower lip. She can taste the cold – dark and peppery on her tongue. Effie is still looking up, and Betsy follows her line of sight. The clouds are low but fast-scudding, and as Effie and Betsy watch, they part to reveal a high arch of sky so black that focusing the eye on it is impossible. It is pinned to the heavens by a trail of bright white stars, shaped like a comet's tail. Betsy often stargazes from her attic window in Saltsburg's Laundry, but she cannot recall ever seeing the stars so clearly defined.

She learned the names of the constellations years ago, sitting tucked in her bedsheets and memorising the patterns marked out in an old cyclopaedia she stole from the Central Library – *Chartford's Cyclopaedia of the Planets and Constellations* – which she still has hidden in the bottom of her wardrobe. She knows that this comet tail arrangement is Salubrious: the health-giver. It is flanked by Sibyl, the teller of the future, and twisting Serpentine, the bringer of doubt. Tonight, she can see no sign of Sibyl, but the tongue flick of Serpentine is just visible, licking out from behind the bank of cloud to their right. She does not like viewing Serpentine, with its winding stardust body: it makes her feel confused and nauseous. Before too many minutes more, she lowers her eyes to the soft white flakes still falling over Copperwell.

They had wondered, when they were sitting on the Observatory roof, whether it would snow properly. Well, here it is: the street is a pale thread under the colossal black sky; the copper pipes and cogs which adorn the front of the buildings sing and spark; every rooftop wears a wedge of powdered snow deep enough to lose a boot in. And it doesn't feel right.

Betsy, Teddy and Effie amble away from The Blackened Lantern, leaving three meandering trails of footsteps behind them.

'Do you reckon it could all be linked?' Betsy asks finally.

'What?' Teddy replies. He ducks his nose into his same old green scarf and Effie thinks again about gifting him a new one for his birthday; she knows he wouldn't accept it on any other day.

'The Shift and the … mistakes the world seems to be making,' Effie offers.

Betsy's eyes grow rounder. 'Yes.'

Effie nods. 'I was thinking the same thing. It can't just be Copperwell that's affected. It's as though something has confused the natural order of things. The shadows, the migration of the insects, the weather patterns. It's all off kilter.'

'The pipe music, too,' Effie says. 'Do you remember, when we were little, how it only played during the working day? But it's been continuous, day and night, for ages now, hasn't it? And getting louder, too. As though it's designed to keep us from hearing something else…'

Betsy grins, pleased with their powers of deduction. 'It's hiding something. It must be.'

'But, what?' Teddy interjects, feeling entirely left out and confused. The girls' thoughts are flitting away from him like zipping birds.

Effie and Betsy turn towards him simultaneously. Their eyes are quite different: Betsy's are hard and sharp and steely grey; Effie's are softer-edged and a muddled hazel colour. But right now, both pairs are identically bright with shared understanding.

Teddy's eyebrows drop into a familiar frown. His face, whether lit with kindness or shaded in confusion, is always wide open. Betsy thinks that perhaps she should like to see his new shadow after all; she considers it would be an exact replica of him, and she would appreciate the reassurance of that.

'That woman!' Effie puts in. 'On Wild Goose Way. What did she say?'

'It's a game,' Betsy recalls.

'They're playing with our lives,' Effie finishes, repeating the woman's words verbatim.

'The Unified Government!'

Teddy lifts his hands in a surrender. He wants the girls to slow down. 'But why would they?' he manages.

The girls do not slow down. In fact, they are pacing along now, driven by the cold, and Betsy and Effie's agitation, and the shock of those frantic moments inside the pub. Their misting breaths reach for the clouds. Their voices echo down the empty street. Teddy trails after them, weighed down by the sinking sensation in his stomach.

'That's what we're going to have to find out,' Betsy declares.

CHAPTER FIVE

Theft

Effie can feel the throb of her own heart as she lies next to Betsy in the dark, trying to keep her exhalations from growing noisy. She can't see anything except black shapes: above, the sag of partially loosed canvas; to her left, the smooth wooden side of the crate, barnacled with rusted nuts and bolts; to her right, the lines and curves of Betsy's slight figure as she shifts and fidgets like a trapped animal. Being trapped is the idea. Or the illusion of it, at least. She had suspected Betsy would not be able to cope with the reality or the illusion, given how restless she is. Effie, however, prides herself on bringing maturity to every situation, and what maturity looks like tonight is stillness. They have to remain still if they are to keep from giving the game away. She wants to angle an elbow into Betsy's ribs, to remind her of the fact, but she is afraid that, if jabbed, Betsy will cry out.

She concentrates instead on the gap between the two pieces of canvas drawn across the top of the crate they have clambered into and watches the light flash through it at intervals. They are being pushed beneath a row of flickering ceiling lamps. The view offers little clue as to how close they are getting.

'Relating to the orrery?' the man who steps along beside them asks again. 'You're sure?' His voice is reedy, flimsy. Effie imagines he looks as flute-like as he sounds: long and thin and awkward. Her thoughts always begin with a sound.

'That's right,' Teddy replies.

Teddy is behind the crate, pushing it through the corridor on its wheeled pushcart. Hearing his voice without being able to see him is odd. Effie realises for the first time what a nice voice he has: gentle and sincere, but sufficiently gruff to persuade this guard that he is old enough to be an independent delivery boy. She feels certain she would believe him, were she on the receiving end of his lies. He dispenses them in a friendly, unhurried way. Though he'd claimed again and again that he could not pull off the deception, he is doing very well so far.

He takes three more strides, then adds, 'Directly to the orrery; that's what the delivery notice said. I imagine it's something delicate, don't you, sir? Expensive, too, given the orrery's worth. Perhaps that's why it said the crate must not be opened by the likes of you or me. Whoever...' Teddy pauses to affect a look at the handwritten label he himself has tied to the knotted rope securing the crate to the pushcart. 'Whoever this Dr Stragglethorpe is, she must be very important.'

A nice touch, Effie thinks, to make the imaginary doctor a woman. The guard, if he was gentlemanly, would be less likely to challenge a female scholar, should one happen to pass through the Observatory today, about whether she was the doctor in question, and whether she knew what was inside the strange crate newly stored in the orrery room.

The guard hums; it sounds like the crackle of a snapped newspaper. 'Dr Stragglethorpe,' he muses. 'Should I recognise her?'

'I couldn't say,' Teddy returns. 'Not my business to know any more about it than what I see written before me.'

In the dark of the crate, Effie feels Betsy smirk at that.

They start to slow, and the guard steps ahead of them. Four strides. Stop. Two back. Stop. The steady creak of a wooden door swung open on unoiled hinges. Effie realises she is holding her breath. They are entering the orrery room. Is it possible she feels Teddy's arms tensing on the handle of the pushcart? Probably not. But she imagines she does.

'Is this it, then?' he asks. And Effie notices that it is Betsy's voice he has been imitating since he arrived at the Observatory entranceway and called for the guard: her intonation; her confidence.

'This is it,' the guard confirms. Guessing by the degree his words fall at, Effie supposes he is perhaps a head taller than Teddy; maybe slightly less. She does not think he would prove much of a threat, if it came to it. They are so very nearly delivered to the orrery room that she feels the task is almost done. Their delivery there, though, is merely the beginning of the plan. She must not relax yet.

'Anywhere about?' Teddy asks, wheeling the girls away from the amber glow of the hallway lights and into a pocket of deeper darkness.

'Just there should do it.'

There follows a rustling as Teddy flicks open a notebook they have filled with invented orders and scribbled signatures, and offers it to the guard. Then, with a few muttered words, he is gone, the guard too, and the girls sit in pressing silence, listening for a stillness they are certain will settle over the building as dawn approaches and the guards and the scholars and the scientists clock off and return to their homes to sleep the day away.

Many hours pass before Effie whispers, 'We should try getting out.'

Betsy starts. Effie thinks that perhaps she had fallen asleep.

'Everyone's gone?'

Effie nods. 'They must have. It's daylight.' She rolls her eyes towards the canvas above them. They can see its colour now: pale, beige. They can see each other's faces: a little greyed, yes, but clearly enough. Betsy nods and shuffles onto her knees. Every muscle in her body aches from being cramped for so long inside the crate. She lines her head up with the gap in the canvas, pushes into a standing position, and turns a full slow circle before clambering out. Effie follows. The orrery room is illuminated by sunlight which blasts in through two ceiling-height windows and in which flecks of dust eddy. Outside, Copperwell's streets are still buried under deep snow and both the light and the room are bitingly cold. Betsy and Effie pad around like the cats Betsy had promised they would be the night they broke onto the Observatory roof. They are captivated by the perfect golden penduluming of an astronomical regulator, which thunders through the empty room like a heartbeat, and the papers scattered across an enormous desk, blackened with hundreds of equations they could not begin to decipher, and the shelves bending under the weight of books and gauges, thermometers and measuring instruments. They are drawn next to the shining horologium, with its intricate mesh of looped circles, its clockfaces within clockfaces, its polished symbols. It is a beautiful confusion of teal-coloured hoops and cobalt lines and gunmetal rings.

'What is it for?' Effie breathes, lifting her hand as though to touch it, but stopping short. It is too magical a thing to touch. It seems to have its own glow, its own energy. Effie could swear she can hear a soothing E flat emanating from it.

'Around the outside,' Betsy begins, indicating by swirling a pointed finger on the air and sending the dust flying on a new trajectory, 'are the twenty-four hours of the day, in Roman numerals. It tells the time, like a normal clock. The smaller circle, with the strange symbols – those are the twelve signs of the zodiac. That part represents the months of the year.' She pauses, tilting her head in consideration of the object. It is twice as large as her own head and much more interesting to look at. 'Then the dial containing the numbers one to thirty.' Again, she draws on the air with her fingertip. 'That shows the age of the moon. Do you see?'

Effie nods, ever the attentive student.

'What about all these other sweeps and marks?'

The horologium is cluttered with lines which burst outwards from a central point like rays of dawn light. There are layers of them. And over and between them, thin silver rods, which twitch, then rotate smoothly around the clock face, then pause and twitch and move back in the opposite direction. Betsy does not know what these are for, but she surmises that they relate in some way to the planets. If the horologium displays the hours, the lunar phases, and the calendar months, it stands to reason that it must, too, show the movements of the planets. Just like the orrery.

As the thickest of the silver rods swings up to the numeral for twelve, a sudden *click* causes them both to flinch, and they whip their heads around in the direction of the sound. Though it does not come again, there is only one place the sound might have originated. On the far side of the room, four black velvet curtains hide something large and square. A table, or a cabinet perhaps?

'Do you think that's it?' Effie asks.

Betsy nods.

They move towards it in unison and, reaching out for one curtain each, draw them back so that two sides of the square are exposed. Immediately behind the black velvet are panes of thick glass. And beyond the glass, an item which is perhaps a yard high and a yard wide, but which seems to pull you to it with all the gravitational tug of the moon. Betsy and Effie lean close to watch the marble planets revolve around the gleaming sun, the bronze cogs slotting into each other and grinding around and around to send the planets on their orbits. Its movements are stately, hypnotic. Its colours brighter than any the girls have ever seen. It is as though each planet and each moon are lit from within, like a person's eyes.

The orrery!

The smaller model that Betsy keeps in her attic room is, surprisingly, almost an exact replica of this, the real thing. She hadn't imagined it would be so accurate. Apart from scale – Betsy's orrery is just a third of the size of this one – and mount – this one sits on a solid walnut plinth – it would be difficult to tell the two apart.

'Yours is powered by clockwork,' Effie says slowly.

'So is this one,' Betsy replies. 'Look at the cogs; they're the same.'

'Yes. But we've been here for hours, Bets. No one has come in to wind it. There's no key. So how did it just click into motion?'

'Perhaps it didn't. Perhaps it was moving all along.'

'But we only just heard it.'

'Maybe we weren't stood in the right place to hear it until now. Or perhaps the movements of one of the other machines have some control over it. Anyway, never mind that now. Do you think we'll be able to lift it?'

Betsy is moving around the glass cabinet, dragging open the other two curtains to find the corner – *yes, there* – with a hinged door and a small silver catch. She hooks the arm of the catch up and swings the glass door open, then stops, to see if something bad will happen. She is expecting a bell alarm to start clanging noisily, or a mob of guards to come rushing in, or the unmistakable clatter of Constabulary horses' hooves on the street below. Silence follows.

'We should bring the crate across,' she says, and all of a sudden, it all seems a hurry. Though Teddy can't return to fetch them until dark, they have stayed hidden too long. They ought to have organised everything ahead of time. And they must both – exhausted by their anticipation and soothed by the ticking machinery – have fallen asleep for a long while in the crate, because already dusk is pinching the edges of the sky. She and Effie dart back towards the crate, grab the handle of the pushcart, manoeuvre it around, then steer it towards the orrery's spotless display cabinet. It is evident that someone looks after the orrery very carefully indeed, and it's possible – isn't it? – that they might return at any time to check on it. Perhaps some of the staff live in the Observatory and haven't had to go home for the day. Why hadn't they thought of that before?

They position the crate as close to the cabinet as they dare, and Effie props open the glass door with a wad of folded paper she finds on the desk so that it will not swing shut while they are easing the orrery out.

'It's going to be heavy,' Betsy warns, pointlessly, as she and Effie reach in to clamp their hands around the glossed round bulk of the walnut base.

'We'll never lift it straight out,' Effie replies. 'We'll have to twist it back and forth between us until it's right on the edge.'

Betsy nods her approval of this plan and, ever so cautiously, they shove the orrery an inch in Effie's direction, an inch in Betsy's direction, an inch in Effie's direction, so that it groans all the way to the edge of the cabinet. With each shriek of complaint from the walnut base, Betsy grits her teeth, and soon she is grinding them painfully together. Her heart is clenched up small, like a fist. Her stomach feels hollow. Effie does not seem to share her panic, but then Effie has always been calmer than Betsy. While Betsy goes screaming towards conflict or excitement without a second's hesitation, Effie stands back a minute, thinks through what she will do, and weighs up the myriad possible outcomes before she acts. Likely she has used this time, as they have eased the orrery closer to the crate, to play through their entire plan in her mind, considering different scenarios so that she will know, if they are faced with a choice, what the best course will be.

'What will we do if we're stopped?' Betsy asks her.

The plan is for Betsy to climb back into the crate to secure the orrery and, come the arrival of the moon, for

Effie, dressed in Teddy's work clothes, to wheel them out through the staff entrance where Teddy will be waiting for them with one of the canal horses and a borrowed cart. Naturally, they have supposed that someone might stop Effie, wanting to check what it is exactly that she is transporting out of the building at the first sign of moonrise. But in the safety of her attic room, Betsy had insisted they could brazen it out; that Effie, possessed of all the confidence of one-fourth of the infamous The Quartet, could call out to anyone looking suspiciously in her direction and simply keep the pushcart moving. *Thanks for letting me in so early. I'll get this out of your way now. Won't be long before its back, good as new*. That sort of thing. But, oh, it seems feeble now, this plan of theirs. Betsy wishes, just for a second, that they had never heard that woman shouting on Wild Goose Way.

Effie ignores Betsy's question and, with the orrery teetering right on the edge of the cabinet now, they slide their hands beneath the base and hope firstly that they have the strength to at least slow its descent, and secondly that the blankets they have lined the crate with will be enough to muffle the thud of its landing.

'On three,' Effie instructs. Betsy grinds her teeth harder and nods. Effie counts them in and, with a simultaneous heave, they free the orrery from its glass cabinet.

Instantly, their shoulders are yanked from their sockets and their ribcages are brought crashing against the wood panels of the crate as they drop with the orrery. It is colossally heavy. They can't possibly hold it. But they keep their hands on it as they tip, grunting, into the crate and the orrery comes to a safe stop in the mounded blankets beneath. Betsy, being the slighter of the two, cannot fight the momentum and tumbles in bodily after it, cracking a cheekbone on the curve of Jupiter. Effie, being some two or three stone heavier, manages to find the floor again with the soles of her shoes and right herself. Peering over the lip of the crate, she can't help but grin at the tangled girl within. Betsy, *humph*ing now, struggles to drag herself into a kneeling position then stands and clambers out with all the grace of a seal stranded on dry land. In her haste, she tumbles again onto the hard tiles of the orrery room floor.

'If you laugh,' she warns, 'I'll get back in and you can push me the whole way.'

Effie lets her tight grin open into an easy smile and shakes her head. 'Come on,' she says, and then they are off, wheeling the pushcart past the glinting horologium and the pounding astronomical regulator, through the double doors of the orrery room, down the corridor under the row of burning ceiling lamps, and into the atrium of the building, where they skid to a halt, whipping their heads this way and that. Their panting breaths echo in the cathedral-like space. The ceiling is impossibly high, arching towards a circular skylight. Orb lights hang from the rafters like ripe oranges, casting their radiance over three tiers of balconies accessed by iron staircases. Each balcony is lined with door after door after door. The ground floor, too. There are perhaps a hundred potential exits from the atrium, and Betsy and Effie have no idea which is the right one.

Something inside Betsy is fluttering now like a trapped bird. She flinches. She is about to start running, indeterminately. But then Effie's fingers are digging into her upper arm, leaving small round bruises, and she fights the urge to drag herself free.

'Wait,' Effie says. 'It'll be the biggest door. To get deliveries through if it's the staff door. For grandeur if it's the scholar's door. We need to find the biggest door.'

'You're right.'

They spin around. The bird inside Betsy is beating at her ribcage.

'There!' Effie is pointing into a far corner, where wide but unadorned double doors have been set in the slanted shade of the lowest balcony. 'Staff. Got to be.'

Betsy nods and they start across the atrium, wincing at the rattle of the pushcart's wheels over the stone tiles. So amplified is the stillness inside the building that their progress is deafening and the girls fall silent, as though their voices could make the din any worse. Betsy, wanting to bring her own kind of order to the chaos, counts their footsteps; every time she reaches ten she begins again at one. Effie lets minor melodies climb around her mind, thinking that they might persuade her racing pulse to fall into their looser rhythms. At some point, the girls have positioned themselves behind the pushcart so that they can steer it with one hand and, with the other, clasp each other tightly.

'Nearly there,' Betsy whispers. It's a stupid thing to say. It's unnecessary, given that Effie can see as well as she can that they are nearing the door. It's risky, given their vow to draw as little attention to themselves as possible, and the glaring obviousness of the fact that in this enormous space everything echoes. She needn't have spoken at all. That is what she tells herself as they fly towards the door. Five yards. Three yards. Closer. They can practically taste the bitter night air.

And then the doors open – inwards.

The man Betsy and Effie almost hit with the pushcart reels backwards, mouth agape, the papers from the files he had been carrying swooping to the floor. He swallows his gasp and finds his breath again, then straightens the knot of his already neat tie.

'I'm sorry,' he begins. 'I didn't…' No sooner have his eyes softened than they harden again. 'Wait. There's not supposed to be anyone—'

'Go!' Effie barks. And they do. They shove the pushcart forward with all their might, and the man in the doorway leaps aside as they wheel over his scattered paperwork, and they are running then along a short corridor and out into the coming night.

'Wait. Stop! Who are you?' the man shouts after them. Effie glances behind to check if he is following them, but he is crouched over his documents, shuffling them desperately back into their stacks. She senses, though, from the way he looks from them to the documents and back to them again, that he will pursue them the first moment he is able. They slam off a single stone step, veer left as planned, judder along the path which surrounds the building and, finally, smashing off it onto the road, they find themselves free of the Observatory grounds. They are just where they intended to be. Soon, they will be safe.

Except… Teddy is not there waiting for them.

CHAPTER SIX

The Copperwell Canal

It was not that it had never occurred to Teddy to wonder where the Copperwell Canal started, or where the boats joined it, or where it ended. He considers that he has wondered about everything a person might, since his father died. It was simply that he hadn't imagined where he might find the answers to his questions. When Edward was alive, he had filled Teddy with stories of all the places the Aur had been sighted: of mountain ranges which touched the clouds; of waterfalls so high that, if you were to stand beneath them, the thundering water might crush your skull; of deserts where only insects and cactus plants survived the arid heat; of woodlands which stretched for thousands of miles, filled with deer and wolves who were wise enough to turn and run from people. They never spoke about the cities. The cities, Edward said, were too full of people's greed to ever be worthy of admiration; their stories were ugly and not worth telling.

Now, however, as Teddy jogs up and down on the towpath and waits for the horse and cart which should have arrived over an hour ago, he wishes he knew more about Copperwell. He is familiar with those rooftops which can be clambered across from the attic window of Saltsburg's Laundry. He knows which of the elevated railways are best to hide under from all those times when he and Betsy have snuck away from Mrs S's anger. He knows a secret place – an abandoned outhouse – behind the soap works where, twice, he kissed Octavia Bennett; and the pubs where Effie's quartet have played their swinging jazz; and some of the houses on The Crescent where, immediately after Edward's death, he had apprenticed as a chimney sweep. He remembers what it felt like to ride through the midnight city before The Order, when the streets were empty, and it was only him and his father's cab horse, Jim. Eventually, he'd been forced to sell Jim, and most days now Teddy refuses to think of his sad, feather-lashed eyes, his rich ginger coat, the way his lips would tremble as he reached out to pluck a carrot or an apple gently from Teddy's palm. But tonight, as the sky marbles from lavender to a deeper navy blue and finally to blackberry, and the first horse and cart does not appear ahead of the first boat as usual, Teddy finds himself glancing along the towpath at movements and sounds – a tossed mane, a soft snicker – which he believes he recognises as Jim's, but which, when he looks again, are simply shifts of the light, tricks of sound. Ghost horses. All that arrives along the canal is the familiar algae stink of his work.

He flicks open his father's pocket watch to check the ticking silver hands. Six o'clock. He is already forty-five minutes late. And he can't understand why. His part in all this was supposed to be simple. He would head to the canal which runs like a great moat, seven miles wide at some points, around the periphery of the city, await the arrival of the first horse and cart, urge the driver from his seat with a flustered account of some emergency in the boat house, then, having ushered the driver inside the ramshackle building and locked the door behind him, borrow the horse and cart for a few hours. He'd been confident in that. He'd calmed himself with thoughts of returning both horse and cart, unharmed and undamaged, to their owner before daybreak. And now… He does not know what will happen to the girls if he doesn't get to the Observatory soon.

He will not learn until much later that the first horse and cart is delayed, this evening, by a simple accident of fate. That the driver, Fergus Drew, was tardy in collecting his usual horse, Freida, from the canal stables because one of the steam locomotives had broken down on the tracks above Sleuth Street and he'd had to run across Copperwell to get to work. Fergus' running, however, is not what it once was, and most of the miles he travelled were covered at a wheezing walk.

By the time Frieda's trotting hooves echo along the towpath, Briny Erwin is striding bow-leggedly towards Teddy, waving one of his big paws.

'What's stirring up, then, Teddy lad?' he asks, when he is close enough to notice the pop of Teddy's eyes, the pale hue of his skin, the way he fidgets from foot to foot. 'You look like you've had a haunting.'

The hollow *clop* of Frieda's hooves grows louder, and Teddy risks a glance into Erwin's wide face. Erwin stares back, as calm and steady as ever. Teddy is sure he can trust him. And what choice does he have in any case?

'Erwin,' he begins. He is mortified by the tremor in his voice and coughs it away. 'Erwin. Do you think I'm an honest person?'

'Well of course that,' Erwin replies, clapping Teddy on the back. Teddy has to brace against the impact. 'Edward James was as honest a man as I ever met, and you're just the same, Ted. You're the truest mirror of your old man.'

'Would you help me, then,' Teddy ventures, 'if I was in trouble and I couldn't say exactly why?'

Erwin's smile drops away and he nods seriously. 'I would, lad. No question.'

Teddy snatches a deep breath, then immediately exhales it. The air between him and Briny Erwin whitens. 'When the first horse and cart arrives,' he says quietly, 'I'm going to take it. I need to get to the Observatory. Betsy and Effie are waiting for me. Or they should be. We're taking the orrery, Erwin…'

'The orrery? What's—'

'A kind of machine. They keep it in the Observatory. It's important. It's—'

'Who keeps it in the Observatory?'

'The Unified Government. They…'

Erwin leans in close. Teddy can feel the heat of his breath, smell the soap that's been scrubbed into his jumper and the smoke from his last cigar. 'You're *stealing* it, you mean? Why on earth, lad?'

'It's to do with the shadows,' Teddy whispers back. 'It has to do with the Unified Government and the shadows. They *did* something. There was this woman – she knew all about it. She'd discovered why the shadows shifted, she said. But the Constabulary took her away before she could speak out. Only we saw, Erwin – me, Bets and Ef. We saw them batter her over the head and drag her away. And all we know for certain is that it has something to do with the orrery, so we're starting there. Will you help me?'

Erwin's enormous chest rises and falls in a sigh. 'I said I would.'

'You don't have to,' Teddy says, still jogging from foot to foot. 'You could look the other way. I wouldn't blame you.'

'No,' Erwin insists. 'No, lad. If you say this is important, I believe you. But no strong-arming this chap when the cart comes up. Leave that to me. We'll go together.'

'But your shift!'

'We'll go together,' Erwin says, clapping Teddy's back again, though on this occasion he lets his hand rest a little longer. 'It's only one night.'

'It'll be longer,' Teddy counters, 'if the Constabulary catch us.'

'Well, then,' Erwin replies. 'We'll best make certain we don't get caught.'

And for the first time since he wheeled the girls into

the Observatory, Teddy feels he can breathe properly. He is relieved when Fergus Drew appears out of the darkness, clutching at his still-heaving chest, and Briny Erwin strides over to converse with him. He says nothing when he sees Erwin pass something into Fergus' hand, then help the smaller man down from the cart; nor when Erwin takes his place and steers Freida towards Teddy; nor as he climbs into the cart and allows Erwin to slap Freida's reins against her rump and urge her towards the Observatory. Now is not the time for questions. First, they have to get the orrery safely to Berliner's Square.

Erwin coaxes Freida into a fast trot and Teddy leans forward on the cart's bench seat as they bump into the cold wind. Freida's white tail swishes in excitement as she turns off her usual route and onto the streets of Copperwell. The cart's wheels rattle noisily beneath them and Teddy balls one hand into a fist and pounds his knuckles into the palm of the other.

'Are you sure they'll still be there?' Erwin asks, as Teddy wills them faster towards the Observatory.

'They have to be,' Teddy replies.

CHAPTER SEVEN

Berliner's Square

Betsy and Effie are in full flight, the pushcart jouncing along ahead of them, the man from the Observatory and a day guard battling the icy cobbles in their wake, when they spot a piebald mare rounding the corner of Dragonfly Way at a rapid trot, her head and hooves held high.

'TEDDY!' Betsy cries and, even in her haste, she has chance to regret saying his name within earshot of the Observatory staff. Granted, they won't have his surname, but it will be something for the two men sprinting after them to report to the Constabulary. 'Don't stop!' she yells, taking one hand from the pushcart's handle to wave it wildly over her shoulder to indicate the chase. 'We'll meet you *at work*.'

Teddy stands and cups his fingers around his ear. 'At work?' he calls.

'Yes. At work.'

Oh, please understand, Teddy, she thinks as the pushcart and the horse cart approach one another. She needs him to create a diversion, to give her and Effie a chance to veer under the archway further down Dragonfly Way and towards the water. The two at her back won't know the way, but Teddy will. It is one of those slivers of the city occupied by the homeless, the outcast, the unfortunate. Along the damp walls of the tunnel which leads to the towpath, beggars sit bundled in stale blankets, drinking poppy-seed tea and scrounging for food. They are filthy. They smell of wet earth and fish guts. But there is honour amongst these people, Betsy knows. She has never admitted as much to Teddy or Effie, but she had lived among them for a short while. She had been abandoned into their midst. She has the proof of it hidden between her mattress and her bedframe.

'Apprehend them!' comes a pompous wail from behind as Betsy and Effie near Teddy and… Is that Briny Erwin? Betsy's jaw clenches. The last thing they need is an adult getting involved, trying to take over, attempting to persuade them that he, by dint of being two decades older than them, knows more than they do about everything. In Betsy's experience, adults are more often than not lacking in imagination, backbone, curiosity and determination: in short, everything which might be required to solve a mystery. And besides, if they're all as clever as they pretend to be, why did they let the Unified Government get away with passing The Shadow Order in the first place?

Briny Erwin, she is adamant, should not be here. And for a full twenty seconds, she believes herself correct in that assertion. But as the pushcart and the horse cart draw level halfway along Dragonfly Way, and Teddy glides past with a salute of understanding, she sees Briny Erwin steer the black and white mare diagonally behind them, cutting off the two men in bellowing pursuit. The bulk of the long-maned horse, combined with the cart, and Teddy and Erwin standing on it waving and hollering, will surely prove enough of a distraction to allow Betsy and Effie to slip away unobserved.

'On the count of three,' she tells Effie in a fierce whisper, 'take a sharp left.'

Effie gives an abrupt nod.

'One… Two…'

Briny Erwin – it transpires, despite Betsy's doubts – is invaluable in transporting the orrery to number eight, Berliner's Square. Not only does he distract the Observatory staff long enough for Betsy and Effie to career through the archway off Dragonfly Way, down the damp tunnel, and onto the towpath, he also steers Frieda around to collect them, lifts the crate containing the orrery onto the cart, and drives them all to Effie's house. Then, with Teddy's help, he carries their stolen goods through the gleaming silence of the towering townhouse to Effie's music room. He is strong and quiet, and Betsy approves of him almost entirely by the time he takes his leave and returns to what remains of his shift on the canal.

'Thank you,' she says, as he climbs back onto the cart and gathers Frieda's reins between his knot-knuckled fingers.

'There you are, Miss,' he replies with a nod. 'Teddy, lad – call on me if I'm needed. And stay safe, won't you.'

‘I’ll try, Erwin,’ Teddy says.

With a click of his tongue, Erwin instructs Frieda to walk on, and as she conveys him away into the darkness, Betsy, Teddy and Effie slip back through the servants’ entrance, across the kitchen, down the hallway, and into Effie’s music room once again.

The room, dedicated to Effie’s double-bass practice, is perhaps five times the size of Betsy’s bedroom above Saltsburg’s Laundry. It contains a shining black grand piano; two double basses, the more beaten up of which Teddy recognises as the one Effie plays with The Quartet; a clutch of carved wooden music stands; a mustard-coloured settee; two spindle-back chairs; a crackling open fire and, set to either side of the fireplace, two white alcoves containing countless stacks of sheet music. A vase of pale-yellow flowers with firework blooms infuses the room with a sweet scent, like ripe strawberries.

‘It’s witch hazel,’ Effie says, when she notices Teddy looking at the strange, spidery flowers. ‘It smells sweet, even in the winter.’

‘It’s not one of our…’ He searches for the word. ‘Anomalies, then?’

Effie smiles gently. ‘No. Just winter flowering. Is the mantis still alive, Bets?’

Betsy, who is wandering around the room, touching the bookshelves then the music stands then the neck of the more pristine double bass with a tentative forefinger, nods distractedly. ‘I snuck one of Mrs S’s potted plants up from downstairs. It just sits in that most of the time, waiting for passing flies.' When she has investigated everything of interest, she slumps down on the settee and sighs noisily. 'Where are you parents, anyway?'

Effie shrugs. 'Father will be in chambers. Mother will be at one of her meetings, I suppose.'

'What meetings?'

'Women's Enfranchisement.'

'What does that mean?' Teddy asks, taking up one of the spindle-back chairs and edging it closer to the fire before settling on it.

'They campaign for women to be given equal rights to men,' Effie replies. 'Voting rights, land- and property-owning rights, that sort of thing.'

'Women *can* own property,' Betsy says. 'Mrs S does. She owns the laundry.'

Effie nods. 'They can. But only if they're unmarried or widowed. If Mrs S were to marry, the laundry would automatically become the property of her husband.'

'No!' breathes Betsy, appalled. 'But she works so hard to run it. That's not fair.'

'That's why W.E. exists,' Effie answers.

It is Betsy's turn to nod then. 'She sounds quite good, your mother.'

'She is... Anyway, what are we going to do about this?'

They all turn to look at the crate, stowed in the corner, against the bottom shelves of the left-hand alcove. It is too large and rough-edged to conceal anywhere in this house.

It is entirely out of place. They ought, Betsy supposes, to dispose of the crate and put the orrery on display: such a shining, expensive-looking object would be unremarkable in a Berliner's Square home; they could hide it in plain sight.

'Let's open it at least,' Teddy suggests. 'See if it's still working after all that.'

Together they remove the canvas from the top of the crate, free the orrery from its bed of blankets, and lift it carefully out. It is heavy and cumbersome, but with three sets of hands to support it, they manage to convey it to the lowered lid of the grand piano and set it down without incident.

The moment it finds itself on a level surface, it issues that same clicking sound that had so startled Betsy and Effie when they were in the Observatory, and the planets ease into their gentle revolutions: they are painted in the exact same colours as the planets of Betsy's smaller orrery, but they seem to spark brighter, as though lit from within. As each planet finds its orbit, so it begins to spin through its own rotation, and before long, every celestial body included on the model, excepting the glinting sun, is dancing in perfect synchronicity. They watch spellbound for a while, until Teddy breaks their concentration with a wide yawn.

'What time is it?'

Effie glances at the clock on the mantle. 'Midnight.'

'Just midnight?' Teddy replies. 'It feels much later. I'd have thought—'

'It was nearer dawn,' Betsy interjects. 'Me too. That's odd.'

Frowning, she goes to the window and considers the scene without. The sky is a high black bridge over Copperwell. The roofs of the townhouses glimmer under a fresh layer of frost. The gas lamps drop their domes of muted light over the ground. The roads and pavements are still mostly white with snow, but footsteps and cab wheels have carved dark paths through it, like lines on a map.

'Are you sure that clock is right?' Betsy asks, looking towards the mantle.

Effie shrugs. 'I don't see why it wouldn't be. It's ticking.'

'But was it ticking when we came in?'

'I … don't know.'

'It really should be nearer dawn.'

'Maybe.'

'Definitely.'

'Stop the orrery again,' Betsy says. She steps back across the room towards it. 'If the clock stops, then we'll know what it does.'

'It can't possibly stop *time*,' Teddy puts in, coming to stand beside Betsy. 'Can it?'

Betsy shrugs. There is, undeniably, something special about this orrery. It has an energy about it – as though it is living.

'How do we stop it?' Effie asks. 'There's no key, like yours.'

'It started on its own when we took it out of the crate,' Teddy observes.

'Perhaps it stopped because we moved it.'

'Perhaps.'

'It did before,' Effie says. 'I didn't think about it, but it stopped as soon as we lifted it from the cabinet in the Observatory.'

'Yes,' Betsy agrees. 'We need to lift it again.'

Though it is impossibly heavy, they position themselves around it without complaint: Teddy to one side; the girls to the other. Teddy counts them in and, on three, they groan as they raise the orrery off the piano lid. Immediately, the planets begin to slow. Within a minute, they have stopped altogether.

They listen for the tick of the clock on the mantle. Nothing.

Teddy shuffles one arm under the orrery and, reaching into his waistcoat to retrieve his pocket watch, flicks it open. The silver hands are frozen: the hour hand points towards the twelve, and the minute hand at the three. The shock of it makes his hair tingle.

'Put it back down,' he says.

The moment the orrery is set, unencumbered, on the piano lid, it resumes its hypnotic movement. The mantle clock, too, recommences its ticking. Teddy checks his pocket watch again.

'Incredible,' he breathes. 'It stops … it actually stops time!'

'But … if the Unified Government has been stopping and starting it, for whatever reason, how hasn't anyone noticed? We haven't noticed.'

'Perhaps they haven't stopped and started it recently,' Effie suggests. 'Or perhaps we can't feel the effect because we're too close to it – sort of at the eye of the storm. Or perhaps it's because we are the ones who stopped it…'

'And maybe we did notice,' Betsy puts in. 'At The Blackened Lantern, when all that snow appeared so suddenly – nobody could explain it. But what if the snow didn't fall all at once? What if the snow fell as normal, but we were under the orrery's spell – sleeping, in a way, until it started rotating again. At the Observatory, too – we slept for such a long time, didn't we? Do you think it's possible, Ef?'

Effie shakes her head, perplexed. 'I think that if this machine can influence time, then anything could be possible.'

Betsy's low-pitched laugh – the singular part of her which reveals any hint of shyness – escapes from between her clamped lips. Seeing her struggle to stay quiet, Effie and Teddy start to laugh, too, and soon they have almost forgotten that they are standing around a secret the Unified Government would have them imprisoned for life – or worse – for unveiling.

The orrery can control time. It is that powerful. What else it might be capable of they cannot yet begin to imagine. The woman on Wild Goose Way, though, had been certain that it held the key to discovering how the government shifted the shadows. The lives of every single person in the Britannic Isles have been changed by this glowing model and might yet be changed again. It is, Teddy supposes, the most valuable item in any of the four continents.

And he, Betsy and Effie have stolen it.

CHAPTER EIGHT

Saltsburg's Laundry

At the poorer end of Hangman's Alley, in the dense, churning steam of Henrietta Saltsburg's Laundry, Betsy leans over an enormous wooden vat of boiling water and, pushing her hair back off her forehead, plunges a long wooden beater into the swirl of clothes. It is just before dusk and low, thick shadows slope across the room from the bottom windows, making shapes on the floor: the barrel-like vat, the drying lines, the shirts and trousers and stockings and skirts suspended from them, Betsy. From the corner of her eye, she glances at her own shadow. Whereas she is nimbly small, it seems larger and heavier tonight. While she stands still, but for the stirring of the beater, it paces back and forth, like a schoolmaster before a blackboard, with calm intent. Can that really be her true self? She feels erratic, as though every one of her thoughts is a winged insect, trapped in the cavity of her skull, trying to find its way out. It has always been this way – apart from when she studies the stars.

She finishes pushing the clothes around the soapy water and, retrieving the scrubbing board, slides it into the vat. The scrubbing board is something like a ladder, with feet which rest on the bottom of the vat and hooks which fit around the rim to hold it in place. It has rungs, evenly spaced, with gaps between for the water to run away through. Betsy uses the beater to fish the first item of clothing from the vat, drapes a red waistcoat over the scrubbing board and, taking up her hand brush, scrubs at it furiously.

There is a reassuring rhythm to her work. Though Betsy laments being trapped in the laundry as often as she is, though she craves crisp outside air while she breathes in the damp sticky warmth of the washing room, she has to admit – to herself – that there is satisfaction to be found in her duties. The repetitive actions, the ache in her spine, the array of clean and colourful clothing which will hang all around the room when she has finished, waiting to be stacked, once dried, into neat towers and returned to its owners. For the first time in her life, Betsy is needed. And the predictability of this process allows her time to dream and invent. But while she used to imagine some new mischief that she, Teddy and Effie might involve themselves in, now she thinks of nothing but the orrery.

'What do you think, Puck?' she asks the orchid mantis.

She has taken to carrying him downstairs on his potted plant to join her in the washing room, having remembered what Effie said about them belonging to the tropical forests of the East, and Puck seems to enjoy the humidity. When the room is quiet, he leaves his plant and flutters from drying line to drying line, basking in the steam which rises from the clothes.

'I mean, the snow never sticks for more than a day or two usually,' she continues. But it is falling more frequently now, growing thicker day on day. Wherever they go in thc city, they are forced to wade through mounds of it. People go about with their skirt-hems and coats lifted between pinched fingers, speculating about its persistence. Colourful woollen gloves, scarves and hats fill Betsy's vats.

'It's got to be the orrery,' – this, she whispers – 'hasn't it?'

The petalled creature, perched on a stiff white shirt collar, shuffles his feet, as though acting out the steps of some strange, stomping dance. Glancing around to make sure no one else has arrived yet, Betsy copies him. Stomp, stomp, stomp. Puck responds with four more steps, which Betsy imitates.

According to the letter of the law, she should not be working. It is not yet dark outside. But Mrs S has never been the type of woman to concern herself with such trivial details as legality.

'What in the four continents are you doing, child?' she asks now, appearing around the washing-room door, her wild ginger hair piled high on her head.

'Stamping the cold out of my feet,' Betsy replies, as indignant as ever.

'Don't give me that! It's a hothouse in here.'

'In here. The same can't be said of my attic, mind. I haven't had chance to thaw yet.'

'Is that so?' Mrs S folds her arms across her wide bust,

raises her eyebrows, and turns out the rounded toe of one burgundy lace-up boot. It is a challenge, that pointed toe. Betsy knows that Mrs S channels all her anger through it, but she feels confrontational today, so frustrated is she by the stupid orrery and her miniscule understanding of it, and she does not back down.

'That is so,' she insists. 'And I reckon, by way of recompense, that you should let me finish early tonight.'

'By way of recompense. Where did you get a phrase like that, I wonder?'

'From Effie,' Betsy replies. 'She's terrible clever.'

'I shouldn't doubt she is, with a father like that.'

Betsy raises her chin. 'She's terrible clever in her own right, actually.'

Mrs S cannot keep from smirking at this. Her rumpled laundry-pile face lifts slightly, and Betsy softens. Having never had a mother, when she imagines things like wrapping her arms around a woman's waist for a hug or lying in bed with a fever and having hot soup spooned into her mouth, it is Mrs S she pictures in the role. Not that either of those things has ever happened. Betsy doesn't need to be cared for.

'Come on, Mrs S. Just two hours. I'll make it up, I promise.'

'One hour, if you can clear all the vats and you get that insect out of here.'

'Puck isn't just an insect!' Betsy protests. Mrs S opens her mouth, but before she can speak again, Betsy continues. 'If I take Puck out, and I empty all the vats, can I go?' She purposely leaves out the bit about how long it might take.

Mrs S gives an exaggerated sigh. 'Fine, child. Though I can't imagine where you find to flit off to all the time.'

The truth is, Mrs S doesn't want to imagine. She doesn't care a jot what Betsy does, so long as she finishes her shift. And lucky, too, because Betsy wouldn't dare admit to grouchy old Mrs S that she, Effie and Teddy have spent every spare minute of the last week crowded around the stolen orrery, trying – and failing – to make it do something, anything, at their direction. Other than knowing that it stops momentarily if they disturb it by lifting it off a level surface and starts again when it readjusts or when they set it down, they are no closer to controlling it.

There are posters up now on hoardings all over Copperwell, offering a reward for information on the unlawful citizens who stole 'an item of historical importance' from the city's Observatory. None of them mentions what that item might be, and none have a particularly good description of Betsy or Effie to offer, beyond the fact that 'two girls' were witnessed at the scene. They do, however, detail 'a tall, strong lad, of perhaps fourteen, in possession of a canal workhorse and cart'. They even mention his 'dark, wavy hair'. The description has been fleshed out by the flute-like man who took Teddy's false delivery.

Though Teddy is not yet fourteen, the canal workers – remembering the night he and Briny Erwin unexpectedly disappeared before their shifts started – would know him immediately. And yet none of them has offered his name to the Constabulary. There is a loyalty amongst the canal workers which Betsy finds herself feeling strangely jealous of. Who would lie for her, beyond Effie and Teddy, if she were thrown in gaol? No one. Betsy Blue has not had anyone to rely on but herself since the day she left the poppy-seed drinkers behind and set off in search of a new life.

She finishes her tasks in record time then rushes upstairs to return Puck to her attic room and change into a dry shirt and pair of trousers. The Quartet is playing at The Stag's Antlers tonight, on the other side of the city, and Betsy and Teddy have agreed to meet Effie after their shifts. Effie, unable to escape school or home for a few days, had sent a note to Saltsburg's Laundry:

I've had an idea, about getting our friend O to act. I won't try it until I see you both.

Naturally, she had been too wise to write anything more obvious. It was possible the Constabulary might intercept a letter. But the mystery of it had left Betsy barely able to breathe with frustration. If Effie has puzzled out how to control the orrery, they are a huge step closer to figuring out what else it does, and what the woman on Wild Goose Way was talking about when she said that the Unified Government had shifted the shadows.

'Be good,' she tells Puck. 'I'll be back once we've worked all this out.'

Flinging somebody else's long red scarf around her neck, she races out of the attic, down the stairs, through the washing room, and out of the back door of Saltsburg's Laundry into a fresh flurry of snow.

CHAPTER NINE

The Sudden Arrival of Strangers

On the towpath beside the canal, Teddy tips back his head and pokes out his tongue to catch the eddying flakes of snow. He can't believe it's still falling. The city is abuzz with talk of how long it might continue. The pipework sings in its newly familiar, clear G sharp. They have checked with Effie: it is always a G sharp rather than the old F sharp now; the shift of tone seems to be permanent. The rest of Copperwell fails to notice: people are too busy working and hiding from the Constabulary and enjoying the snow to worry about something so small as the tone of the weather pipes. The barges bring more wood into the city – they're having a terrible time cutting and drying enough of it, Teddy hears – and smoke puffs from every chimney, and families out having snowball fights or snowman-building contests under the moon know that soon they will be able to huddle round a burning fire to warm again. It brings happiness, the snow – despite the initial fear which accompanied its strange and sudden arrival. It's a distraction from the drudgery, the lack of silver, the darkness. It illuminates the nights.

Teddy glances along the line of lights strung over the water and notices that the next barge carries another wood delivery.

'How can there be so many deliveries,' he says, 'when the city is short of almost everything? Do you wonder about that?'

At his side, Octavia shrugs. It seems to Teddy that all she does these days is shrug; it is all she has the energy for. Her eyes are sunk into the bones of her face, so that they appear dim and dark. Her head looks too large atop the thin stem of her neck. She had started off slight, but she is fast becoming skeletal. Teddy has been lucky these past months that he's had so many of his father's belongings to sell or exchange for hot broths or baked potatoes in the market. After all, what does Teddy need with a roomful of anything. He is only one boy. He is in need of no more than one bed, one chair, one warm blanket.

The two-roomed cottage Edward and his son had once occupied, directly behind the stables, had been a perk of the cab driver's job. When Edward died, Mr Hanberry – the owner of the stables, the cottage, and a very grand house on the Crescent besides – had informed Teddy that, though a new cab driver would be employed to replace Edward, the man would be permitted one room in the cottage. Teddy was to keep the other until he was fifteen and could make his own way, on the condition that he worked to put food on his own table. It was a shame he was not old enough to take the cab driver's job himself,

Mr Hanberry had said, but perhaps – at this point, he had grasped Teddy's hand in a shake and given it a squeeze – Teddy James was meant for another purpose.

Teddy had not paid particular attention at the time to Mr Hanberry's condolences. He had assumed the statement nothing more than a kindness. But now, he wonders.

Might his purpose be to help Octavia? Given that he has a warm room and enough food, he could do more than just put extra crates into her stack. He spends more time on Hangman's Alley and Berliner's Square than he does at home. Why not offer Octavia his room?

'Octavia?' he begins, slowly. He doesn't know how best to broach the subject. 'Where are you living?' Before the shadows shifted and The Order was passed into law, this would not have been an awkward question. Nobody felt the need to conceal their situations then. But since Prime Minister Bythesea started offering rewards to those inhabitants of Copperwell who were willing to spy on their neighbours, to report a shadow accidentally revealed and glimpsed, simple facts have been transformed into secrets.

'The towpath tunnel off Dragonfly Way,' Octavia returns, without looking at him.

He knows the towpath tunnel, of course. It is the very same tunnel Betsy and Effie used as an escape route the night they stole the orrery. It is one of the most unfortunate places in the whole city.

'Since when?'

Octavia shrugs again. 'I don't know. Two months. Three.'

He decides then, for certain, that he will let her have his room. She needs it more than he does. But he doesn't have chance to make the offer before the barge glides alongside them and the canal workers surge forward to begin lifting free the crates of wood. Dust rises around them and settles with the snow on their newsboy caps, their eyelashes, their shoulders. Above the dust and the canal lights and the chatter, bats flit through plum-purple clouds. The moon is not visible tonight. The canal is a gutter of deeper darkness cutting through Copperwell. Everything is half concealed, but Octavia's pale face glows – sad and pinched – from under her cap, and Teddy cannot stop looking at it.

And perhaps that is why he does not notice the figures – lumpen black outlines against the snow clouds – poised on the gunwhale of the barge. Or the fact that it is not Fergus who steers Frieda along the towpath, but another, bulkier man. Afterwards, when he has too much time to think, he will even suspect Octavia, imagining that she had seen what happened when they fled the Observatory through the tunnel and, in exchange for a good meal perhaps, had told the Constabulary exactly where they could find Teddy James – the boy so vaguely described on the posters.

But in truth, he knows that Octavia is not to blame. A minute later, and it might have been the bats which caused him to turn away from the barge. It might have been the anticipation of another barge chugging down the river. Really, the cause is of no significance. All that matters is that, as the barge passes, Teddy turns his back to it, and the moment he does, so two quick figures leap from it onto the bank and knock him to the ground.

He lands with a groan, winded and confused. He kicks, but his boots find only air. He throws his fists, but two strong hands seize his wrists and wrestle him still. Teddy won't submit, though. He flails his body like a fish dragged ashore. Teeth clenched, he flips and writhes. There are two more hands clamped around his ankles and, though he strains and twists, the man at his head and the man at his feet work together to roll him onto his back. Snow covers Teddy's face, freezing his lips, and his view now is of the sky: the purple clouds; the falling snowflakes; the spiralling bats. And, closer to, a man's head, concealed behind a black mask. And a man's wide body, hunched over him. And a man's fist, being drawn back, ready to strike him hard across the jaw.

Teddy hears the crack of his jawbone a split second after it seems to burst under the man's punch. He sees his newsboy cap, arcing away and landing in the snow some yards away. He feels the trickle of blood from his nose. But he does not lose consciousness and that, perhaps for the first time in his whole life, makes him feel brave.

Adrenalin keeps him fighting as the man at his feet shuffles up to kneel on his chest, and as something is pulled down over his head and he is blinded, and as more hands appear and lift him, kicking, twisting, heaving, grunting, through the air and dump him onto what he presumes is the back of a cart. As he thumps against the wooden slats, his hearing returns to him. All at once, he becomes aware of men shouting and scuffling, a horse's high-pitched whickering, the uneven drop of anxious hooves, wheels grinding over gravel, a girl screaming… Octavia! He holds his noisy breath to listen more carefully. Yes, it is Octavia, but her screams are growing fainter. Teddy is being driven away from her. They don't have her. They have left her on the riverside, where Erwin or Trudy will look after her.

Finally, he exhales. And that's when he feels it: the spear of pain thrusting again and again through his jaw; the contorted agony of having been bound with ropes, with his hands pinned behind him and his arms at the wrong angles; the torment, in his stomach and heart and throat and eyes, of true fear. He's going to gaol – he knows it. They're going to lock him up for the rest of his life. He's never going to inhale the stink of the canal again, nor put his palm to the hot neck of a horse, nor leave Copperwell in search of the Aur. He is never going to do his father's memory proud. Bellowing, he thrashes against his restraints, but this achieves little except to bump him pathetically along the wooden base of the cart. Teddy James, criminal. That's what they'll write on his gravestone. And he doesn't deserve it. He was only trying to shift the shadows back.

'Betsy!' he screams. 'Betsy!' Though he knows she will

not hear him. She will already be at The Stag's Antlers, listening to Effie play her trickling jazz. She will be smiling and singing along. Her life, and Effie's too, will continue without him. Tears prick behind his eyes at the thought, and though his face is hidden within a sack, he concentrates hard on swallowing them. He cannot let anyone see that he's been crying when he reaches gaol.

He opens his mouth to shout again, to channel all the energy he might waste crying into drawing attention to his predicament. He has, after all, been kidnapped. He needs anyone and everyone to notice. Drawing in the deepest of breaths, he summons all the fury he possesses, and—

With a jolt, something heavy meets with the back of the cart, tipping it up by five or six degrees. Teddy slides wildly towards the new weight and, as he clunks to a stop, he hears it speak.

'Teddy,' the voice says, and Teddy knows immediately who it belongs to.

CHAPTER TEN

The Black Fox

Betsy and Effie spill out of The Stag's Antlers and onto Inca Street, where another snowball battle is taking place. On one side, a group of five women gather up fistfuls of snow, pack it, and fire it furiously at the five men on the other side. The men return fire without reserve, and the women, when hit, shriek before bending to make another snowball. They are hampered, of course, by their skirt hoops, which cause their wool dresses to stick out about them by at least a yard. They look, Betsy thinks, like a posy of flowers. Each bloom is a different muted colour: green, violet, blue, crimson, yellow. The skirt hoops swing madly as the women bend down and spring up again. Ridiculous.

'Better if they'd worn some trousers,' Betsy says.

Effie sends her a sideways smile and says nothing. They have argued enough times about women wearing trousers – which Betsy insists is practical but which Effie has been brought up to view as an indicator of low social class – and Effie refuses to get into all that now. The canal workers, the chimney sweeps, the street sellers, the factory workers – they all wear trousers. But the schoolteachers, the Unified Government workers, the university scholars, the musicians of the Imperial Orchestra – they do not. Even the female servants on Berliner's Square would not think to don a pair. And Effie's father would pop an artery if he saw his daughter wearing them.

'I thought he'd be here by now,' Betsy continues, glancing up and down Inca Street. They are plenty of people, walking or standing outside pub doors to talk or playing in the snow – they've already forgotten their initial fear of it – but Teddy's lean, loping figure is not amongst them.

'Do you think we should go without him?' Effie asks.

Betsy bobs her shoulders. 'He can catch us up, I suppose.'

They begin the walk along Inca Street towards The Strand, which will eventually curve them towards Berliner's Square.

'Do you really think it will work, Ef?'

'I don't know,' Effie replies. 'But I noticed the change when I played a certain scale—'

'Which scale?'

'Do you know the scales?'

'No. But it might matter, some time.' Though she'd scoffed when Teddy had asked about the notes of the weather pipes, she'd been wrong to. Knowledge is something you ought to collect, whether you can see any immediate purpose for it or not. Knowing the name of this one scale might lead her to a second, a third – just as learning the name of her first constellation from *Chartford's Cyclopaedia* had led her to an understanding of so much of the night sky.

'G sharp harmonic minor,' Effie says.

'G sharp. The same as the snow music?'

Effie nods.

'Do you think that's important?' Betsy asks.

'It might be.'

They have reached the site of the snowball battle now, and shuffle closer to the buildings behind the gentleman's team – an apothecary, a milliner's shop – to walk by. There, they sidle past an older couple, arms linked, who cower under the onslaught of icy missiles. The man wears a top hat and carries a cane. He leans over his fur-coated wife and, past the bristles of his moustache, grumbles, 'Nothing but jazz and hijinks, this damn city.'

Effie nudges Betsy and Betsy smirks.

'It'd be a pretty miserable place otherwise, don't you think?' Betsy offers.

The top-hatted man answers with a flick of his eyebrows and nothing more, and the girls try not to laugh too hard until they are out of earshot. They pass the dressmaker's shop without glancing at the colourful velveteen gowns poised behind the pipework and the glass. On the other side of the window, a single lonely shop girl bends over her sewing, her head nodding with exhaustion.

'And the faster you played...' Betsy says, inviting Effie to continue with the explanation she had begun before The Quartet had started their performance.

Effie nods. 'The faster the planets rotated,' she confirms. 'I didn't think about the music at first. But I noticed them speeding up while I was practising my scales, so I slowed down, because I was distracted, and as I slowed they slowed too.'

'You're sure it was the music? Did anything happen? Anything else, I mean?'

'I don't know,' Effie replies. 'I sped up once more, to see if it really was happening, and it was, but only on that one scale – G sharp harmonic minor. The orrery responded to those notes specifically. But I couldn't keep doing it, speeding it up and slowing it down, in case it was having some effect. I didn't want...' She lowers her voice and glances about to check they are not being eavesdropped on. Betsy checks with her. '...to interfere with time again,' Effie continues, obviously satisfied that there is no one around to hear her. Betsy, however, raises her hand to shush Effie. Behind them Inca Street is busy with revellers, but in front of them, on the otherwise empty Strand, there is a movement. A soft pattering through the snow. A fleet shadow crossing beneath the lowered illumination of a gas lamp. A tail tip brushing the ground.

'A fox,' Betsy whispers. The fox pauses just inside the cone of light, its left forepaw lifted in curiosity. They have seen them rarely, and Betsy and Effie know that in Eurasia, the foxes are gingery red; in The Antart, they are pure white; in Amerikk, they are a light sandy brown; and in Africa…

'A black fox,' Effie breathes.

The fox turns its pointed nose towards them, its peaked ears flicking forwards. Amber eyes stare out from soft jet fur, considering whether the girls are friends or foes. Betsy slowly reaches out and touches Effie's wrist.

'Have you ever seen one?' she whispers.

'Never.'

'They're not supposed—'

'To be here.'

Betsy is thinking about what Teddy said the night the snow almost trapped them in The Blackened Lantern past dawn. Something from East Eurasia, something from The Antart…

The fox hears the disturbance before either Betsy or Effie. Whipping its head around, it flows away into the night. Betsy tries to keep her eyes on it, to track which direction it takes, but it disappears easily despite her best efforts. Her fingers are still around Effie's wrist, and Effie is using her free hand to drag at Betsy.

'Betsy! Quick! It's out of control.'

Betsy spins around and sees, finally, why the fox has fled. The snowball fight has been shattered. People are leaping back onto the pavements to either side of Inca Street, grasping each other tight against the weather pipes and yelling in fright. The mounded snow bursts up from the cobbles like fireworks as one of those shining new clockwork carts veers chaotically through the crowds towards Betsy and Effie.

The first clockwork carts appeared in the city perhaps three years ago, but no one much likes them, given that they scare the horses, and no one much uses them, knowing how unpredictable they can be in bad weather. They have been said to tip clean over in strong winds. And it is obvious, as this one hurtles along Inca Street, that the little vehicle cannot deal with the deep snow. Its central front wheel shakes as though it is about to pop loose. It jolts to left and right, swerving unpredictably. The cogs mounted on its high-sided metal panels click desperately as they grind faster and faster. Steam pumps out of the copper pipe which sticks up from the cart's roof and trails behind it like a flimsy white party streamer. The cart's fenders, which have been painted a rich cardinal blue, gleam under a layer of melting frost.

'Betsy!' Effie shouts, and Betsy realises then that she has been standing, motionless, right in the path of the approaching cart. She is sure, though – she leans forward, straining against Effie, and squints – that she recognises the man who is driving. Yes, she definitely does. The man behind the wheel hunches forward, his jaw tightly set and his eyes narrowed as he urges the vehicle to travel quicker. Snapping free of Effie's grip she takes off, running towards the careering vehicle.

'Erwin!' she calls back to Effie. 'It's Briny Erwin.'

She knows, somehow, by his erratic driving, by his wild expression, that something is badly wrong.

CHAPTER ELEVEN

Queen's Parade

When the girls are safely aboard the clockwork cart, tucked into the small leather seat behind Briny Erwin, and they have started their way across Copperwell in the opposite direction, away from Berliner's Square, Erwin's driving settles into a steadier rhythm. The cart stops slipping and sliding about in the snow and trundles quite comfortably back down Inca Street, past the Duke's Theatre on Holloway Road and its usual queue of fur-coated visitors, and onto smaller, darker streets: Rose Terrace; Limpet's Lane; Judge Marlow's Way. Here people live in closer quarters than they do in the rest of the city. Here, chamber pots are emptied into the gutters and children play barefoot in the streets. Here, there is always a dog barking and a door slamming and a just-drained ale glass being smashed. The copper pipes, cogs, wheels and whistles which front the buildings are patchy: in some places removed to be sold or put to other purposes; in other places, dulled to a jade green where they have not been kept clean and the Unified Government has refused to replace them. This is Swindlers' Quarter.

The snow music is more muted here, and Effie is

conscious of the noise the cart makes as it slows into narrower bends. Instinctively, their conversation has grown hushed.

'You're certain it was the Constabulary?' Betsy asks again.

It's a question she has repeated in every pause since Erwin started explaining what happened. Effie is impressed by the man's patience as he says, for the umpteenth time, 'I'm afeard so, Miss.'

'But…' At this, she trails off, looking sideways out at the buildings they pass. Effie thinks she is most likely hiding her tears.

'I'm not sure what we can do, Mr Erwin,' Effie offers.

'Just Erwin,' Erwin replies. 'Only name I claim. No Mr. I never earned any Mr. But, anyway, I know who you are, Miss. Didn't I see that house of yours that night? You're Chief Justice Hart's daughter – only one he has, far as I know.'

'That's right,' Effie answers, leaning forward to speak into Erwin's bulky shoulder. She trusts him. It was evident that Teddy did, the night they stole the orrery, and he has not betrayed them since, though he could quite easily have reported Teddy and taken his reward. Effie is certain he needs the silver, given that he wears the same stale burgundy woollen jumper and grey flat cap every time she sees him; and that he smells a little salty, like river water; and that he works on the canal, where the more desperate of Copperwell's poor tend to gather. 'I am Chief Justice Hart's daughter, and I am his only child, but I can't ask him to have Teddy freed. If I did that, I'd have to tell him about the orrery, and if he knew about that… We need to hold on to that orrery, Mr … Erwin. In secret. Until we can figure out how it works and what we should do with it. And I can hardly ask my father to have Teddy released by admitting his guilt. I don't know—'

'I do,' Betsy interjects. Her voice is thick, gluey, unsteady. She chews at her bottom lips between words.

'What?'

'Will you do anything?'

'For Teddy, yes.'

'Even if it might get you into trouble with your father?'

'If it would work, yes.'

'Then I say you just walk in there, bold as you like, and say "I'm Chief Justice Hart's daughter and I have come to find out why my good friend has been wrongfully imprisoned."'

From the front of the cart, Erwin speaks gently. 'It might be enough, Miss.'

Effie shakes her head. It wouldn't be enough. 'I could be anybody.'

'Oh no, Miss,' says Erwin. 'It's apparent just to listen to you speak that you're born of wealth – if you don't mind my saying. You're an intelligent girl. I reckon if you were to appear confident enough, they'd be too afeard to challenge you. After all—'

'They wouldn't want your father to come in your place,' Betsy finishes.

Erwin cocks his large head. 'True enough.'

'You want me to threaten the Constabulary,' Effie says. Her voice does not rise into a question; it is monotone, resigned. She knows what she must do to save Teddy from a lifetime rotting away in gaol. She must risk the position of the Hart household, for there is no way Chief Justice Hart could continue in his role as the reigning judge of Copperwell if Effie's deception were discovered.

'Not threaten,' Betsy insists. 'Not directly. Just … let them reach their own conclusions.'

There comes a sudden tightening at Effie's throat. Her breaths want to come more rapidly, but she won't succumb to hysteria. She won't let Teddy down. She lengthens her spine and sits up straighter on the tiny leather seat, trying to appear dignified despite the bumping of the cart. Retrieving Teddy, finding out what the orrery does, helping shift the shadows back – all this is bigger than Effie's own circumstances. Fear cannot come into it. She has a job to do.

Copperwell's solitary gaol sits at the furthest end of Queen's Parade, in Lawmakers' Quarter. It is an enormous, gothic building which looms over the Constabulary's headquarters, the solicitor's chambers, the inky offices where the *Copperwell Gazette* is written and printed, the city's largest church, and the Unified Government's Postal Services Bureau. The gaol's stonework is deep grey and dirty, and, with every glance at it, a person might see a different pinnacle, a higher flying buttress, an uglier gargoyle, a more impressive oculus. It was chosen, Effie supposes, to be imposing – so that those prisoners being escorted in through the arched wooden doors would feel themselves small and insignificant. She feels small now. It is a sensation she is unaccustomed to, given her broad hips, her strong legs and large hands; given, too, that she is the only child of one of Copperwell's wealthiest couples. It is not easy to feel insignificant when you have a private tutor, and a staff, and a specially designed music room all to yourself. It is impossible to feel invisible. That was why Effie had insisted that The Quartet play in masks – so that she could, for once, be anonymous. Now, as she steps through the vaulted entranceway of the gaol, and as a pair of squabbling crows yawp from one of the pinnacles above and moonlight greys her way, she cannot imagine why anyone would listen to her.

She reaches the kiosk besides the doors and, as she does so, a wooden panel is slid open with a bang. A small, wan chin and mouth appear. Overhead, the crows startle at the sudden noise and flap raucously away.

'Yes, Miss?' says a whining, from-the-nose voice. 'What can I do for you?'

Effie summons a deep breath and makes sure her shoulders are set back. 'I'm here on behalf of my father,' she replies, being careful to speak slowly and clearly. 'A friend of the family, a young man, has been brought in in error. My father asks that he be released immediately; he cannot come in person today.'

'Is that so?' The mouth cocks to one side. 'He sounds to be an important chap, your father. I wonder that he should be too busy to come himself, if this prisoner is so special to him.'

'I assure you he is,' Effie says. 'Too busy by far, I'm afraid.'

'Hmm,' says the sneering mouth. 'And the prisoner's name?'

'Teddy. That is, Theodore James.'

'And your name, Miss?'

At this, Effie forces herself to pause. She needs the guard to be listening intently when she next speaks, so that he will realise the full weight of her words. She counts to five in her mind.

'Euphemia Hart,' she says finally.

Immediately the guard's manner changes. There comes a shuffling, and then the wooden panel is opened fully to reveal a sunken, narrow face, housing a pair of darting blue eyes.

'Hart,' he says. 'I'm sorry, Miss Hart. I didn't realise it was you. I couldn't quite see you, you know, from...' He licks his lips, indicates the gap in the front of the kiosk with a bony finger. 'Not that I would have known you right away. Perhaps not. Although I have seen your photogram in the newspaper a time or two. He's very proud of you, your father, isn't he? Of your musicianship? I read you were on your way to the Academy.'

'I decided against it,' Effie answers. 'I thought it better

to remain here, where I might be more help to my father. I am to train under him.'

'Is that so?'

Effie nods, not daring to test the lie on her tongue for a second time. She hardly knows how she mustered it so fluidly.

'Well, well,' the guard says. 'Wouldn't that be something? A female Chief Justice!'

'If I prove my worth, of course,' Effie replies, imagining that the self-deprecation will endear her to this man, when what she really wants to say is, 'Why shouldn't there be a female Chief Justice? In fact, why hasn't there been one before?' They are the questions Betsy would ask.

'Of course, of course,' the man mutters. 'Listen, what was your friend's name again?'

'Theodore James.'

'Right you are. Wait there a moment.'

And then he is on his feet, disappearing into the depths of the gaol, and Effie tries not to cry with relief that she has not yet been ushered inside this monstrous building. She risks a sideways glance towards the spot, further down Queen's Parade, where Briny Erwin has stopped the clockwork cart. He and Betsy sit inside it still, watching. She can feel their eyes, though she cannot see them in any detail. The cart and Erwin are bulky black shapes in the darkness. Betsy is completely concealed. Effie fights the urge to turn and run back to them, away from the hideous gaol and the cold, creeping feeling it leaves around her neck; away from the fear she has for Teddy, trapped inside; away from her own deception. To keep herself from moving, she imagines her way up and down the melodic minor scales: C minor, F minor; she has always preferred the softer sound of the flats to the sharps.

Perhaps five minutes later the guard returns. First, Effie hears his footsteps, light and languid. Then his torso appears, framed in the kiosk opening. Finally, he ducks into view.

'Sorry, Miss Hart. We've no Theodore James here.'

Something inside Effie – something heavy but hollow – plunges. He has to be there. Where else could they have taken him? Unless it wasn't the Constabulary at all. Hadn't Betsy kept asking, thinking it could have been… Who?

'Teddy, then. Perhaps he said his name was Teddy.'

The guard shakes his thin, equine head.

'When did you say he was brought in?'

Effie concentrates hard on the words. Her tongue is thick and honey-stuck. 'Tonight.'

'I can't help you then, I'm afraid, Miss.'

'But…'

'No one brought in tonight under the age of forty, Miss. He's a young chap, isn't he, your fellow?'

Effie nods mutely.

'Then he ain't here,' the guard concludes. 'You must be mistaken. Although, I'm sure that's a good thing. You wouldn't want your friend in here, Miss. Not for a minute.'

Betsy is already clambering out of the clockwork cart as Effie reaches it.

'He's not there, is he?' she hisses. 'I knew it. The Constabulary would have made a scene about taking him. The same way they did with the woman on Wild Goose Way. They weren't quiet about that, were they? They didn't sneak. It's not their style.'

'Girls!' Briny Erwin warns in a low growl. 'Back inside, please. Discuss this while we're moving.'

Betsy and Effie climb obediently into the cart. Erwin grabs the little gold handle in his roughened paw and winds it around and around until the cart puffs into life, then steers them in the opposite direction along Queen's Parade, leaving the gaol behind. The snow swirls thicker and faster. The snow music chimes out a muted G sharp, its intensity softened by the lowering clouds. It's lucky for Effie, Betsy and Erwin that the clouds have dropped so heavily over the city, for their weight is extending the night. Though dawn is approaching, and the streets are now grey and deserted rather than black and busy, they might steal another hour before they must go indoors and wait the day away.

They drive in silence, none of them sure where they are going, but all equally keen to get as far away from Copperwell Gaol as possible. Betsy presses her forehead to the side window of the cart and stares out at the buildings they pass: their pipework gleams all the brighter in the half-light. The gas lamps are turned down so far that they are only tiny sparks, like fireflies caught in glass jars. At first glance Copperwell is beautiful, but Betsy knows better than many about the ugliness that beauty conceals. She has been an orphan for so long, she cannot even remember her parents' names. And now Teddy, an orphan too, the closest thing she has to a brother, is lost. What if they never find him? What if—

'Stop!' she barks. 'Stop, Erwin. Please.'

Betsy and Effie grasp the sides of the seat as Erwin swings the cart to a halt. He spins around to face them. 'What is it? What's wrong?'

Betsy shakes her head and lifts a forefinger to her lips. When Effie and Erwin nod, agreeing to remain silent, she uses her pointed finger to direct their attention out through the window and towards a gate which leads into one of the city's mapped gardens. There, the fox sniffs at the ground, checking the spaces between the iron railings, its ears twitching at sounds inaudible to the humans who watch it, its tail tip flicking as though it is a sensor for approaching danger. Betsy wonders at why it has not scarpered at the sound of the cart, but she is glad it hasn't. She had wanted a better look at it.

'A black fox,' Erwin mutters under his breath. 'Never thought I'd see such a thing. What do you suppose it's doing here?'

'I don't know,' Effie answers. 'But it's not the only—'

'First there were the mantises,' Betsy interjects. 'Then the snow. Then the fox. And—'

'Slow down, Miss,' Erwin says. 'I haven't the first clue what you're prattling about. Firstly, what's a mantises?'

In whispers, as they watch the fox inch along the railings, snuffling and then lifting its head to check up and down the street and then pawing at the ground, Betsy and Effie take turns to explain to Erwin about how the arrival of the mantises and the relentless snowfall have led them to the beginnings of a theory – as yet incomplete – that oddities from all the four continents are making their way to Copperwell. Sighting a black fox, only ever before seen in Africa, had been another clue. But of what? They hadn't slotted it all together yet, they admitted, but there must be some link…

'Look!' Effie points to a spot, a little further along the pavement, where a second vulpine face is peering out from between the railings. The second fox undulates through the iron bars and the two touch noses briefly, before bowing into a game: their amber eyes flash in the early morning light as they spring up on all four legs, pounce, tumble over and around each other, open their jaws like scissors and pretend to bite. Their tails swish. They appear both completely at ease and entirely out of place. And thin – as though they have been without sufficient food for weeks.

'Do you think they'll stay?' Betsy asks Erwin. Despite all her long-held beliefs about the incompetence of adults, Briny Erwin has earned her admiration. He wants to find Teddy as much as she and Effie. She values his opinion.

'Haven't the first clue, Miss. But I do hope so.'

'Why do you say that, Erwin?' Effie asks.

He sighs. 'Well, I just think… Haven't you noticed how… I don't know quite how to say it. But I think that, for some time now, Copperwell has been dying.'

'Dying?' Effie's eyes grow rounder.

'In a manner of speaking. Everybody working harder and harder, but growing ever poorer. And then the shadows. And being forced to live in darkness. It doesn't seem the right direction for a city to be going to me, Misses, that's all. But then again, I ain't never been smart enough to know a sniff about politics.'

'How would a pair of foxes help with any of that?' Betsy asks.

Erwin gives a heavy shrug. 'They're new life, I suppose.'

'Like Puck,' Betsy says to Effie. 'New life.'

And the repetition of the word sparks something in Effie's mind.

'Erwin,' she says. 'Take us to Berliner's Square, please.'

'Of course, Miss.' Erwin turns back towards the front of the cart, grabs for the little handle. 'It's been a long night, an upsetting one, and we can always try again tomorrow—'

'No. It's not that I want to go home. I just… I have an idea. About where Teddy might be.'

CHAPTER TWELVE

A Developing Plan

In the kitchen at the rear of number eight, Berliner's Square, Millicent Shaw, the kitchen girl, hums to herself over the crash of the tap as she runs scalding water into the huge ceramic sink and drops tankards and dishes into the steam. Though she is nearly twenty years old, Millicent is slight and short, and she can hardly see over the taps and out through the window before her. Or rather, the angle she sees out at shows her more of the sky than of the back yard. As such, she does not notice the back gate easing open, nor the three figures who slip stealthily through it. She knows nothing of the fact that she is being watched until a missile slams into the glass and sets the windowpane rattling. Shrieking, she drops the tankard she is holding, then winces as it meets the edge of the worktop and cracks, sending shards of china all across the kitchen tiles. Twisting the tap closed, she tiptoes over the splintered china towards the door and wrenches it open. The cold dawn air makes her breathless, but she swallows hard and stands tall, determined not to cough or shiver.

'Who's there?' she calls. The apple which had hit the

window spins across the flagstones, red and dense as a heart. 'Answer me fast, or I'll call the Mr.' Her hand is a claw around the doorframe. She is ashamed that her breath is trembling from her. 'All right, then, but I should warn you, the Mr here—'

'Millie!'

Millicent glances about, trying to locate the whispering voice.

'Millie. It's me. Listen – I need you to be quiet.'

This time, given more of a chance to trace the sound, Millicent follows it to the woodstore. In the rising grey light, she can just make out the bundled shape of Miss Hart, crouched behind the slatted structure. Miss Hart, and somebody else, too. Somebody large.

'Miss!' Millicent hisses. 'Are you all right?'

'Of course,' Effie whispers back. 'I just need to know, before I come in, is my father at home?'

'No.' Millicent gives a rapid shake of her head.

'My mother?'

'No, Miss.'

'Mrs Steckler?'

Mrs Steckler is the housekeeper: a looming, glassy woman whom Effie wouldn't dare anger.

'No, Miss,' Millicent answers.

Effie exhales properly for the first time in many hours, then stands and scuttles across to the kitchen door. She is followed closely by Betsy and Briny Erwin, who strides after them at a strange forward hunch, as though trying

– and failing – to make himself smaller. When she nears Millicent, Effie reaches out to give her arm a squeeze.

'It's nothing to worry about, Millie,' Effie insists. 'It's just … I've been planning a surprise, and didn't want them to know I'd…'

'No need to explain, Miss,' Millie answers. 'And no need to keep whispering, neither. Ain't nobody here but me. Mr Bellamy left over an hour since.'

Mr Bellamy, the butler, is so old and slow that Effie wouldn't have worried if he'd seen her stroll directly into her father's study – which is exactly what she intends to do. Bellamy has retained his position at the house because the Harts are too kind to retire him. Effie knows that whenever he speaks to her father he takes so long to stutter through each sentence that Chief Justice Hart has lost interest and moved on before Bellamy has made his point.

'Millie,' Effie replies. 'Would you mind putting the kettle to boil, please? We'll be going back out shortly and it's terribly cold. We could use some flasks.'

'You're going back out, Miss Hart?' Millie replies, her eyes popping at the thought. 'But … it can't be more than half hour until dawn. You'll be caught.'

'Don't worry. We're not going far.' Effie's mind is whirring now with realisation after realisation, connection after connection. Ideas are slotting and turning into each other as desperately as the cogs that power Erwin's clockwork cart. She needs to remain at home for as long as it takes her to find the file in her father's study which relates to the U.G.G.P.P. – a place she has known about, vaguely, forever, but which she has never had any great need to think about. Once she has the file, she will have Erwin drive them back to Hangman's Alley, where they will be able to discuss her plan without being disturbed. Mrs S won't question Betsy's whereabouts or mischiefing unless she misses a shift. And in Betsy's attic room, they will be able to consult *Chartford's Cyclopaedia* and put Effie's new theory to the test.

She gives Millie a reassuring nod, then leads Betsy and Erwin through the hushed hallway towards the music room. Pushing open the door, she stops to whisper instructions to them. 'I need to find some paperwork,' she explains. 'Erwin, would you be kind enough to pack the orrery carefully back into its crate. Pack it tight, so that the arms can't move. Betsy, I need you to get my double bass into a case, any case. Then go back through to the kitchen. Don't try to hide what you're doing. We don't have time. Just take the orrery and the double bass back through to the kitchen and I'll meet you there with the papers we need.'

With silent nods of agreement, Betsy and Erwin step into the music room and busy themselves with their tasks. Effie turns and runs down the hallway, up one carpeted flight of stairs, along the landing and in through the unlocked door of her father's study. The air inside is undisturbed, heavy. This is Jeremiah's private space. He has never barred Effie from entering – there has never been any need to keep secrets from her – but she has always understood that the files, documents, contracts and textbooks stored in this room are deeply important, not to be touched. The study is no playroom. She finds herself tiptoeing, therefore, over the plush burgundy carpet towards the huge captains' desk, her breath held. If he comes home now, what will she tell him? She'll have no choice but to explain everything, she supposes, and what then? Her father is employed by the Unified Government. He couldn't accuse them of manipulating time. And that, Effie concludes, is exactly what they have done: they have found a way to alter the way the orrery moves and, in doing so, they have confused the workings of the planet. It is the best way to explain the still-falling snow, the sudden arrival of the orchid mantises, the starving black foxes who have travelled so far from their proper home – across oceans on steamships perhaps? When Betsy had said, offhandedly, that maybe they should look out for something unexpected from Africa, none of them could have imagined this. The concept is huge, too big for Effie to voice. She thinks perhaps that she'll need to wait for some other clue – a confused creature stumbled all the way from Amerikk, or an abrupt change in the weather – before she is brave enough to risk explaining aloud what is clattering around her brain.

But on the other hand, she cannot possibly delay. Not if Teddy is where she thinks he is.

She slides out drawer after drawer, flicks through

folder after folder. She grows increasingly frantic as the glow of lilac morning light spreads through the window. Her eyes flicker over pages of impenetrable text. And then she glimpses it – the title she has been searching.

The Unified Government Gaol for Political Prisoners.

She snatches up the folder, stuffs it under her arm, and flees Jeremiah Hart's study, leaving the drawer and the door wide open behind her.

CHAPTER THIRTEEN

A Rescue

'I've just never seen anything like it,' Briny Erwin grunts, leaning forward again to gently poke at Puck, who is resting in his potted plant. Puck responds by lifting his front legs and pincering them around the tip of Erwin's pointed forefinger. Erwin emits a low, rumbling sound which Betsy assumes is a laugh. 'It looks like a flower with eyes… And it flies?'

'When the fancy takes him,' Betsy answers.

They have been huddled in Betsy's attic room above Saltsburg's Laundry since dawn, pouring over *Chartford's Cyclopaedia* and, without quite finding the answers they are seeking, exchanging theories about the orrery. They would sooner be having these discussions on their way through the city, but they have to wait for darkness to fall. Thankfully, since it is January and snowing constantly, the daylight hours have been short and dim, and now, at four o'clock, Betsy, Effie and Erwin are almost ready to squeeze into the clockwork cart and make their trundling way towards Stag's Circus, on the westernmost edge of Lawmaker's Quarter. The orrery and the double bass have already been stowed beneath the small leather passenger seats and take up so much room that when the girls get in, they will have to sit with their knees pulled up to their chins.

'Bring him with you,' Effie says. She has been pacing back and forth on the other side of Betsy's bed for upwards of half an hour.

'Puck?' Betsy asks.

Effie nods: a strange, rapid nod that's nothing like her usual way of moving.

'Why?'

'We might not be able to come back, Bets.'

Betsy considers the little mantis, perched in his usual place. She's never been responsible for anything but herself until now – not a cat, nor a spine-hog, a dog, nor a hawker owl – and though she wouldn't voice the thought, she does love Puck. 'He'll be all right for a while. He doesn't need much and—'

'We might not be able to come back, ever,' Effie insists.

Betsy pushes herself up off the bed to stand. 'Ever? But…' She is not so attached to living in a dusty attic above a laundry, leaning for hours into vats of steaming water to scrub filth from other people's garments and being shouted at by Mrs S, that she would mourn the place. The sole thing to miss here is Madam Bee's soft black fur and recumbent attitude. Everything else – her hopes, her independence, her learning – she can take with her. She has always ensured that she remain a portable kind of person, so that whenever opportunity came, she could take it. But surely

Effie couldn't leave Berliner's Square forever. Her mother and father, Mr Bellamy and Millie, even Mrs Steckler, care more for Effie than anyone ever has for Betsy. Effie cannot abandon that, or The Quartet, or her studies. 'Nobody ever leaves Copperwell. And you… Your parents, Ef.'

Effie's mouth trembles into a sad smile. Tears brighten her eyes, but she manages to keep from breaking into a sob. 'I've stolen from the Unified Government, fabricated official business at the gaol, taken confidential paperwork from my father, the Chief Justice!' Disbelief lends laughter to her voice as she counts her crimes off on her fingers. 'We're about to break Teddy out of a gaol most people don't even know exists. At the least, I'll have lost my father his job. At the worst… We can't be sure, can we, exactly what will happen when we speed up the orrery? The damage we'll cause…'

'Seems to me you ain't got much of a choice, either way, Misses,' Briny Erwin offers into the new silence. His voice is as slow and even as the plod of a trusty cab horse. 'That woman on Wild Goose Way, she wouldn't have let the Constabulary haul her off if this wasn't truly important. And we've all noticed the changes happening around here. You girls are right – there ain't nothing natural about it. And, the posters asking for information about "the boy who stole from the observatory" are everywhere now. They're calling him an enemy of the Unified Government, our Teddy. Seems to me that the sooner you get yourselves away from Copperwell, the better. The Constabulary is more ruthless now than I've ever known them, Misses. There'll be no safe place for Teddy here now.'

'You're right, but…' Betsy pauses, realising the truth of the words she spoke just minutes earlier. She repeats them, slowly. 'Nobody ever leaves Copperwell… Do they, Erwin?' She fixes her attention on the older man's hooded eyes. How old is he? Thirty-five? Forty? He must know someone who has left, travelled to one of the other three continents, or to another country within Eurasia. Parts of Eurasia are vast and wild, but there are cities, too, and coastal towns and farming communities and canal dwellers and mountain clans – they've learnt about them, vaguely and mostly through rumour – and all of that is separated from the Britannic Isles by the narrowest waterway. Just as Copperwell is isolated from the rest of the Britannic Isles by just the canal. And yet there are no regular boats out of the city.

'The ferry crossings were stopped when I was a lad, Miss,' Erwin answers.

'But why?'

'It was said the rest of the country had grown too unsettled, too dangerous, to travel through freely,' Erwin answers with a heavy shrug. 'Copperwell being cut off by the canal made it a place of safety. Leastways, that's how the Unified Government framed it.'

Betsy leans forwards. She is aware that Effie has finally stopped pacing. 'Did everyone accept it easily?'

Erwin shakes his weighty head. 'Not at first,' he replies.

'But then I suppose that, given enough time and enough persuasion, people will accept pretty much anything.'

Betsy turns to grasp Effie's arm. 'It's just like the shadows!' In her excitement, she is speaking in a hissed whisper. 'First, they put a border around the city without consulting anyone, then they persuaded people that it was for their own safety. Now they're limiting the time we can spend in the outside world by shaming us into hiding our shadows. And, really, who ever thought it was a bad thing, when the shadows first shifted? Nobody was trying to hide them until The Order was passed, were they? It's the consequences of revealing them everyone's afraid of, not the revelation itself. The four gods, Ef, they're turning Copperwell itself into one big gaol.'

Effie takes a deep in-breath, as if she is about to speak, but stops. Her father is an employee of the Unified Government, and she knows he would have no involvement in a scheme like this. He became the Chief Justice to do good. Besides, she cannot understand why they would do it? What benefit is there, to trapping a city?

'It makes sense, Miss,' Erwin offers, with a sad cock of his head, when Effie manages nothing more than to stand with her mouth opened like a fish. 'Look at how it's been these last few years. People all about getting poorer and poorer, but the Unified Government still having all them fancy buildings to keep and warm and staff, still having their ceremonies and their posh dinners. There's only so much wealth in any city, and the Unified Government won't have been willing to give up their share to put dinner on the tables of the likes of Briny Erwin or Betsy Blue.' He thrusts a finger at his own chest, and then in Betsy's direction. 'You can't drain silver from the poorest without risking revolution, though, can you? So why not gradually take a freedom away here, a right away there? Soon enough, you've got a population without the strength or the unity to revolt.'

Control. Of course! It's been about control from the start. All anyone's shadows were revealing was their truest selves, and what's wrong with that?

'Then I don't ever want to come back,' Betsy says, crossing her arms tightly over her chest and jutting out her chin. 'I don't want to live somewhere like that.' She strides towards Puck's potted plant, scoops the little creature up, settles him in the crown of her curly hair, then snatches her small-brimmed hat from where it hangs on the mirror frame and carefully places it over him. Next, she retrieves *Chartford's Cyclopaedia* and shoves the cumbersome weight of it into her old leather satchel. Immediately she realises it's too heavy, removes it again with a sigh, and packs a couple of pairs of trousers, some warm wool socks, a shirt, and two knitted jumpers. Then she glances around the room. 'That's it,' she says. 'I'm ready. Shall we go?'

It takes nearly two hours for them to reach the corner of Stag's Circus – a long, crowded street, which curves gradually away into smallness, like the whorl of a shell.

The buildings are not so impressive as those on Queen's Parade, though mostly they stand four storeys high, with grand front steps and their very own gas lamps. They remind Betsy of the houses on Berliner's Square, but whereas those houses are built from pale stone, the stone here is the deeper grey of the sky on a rainy day. The trees which line the pavement reach into the clouds like knotted finger bones. A shudder crawls up the back of Betsy's neck. She cannot imagine Teddy, with his bouncing lope and his emerald scarf and his bright brown eyes, here, in this dull, dark place. She thinks of a sunflower, dragged from the earth and tossed into a rain-filled gutter to shrivel to nothing.

Briny Erwin slows the cart and they trundle along, each peering out through the windows in silence to read the carved name plaques mounted beside the entrance doors of each building. Havill Hall, Sunderland House, Cantonville Manor. Perhaps deliberately, they give no indication of the business being conducted within. What did they expect – to discover a sign helpfully directing them to the Unified Government's Gaol for Political Prisoners? Wherever Teddy is being held, it will be hidden. They shouldn't have even known to come to Stag's Circus were it not for Effie's father and his secret documents. So deep is Betsy's dread now that she feels cold, itchy, as though her limbs are nothing but pins and needles.

Except for the puffing of the clockwork cart, the street is quiet and almost empty. On the opposite pavement, a lone man strides after the tap of his cane, his face invisible beneath his hat, his coat collar pulled up around his neck. Betsy holds her breath as he passes them by without a glance. The snow clouds are so thick that no glimmer of moonlight peeks through. The world is flat and monochrome, except for the low flicker of the gas lamps and the occasional overhead flit of a bat disturbed from its slumber.

'We're never going to work out which building it is,' Betsy whispers.

'I think we should just do it,' Effie replies.

'Here?'

In the gloom, Betsy studies Effie's eyes: they gleam like dark pearls. She is scared. Scared but determined. Just like Betsy.

Effie points down the street: beyond a closed-up cocoa and pastry cart, in the umbra beyond the nearest lamp, is the turning into a narrow side alley. The blackness seems denser down there. Betsy nods.

'Erwin. Would you help us with the orrery?'

Erwin gives his usual weighty nod, and the three proceed at length to shuffle the unwieldy crate out of the cart, onto the pavement, and into the alley. Betsy checks up and down the street again and again, but no one appears. They duck into the shadows, ease the orrery free of the crate, upend the crate, secure it by packing the mounded snow around it, and, at length, settle the orrery on top of it. It sits then at waist height, where they can readily observe its movements.

'Do you think it will happen quickly?' Betsy asks, as Effie unfastens the case of her instrument and draws the enormous double bass free. Betsy often wonders at Effie being able to manipulate the thing, given its size and weight, but then she has always known Effie to be powerfully strong. She might have been a muscle woman at the Duke's Theatre, should the fancy have taken her.

'I think so. It seemed to, before. Though I wasn't looking out for it then, of course. We'll just have to wait and see.' She runs a block of yellow resin up and down the length of her bow with thoughtless expertise. 'Are you ready?'

Betsy shrugs. 'Suppose so.'

'Erwin?'

'I'd better keep a watch out, I reckon,' he replies, before lumbering to the corner where the alley opens onto Stag's Circus and leaning against the frozen wall in as casual a manner as he can.

He needs a pipe, Betsy considers, to make him look truly unremarkable – a chap out for a smoke – but it will have to do. She fixes her eyes on the orrery, which is just beginning to swing back into its usual rotations after the indignity of being packed into the crate again. The indignity, Betsy thinks: a funny way to think about an object, and yet it seems to fit. The orrery gives off an air of disgruntlement as it feels again for its rhythms, its jewel-bright planets glinting through their orbits. The clockwork gives off its familiar, comforting whir and click. And that is all Betsy hears as she stares at the object, the whir and click, the whir and click, until Effie drags her bow over the string of her double bass and entices it to sing along the G minor scale. It seems to Betsy that the orrery falters then. That, if it were an animal, it would have peaked its ears to listen. For a fraction of a second, it actually pauses. Then, with renewed intent, it resumes its rotations and, within a minute or two, begins to speed up.

'It's working, Ef,' Betsy breathes.

Effie had explained her theory to Betsy and Erwin over and over in Betsy's attic room. The orrery, she said, wasn't *showing* the motions of the planets, it was *controlling* them. And music was the key. A certain sequence of notes and the orrery could be manipulated. And the Unified Government had discovered that. With the orrery, and all the other instruments held in the Observatory, they would be able to alter the orbits of the planets around the sun, tilt the world a degree further on its rotational axis, move the moons. They might even be able to change gravity! They had interfered with the natural order of the world. Meddled. That was why the snow wouldn't stop, and the black foxes had appeared. In trying to control life, they had attracted new life. *But why?* Betsy had asked. That, Effie hadn't worked out yet, but she knew she was right.

'Look...' Effie continues exploring the notes of the scale, but rolls her eyes up to indicate the snow, which is already falling thicker and faster.

'Keep playing,' Betsy says. 'Quicker.'

Effie obliges. A new layer of snow is settling itself on the gleam of her hair, on her tweed coat.

'Quicker again,' Betsy urges.

This time, it is the wind that responds: suddenly the snow is being tossed about in every direction by a gale which rattles noisily down the alley. Betsy presses a palm over her hat, to keep Puck safe, and tips back her head. Above, between the rooftops and the low clouds, bats hurtle on the unexpected gusts, shrieking in terror. Hold on, Betsy thinks. Here we go.

By the time the Constabulary attempt to march the midnight prisoners along Stag's Circus, Copperwell is in chaos. The storm sweeps into the city from who knows where: snow turns to sleet then rain; the rain ceases and the air crisps; the wind whips and wails. The moon hauls itself above the clouds, then dips between them again. The sun flashes out and in with the rapidity of lightning strike. People scream as windows smash under momentary attacks of violent hail. Chimneys are toppled and crash to the pavements, where their stones smash and shoot between the hooves of skittering horses. Cab horses take flight and clatter over the cobbles, whickering in terror. Crows and pigeons tussle for shelter along the window ledges. Dove hawks wheel above, stealing the opportunity to snatch up easy prey. The Constabulary thunder along Stag's Circus, frantically blowing their whistles. Prisoners roar as truncheons are brought down against their backs and legs and heads. Erwin has backed down the alley a little way and stands now braced to fill the space from wall to wall, in case any passerby should charge in Betsy and Effie's direction. And Effie plays through it all. She has entered into conversation with the orrery, and it answers her music with spin after spin after spin, more readily than it ever must have for the Unified Government, for the change has never been this dramatic before. Faster and faster it goes, until Venus and Jupiter and Mars are whirs of sparking colour.

The weather shifts again and an enormous moon lights the sky overhead with a silver-white glow. The wolf moon, Betsy thinks. But, no: they have already seen the year's wolf moon. And it is not time yet for February's snow moon. How then… Unless… They cannot be moving time so quicky! They cannot have spun through a full year!

'Effie,' Betsy says. 'Stop now. It's enough.'

Effie draws her bow more slowly through each note, gradually easing the orrery with her. Immediately, the planets begin to calm. The weather settles. The moon remains fixed above them. On Stag's Circus, however, shouts and thuds can still be heard: the chaos is continuing, as they had hoped it would. Sneaking towards the end of the alleyway, Betsy, Effie and Erwin peer around the wall and watch as a gang of prisoners, free from the Constabulary's control now, dance along the street. Some leap into clumsy pirouettes. Some skip back and forth like children just freed from a classroom.

Some grab each other's hands and whirl around as though they are performing the waltz. And, under the glare of the full moon, their shadows are clearly visible: younger versions of some prisoners cower, frightened, on the cobbles; larger versions of others square up to nothing, ready for a fight; some shadows remain completely still as their owners spin through their invented routines, while others pace back and forth like animals trapped in a cage. They cannot move apart entirely from the humans who cast them. They remain connected, always, at the feet. But they are, undeniably, distinct. They are revelations. Betsy understands then, for the first time, both why the shifted shadows are so feared and why they are so beautiful. It is because they do not allow anyone to pretend; they do not permit a person to hide from themselves. They are made from truth.

'If the Unified Government has been doing this all along,' Betsy breathes, 'how haven't we noticed? There've been no storms like that one, no days or night sped up to last less than a minute. That was scary, Ef.'

Effie shrugs. 'Perhaps they did it more gradually. Or used a different instrument. Perhaps something about the room it was stored in quietened the effect. I don't know.' She ducks her head around the alley wall again. 'Do you think it will be enough of a distraction?'

'It'll have to be.'

'I'll get everything back into the cart,' Briny Erwin assures them. 'You two go on and find him, won't you.'

And, with a quick clasp of hands, they take off running onto Stag's Circus, past the rioting prisoners, and in the same direction as the one constable who, deciding that those men they have paraded through the city in shame are lost to them now, has seen fit to aim for the relative safety of his workplace. It is helpful to Betsy and Effie that this particular constable is reckless and noisy in his panic. They hurry closer behind him than they had supposed they would be able, racing from tree trunk to lamp post to tree trunk and keeping him all the while in their sights. They do not glance down at each other's shadows as they move in and out of the moonlight. There is no need. They know each other. Betsy knows that Effie is bolder and braver than might be suggested by her fancy clothes and the low angle she holds her chin at whenever she is not playing music. Effie knows that Betsy's showy confidence will be more delicate and thoughtful, faltering even, in silhouette. Tonight, though, they are both made strong and fleet and fearsome by their love for Teddy. As they dash up a steep set of front steps behind the frightened constable, their shadows are giants.

When the constable flings open the entrance door of Grenville Manor and flies through, Betsy and Effie are right behind him. Feeling someone on his tail, he moves quicker, opening door after door and failing to secure any one of them behind him, such is the depth of his terror. Betsy and Effie chase him further into the building, which seems to them a labyrinth of dark hallways and windowless rooms they might never find their way back out of. When the constable takes a sharp right, disappears through a heavy door, and slams it shut with a thunderous thud, they keep running. Increasingly, they pass constables who are rushing out of offices and holding cells, pulling on their coats and helmets, clutching for their whistles and truncheons. Their eyes bulge when they spot two girls, rushing through the hallways, but they haven't the time to stop and question them. Two young girls pose far less of a risk than fifty midnight prisoners loose in the street.

As the building empties, Betsy begins to shout. 'Teddy?' she hollers. 'Teddy!' And between the beats of her feet against the tiles, she hopes to hear her own name shouted in response. But there is only the echo of hers and Effie's footsteps and the panting of their breath.

They reach the top of a staircase and hesitate. Narrow stone steps curl down into darkness. There are no gas lamps down there.

Betsy raises her eyebrows in Effie's direction.

'They have to be keeping them down there,' Effie whispers. 'They have to. Don't you think?'

Betsy nods.

'Then let's go.'

Effie grasps Betsy's wrist and begins the descent, but Betsy does not move. The skin at her wrist burns as Effie accidentally drags at it. Two steps down, Effie stops.

'What is it?'

'Don't know… It just…'

Effie's eyebrows wrinkle into one tight length of twine. Her big, round eyes can hide nothing. She is disappointed and angry. 'Teddy might be down there,' she says, and her voice is no different, but Betsy knows. She can feel a hot wave of fury pulsing from Effie. She considers the staircase again: it is nothing much more than a hole cut into the floor; it undoubtedly leads to a basement.

'Teddy and what else?' Betsy hisses. She is imagining walls running with damp; rats with gleaming eyes and quick tails scuttling in wet corners; the groans of men who, confined to darkness, have gone steadily insane. There might even be bodies down there, chained to the walls and starved to skeletons. A shudder spreads across Betsy's back.

'What does it matter?' Effie insists.

'It doesn't.' Of course it doesn't. It's Teddy. She would leap from a clifftop to save Teddy or Effie. Betsy shakes out her arms and legs, as though she is preparing to fight in a boxing match. She tilts her head from side to side. 'No. It doesn't.' Her feet are heavy, but she coaxes one off the floor; she takes one forward step.

But she is prevented from having to force herself to go any further, because before she and Effie can proceed down into the dark, there comes a sound. A fast, rhythmic thumping. It is reminiscent of the sound of an army on a march. You could almost count time with them: one-two-three-four, one-two-thr—

'There's somebody coming up!' Betsy breathes, hauling Effie back up the top two steps. 'Come on.'

Hands locked, they hurtle a short distance along the hallway, and, finding a doorway to hide in, press themselves against the polished wood of a windowless door. The sustained thumping is interrupted by voices as people spill out from the staircase and into the hallway. It is apparent from the noise that they move as one, rather than spreading into the various hallways they might have chosen, and that there are women amongst them. Why shouldn't there be? Betsy wonders now. Why had she assumed there would be men but not women imprisoned below? Haven't Betsy and Effie wronged the government just as badly as Teddy? The prisoners now charging along the abandoned hallway of the Gaol for Political Prisoners might not be criminals at all. They might simply be people who were trying to do the right thing. They might be people just like Effie and Betsy and Teddy. Betsy cannot think now why she had been too scared to descend those stairs. Who did she possibly imagine could have been waiting at their bottom except individuals in need of help? The Order has made her suspicious and fearful, and she doesn't like it one bit. She is going to do better. She must. She will find a way to help these poor souls, and she cannot do that while she is hiding here like a coward.

With a nod for Effie, she takes a deep breath and steps out into the hallway. And there, moving with the fleeing crowd, his bunched fists punching the air with each desperate forward pace, a green scarf flying behind him, his eyes bulbous and haunted in his paled face, is their Teddy.

CHAPTER FOURTEEN

Into the Wild

They do not slow until they reach the clockwork cart, which Erwin has kept running on the street outside. Effie wrenches open the door and they pile in – Teddy, then Betsy, then Effie.

'Go, Erwin!' Betsy yells, but she needn't, for Briny Erwin is steering them wildly away from the Gaol for Political Prisoners before Effie has even managed to slam the door. The little cart, overloaded now with four frantic people, the double bass and the crated orrery, swings and tilts at dangerous angles; the copper pipe puffs desperately; the side-mounted cogs turn so fast that they clack like chattering teeth.

'Erwin!' Teddy says, reaching into the driver's seat to clamp his right hand around the older man's bicep. His left hand is still fastened to Betsy's, as it has been since the moment they spotted each other, and he makes no move to free it as he slumps back against the leather-cushioned bench and releases a long exhalation. 'I thought I'd never see any of you again,' he mutters. Amongst the shouts of the midnight prisoners Erwin is swerving around and the whistles of the Constabulary and the whickering of galloping horses, only Betsy hears him, and she squeezes his hand tighter. She pretends that she cannot see the sheen of his tears.

'Right, then, you three,' Erwin grunts. 'Grip on tight now.'

And Betsy laughs because they are already white-knuckled with gripping each other and the seats, and they bang shoulders as they slide from side to side, and Effie starts to laugh, and soon they are all laughing and crying and none of them can quite say why.

'Where will we go, Erwin?' Betsy asks when they have wheeled off Stag's Circus and onto unfamiliar streets. This part of the city is quieter, though no less chaotic. The wind has loosened roof slates which drop into the path of the cart and burst into shards. Dustbins roll on their metal rims. A cat streaks in front of them, ginger tail bushy with fear. Such a storm cannot be stilled instantly. When the Unified Government manipulated the orrery, they must have done so far more cautiously than Effie did.

'Across the canal,' Erwin shouts.

'But … how? You said there were no crossings.'

'There ain't. Don't mean we won't have to find one. You said it yourself, Miss. There's no place in Copperwell for any of you now.'

'You'll come with us, though, won't you, Erwin?'

'Not me, Miss.' Erwin shakes his head. 'I'm an old man. There's nothing for me except what I know.'

'That's not true!' Teddy lurches forward to speak into

Briny Erwin's ear. 'We need you. We don't know what's out there.'

'I don't, neither,' Erwin returns. 'That is, I know of two things, but they're waiting for you, not for me.'

'What are they?' Effie asks.

'Freedom,' Erwin says, throwing a grin back at them. 'And adventure.' And his voice is full of mystery and impossibility and wonder, and it sounds to Betsy like the song of the stars and she knows that what they're doing is right. They will take the orrery out of the city. They will keep it out of government hands. They will uncover the game the woman on Wild Goose Way warned them was being played and put a stop to it. Betsy has been gazing into the sky for as long as she can remember, searching for her purpose, and she supposes now that it is to be found in the secrets of the orrery.

They ride in silence a while, each lost to thoughts of unknown lands and the trials which might lie ahead of them.

Above the rooftops, pale blue hints of morning the orrery has dragged from another time throw the chimney stacks into relief. Along the ridges ravens hunch against the weather. They are joined by mockingbirds, turtle doves, sparrowhawks – species which have never before flocked to Copperwell. Betsy scours the kerbs and the hedgerows and the basement flat railings for another glimpse of the black foxes.

When Briny Erwin slams a boot down on the brake

pedal and the cart clunks to a stop, she very nearly smashes her forehead against the window, but she manages to brace herself well enough that only her nose bumps the glass. Righting herself, she peers around Erwin to locate the problem. There, standing in the middle of the road, her hands spread before her as though she intends to stop the vehicle with the weight of her tiny body alone, her palms eerily white, her eyes huge in the glare of the cart's central headlight, is Millicent Shaw, the Hart's kitchen girl.

'Millie!' Effie grapples for the handle and, stretching one foot out of the cart, stands to speak over the shield of the door. 'What are you doing?'

'I followed you, Miss. I…' Millie pants between words. She is evidently exhausted. 'I had to tell you…'

'What, Millie? What is it?'

'Your father, Miss. He's been arrested.'

Millie manages to bundle herself into the cart next to Briny Erwin and crouch on her knees, her back to the road they are travelling, to explain to Effie and the others what had happened at number eight, Berliner's Square. Through jolts and pauses, they learn that Constable Pridmore, Chief of the Copperwell Constabulary, had arrived on the doorstep accompanied by two of his junior colleagues.

'Huge, the pair of them,' Millie says, wincing as Erwin takes a corner too fast and she collides bodily with him.

Chief Justice Hart had, naturally, allowed them in and sat with them in the parlour. Millie had been eavesdropping from the hallway – 'Given how odd you'd been behaving, Miss Effie, I was curious!' – and had deciphered snippets of the discussion. What she knew, though, was firstly that Pridmore had accused Jeremiah Hart of concealing on the property an item of vital importance to the Unified Government; secondly, that he had been instructed to return it forthwith; and thirdly, that when he denied any knowledge of such an item, Chief Justice Hart had been arrested on the spot and frogmarched out onto Berliner's Square for all the neighbours to see.

'Your poor father,' Teddy says. 'How would they have known?'

'Known what?' asks Millie.

Effie's eyes narrow; she is thinking something through. 'Where did they take him?'

'Gaol, I imagine,' Millie replies. 'I can't see where else—'

'Except that nobody would have known we'd brought the orrery into the house. We moved it concealed inside the crate, both in and out. Nobody would see an old wooden box and assume that a priceless orrery was hidden inside, unless they knew exactly what they were looking for. Perhaps the Constabulary know I'm responsible, and they want him to give me up. Or perhaps they think it's one of the staff, or my mother and her Women's Enfranchisement friends. Either way, my father won't tell them anything. He doesn't know anything, but even if he did, he wouldn't...'

'You want to go back, don't you?' Betsy says.

Effie is silent for a spell. She thinks of the canal they are racing towards, and her father being accused of theft and treason, and her mother's rage at the Constabulary for treating her husband so poorly. 'No,' she replies. 'My father is innocent. He'll be all right.'

Teddy puts a hand over Effie's. 'Just because he's innocent, Ef, doesn't mean—'

'It has to, Teddy,' Effie says, her eyes fixed firmly on the view through the clockwork cart's tiny front window. 'He is innocent, and it will be proven in court, and we must not get distracted from our task.'

'You'd really leave,' Betsy asks, 'knowing what could happen? You have to be certain, Ef.'

Effie nods her head resolutely. 'This is more important than just one person, one family. Getting the orrery out of Copperwell might mean that everyone would be free again. Free from The Order, and fear, and the Constabulary. It's worth the risk.'

And because it is evident that Effie will not be dissuaded from her standpoint, they continue the rest of the way to the canal in silence.

When, thirty-five endless minutes later, they clamber out of the little cart onto a damp, dark stretch of the towpath, the sky is calmer. The canal, though, is a different matter. The water is brimming, churning, black. No lamps are strung out to guide the barges, which perhaps don't come by this route at all. Betsy glances left and right, searching for a way across, but there is no bridge, no old boat they might requisition… All she sees is an expanse of murky water, thundering into invisibility. They will never make it across.

'Far as I know, this is the narrowest part of the canal,' Erwin explains at a grumble. 'Half a mile, bank to bank. It's your best chance.'

'But how can we… We can't swim…'

The heavy stink of algae and disturbed mud clogs their mouths and noses.

'You can!' Erwin insists. When he turns a second time to look back in the direction they have travelled, Betsy follows his gaze. She can see two broken-down old huts set just back off the towpath and the road they have raced down. The rest is swallowed by the night-time dark which still hangs over Copperwell. But then she tilts her head, and she catches the sound at the same time as she notices the grimace on Briny Erwin's face. A rapid four-beat. Metal on cobblestones. The Constabulary!

'The doors,' she says, taking off suddenly towards the huts. 'Tear off the doors. We can use them as rafts.' Reaching the first hut, she pushes her fingertips between the door and the frame and drags at it with all her body weight. Within seconds, she is breathless, but Erwin soon arrives at her side and, with two enormous heaves, wrenches the door off its rusted hinges. Teddy, Effie and Millie free the other, and then they are running towards the water, setting the doors afloat, balancing the orrery and

Effie's double-bass case on top of them, trying desperately to keep both items still while Teddy pulls his scarf across their width and attempts to secure them. It is precarious, but it's the best they can do.

'A rope,' Effie says. 'We need to tie ourselves to them, too.'

Erwin lumbers back towards the huts, disappears with a grunt, and emerges moments later clutching knotted tats of frayed green fishing rope.

'Around our wrists,' Effie says, holding her arm out for Erwin to make the loop. Betsy and Teddy copy her. 'And then around the door handles. We'll drag them across.' Erwin finishes tying the ropes around their wrists then slings the spare lengths over the orrery and the double base case and roughly knots them.

'What if we're not strong enough?' Teddy protests.

'The water will help us,' Effie replies. 'Come on.'

The four-beat of huge horses' hooves grows louder, echoing down nearby streets. They can't be more than two minutes away.

'Come on!' Effie is already wading in. She does not react to the stabbing cold. She is focussed entirely on what she must do.

Betsy and Teddy plunge in after her. Immediately, Teddy's teeth begin to chatter, but Betsy grasps his hand and urges him on. Though she is by far the smallest of the three, Betsy is tough as gristle; she will not show anyone that her muscles are already trembling, that her bones are aching.

'Quickly,' Effie orders. Teddy fumbles with the rope and the door handle, trying to tighten the knot. The water is around his waist now and beginning to drag at him. He strides on through the silt, his feet slipping and twisting. Two steps further and there's nothing else for it but to swim.

'Ready?' he calls, eyeing Betsy and Effie carefully. Betsy is already neck deep. Effie, slightly taller, is just on the cusp of losing her shoulders to the flow. The girls nod. Or shake. Teddy cannot tell which for certain, but they're too far in now to change their minds. There's no choice but to try for the opposite bank. With a shove, he pushes the door out into the canal and begins to kick with all his might. The sky is the exact same colour as the water, and he hardly knows what he is aiming for, but he does know that, wherever they wash up, they will find themselves in the strange and unknown world outside Copperwell. He really will become the explorer he has dreamt of being. And who knows what they might find outside the confines of the city. He kicks harder, driven on now by a sudden swelling excitement. He cannot understand why he had worried about any of them not being strong enough to steer the rafts across the canal. Who could be fiercer than Betsy Blue, who has fended for herself for as long as any of them remember? Who could be stronger than Effie Hart, who has chosen what is right over her own family? Who could be braver than Teddy James, who has lost his mother and his father and Jim, but who has never given up his hope?

He knows, all at once, that they will reach safety. He opens his mouth, to reassure Betsy and Effie… And that is when he hears the clatter of horses being abruptly reined in on the towpath. The shouts of Erwin and Millie, lost amongst louder, harsher voices. A singular splash.

Erwin is struggling after them, his heavy arms arcing above the water and slamming back below arrhythmically, his head thrashing from side to side, his mouth gaping and pink against the thick hair of his beard. It is obvious he is not a strong swimmer.

'Faster,' he gasps, as he draws alongside them and shoves at the makeshift rafts. 'They'll … be in … after you. Faster.'

On the tow path, Millie is clawing and screeching and writhing as the three pursuing constables lift her clean off the ground. They toss her easily aside and she lands with a sickening thud. But within seconds she is back on her feet and charging towards them, cackling with laughter, biting, screaming. She fights like a wildcat, doing anything she can to distract the constables who would surely otherwise have dived straight into the canal after Erwin.

'Don't look,' Erwin insists. 'Don't … look back… Just … forward…'

Betsy, Teddy and Effie obey. They look away from the place where Millie is fighting like a warrior, and they haul and kick and cling desperately to their rafts. The flow of water is too much and their muscles burn, but they battle on, never looking back. Even when Millie's screams and curses fall silent, they do not look back.

'Do you … see it?' Briny Erwin splutters. 'Look. Do you … see?'

Teddy squints into the darkness. In the distance, a lumpen shape is just coming into view. A long, uneven mass, stretching along the horizon. And from it, deep grey pillars rise. Hundreds of them. Trees! The opposite bank is in sight.

'We're nearly there!' Teddy yells. 'Hold on. It won't be long.'

To his immediate right, he can hear Betsy growling with the effort of surging onwards. He turns to glimpse Effie, her hair strewn awkwardly across her face as she paddles desperately ahead of her raft, dragging it in her wake. And Erwin…

'Erwin?'

Teddy swings his head around.

'Erwin!'

Betsy and Effie, too, slow just enough to look around. Suddenly, none of them can spot Erwin.

'Erwin?' Teddy bellows, so that his cry carries on the frozen mists.

And only then does the man answer. His voice is smaller than it ought to be. Already he is some way further down the canal. The drift is drawing him away, and he can do nothing but let it take him. He is heavy. He is not a strong swimmer. He has given the last of his power to pushing the rafts out of harm's way. Water plashes over his huge, bull-like head. It spills into his open mouth.

'You're all right … Teddy lad,' he calls. 'Go on, now… Go…'

And then, with one final gasp, the water swallows him and Briny Erwin vanishes.

CHAPTER FIFTEEN

The Forest

The forest is deep and black and unknowable – a whole world built from the screeches of invisible creatures and shapes which shift without warning. Betsy, Teddy and Effie walk and walk, taking turns to drag the rafts containing the crated orrery and the double bass behind them over the snow, and never knowing whether they are moving away from the canal, or back towards it, or round and round in endless circles. They shiver inside their soaked clothes, but they cannot possibly build a fire while it is still dark and risk giving away their position, so they try to forget the way the cold makes their bones ache and their heads thump and their jaws clench. They follow the bumpy spines of narrow paths, and the smell of fresh falling snow, but no landmark emerges to show them the way.

The way to where, in any case? Their plan took them so far as the opposite side of the canal. All they can do now is struggle over tangled roots, scratching their frozen hands and legs and faces on claw-fingered branches, until they figure out what to do next. The trees are so tall that they bend into each other, their topmost leaves conspiring to make a canopy which obscures the sky. The moon is an occasional pearly glimmer; it drops over the forest floor in strange, unpredictable patterns – stars and rhombuses, pyramids and crescents – which look like fragments of treasure. Attempting to warm herself up, Betsy hops quietly from one accident of light to the next, as though they are clues, leading her towards an answer to the question she is too frightened to voice: *What will we do now?*

Beneath their feet, the ground is hard and littered with curled marmalade-and-crimson-coloured leaves – the autumn and deepest winter come together. What had the Unified Government hoped to achieve by confusing the seasons, by letting the people of Copperwell fall further and further into poverty, by shifting the shadows? They must have been engineering something colossal to interfere with the natural order like that.

Effie, who is leading the way for the moment, stops suddenly and holds a hand up high.

'Can you hear that?' It has been so long since any of them has spoken that her voice sounds too loud. It is claggy with the tears they have all been privately shedding: for Erwin; for Millie. Betsy worries that they might never discover what has happened to those two brave souls.

They pause and wait for the call to sound again. It comes twice in quick succession: a light, mellifluous trill, slowing into a single sustained note. Effie knows it to be a B flat, but she doesn't mention the fact. It is irrelevant. The sound is recognisable enough.

It belongs to a hickory bird.

None of them can see the sapphire flit of the little creature's wings in the dark, nor the lavender gleam of its bead-like eyes, but they know the call well enough from visits to Copperwell's Zoological Gardens. The hickory bird hails from Indochina: it has shining blue wing feathers and a silver-streaked tail, bright purple feet and a rose-pink bill. There are no wild examples in the Britannic Isles. Or there *were* no wild examples in the Britannic Isles. Like the orchid mantises of East Eurasia and the black foxes of Africa and the Antart snow, the hickory bird is lost.

They wait, listening past the symphony of clicks and creaks the trees play, to see if the call is answered. It is faint, far-off, but eventually they hear it: a fluting trill followed by a long falling note.

'Sounds like it's miles away,' Betsy whispers.

'How far do you think this forest stretches?' Teddy replies.

Effie glances around, as though she might find some indication of distance or direction, carved into the tree trunks. 'All the way to the coast, I'd imagine. To the south, at least. To the north…'

'Which is the nearest city?' Teddy squints, trying to recall his geography lessons.

'Coalbrook,' Effie says. Information has always lodged easily at the tip of her tongue. 'Sixty-three miles north-west of Copperwell.'

'We'll never walk that!' Betsy blurts. The thought

of just how far the forest stretches makes her stomach churn. 'Especially dragging these damned things behind us.' She gives the crate a half-hearted kick, making sure not to strike it hard enough to damage the orrery within. She would not risk that for anything. What she will not admit to the others, though, is that her instinct to protect the orrery is not founded entirely on the urge to right the Unified Government's wrongs. Nor is it based solely on a determination to help that poor woman on Wild Goose Way, though her face has haunted Betsy every time she has gone to her attic room to sleep off her laundry shifts since. More than that, she feels protective of the orrery – as she might Madam Bee or Puck. It feels … she thinks that perhaps… The orrery seems to have a soul.

'What option do we have but to walk?' Effie returns.

Teddy slumps down onto the crate with a sigh. 'We don't even know if we're going in the right direction.'

'Then we keep watch for an air-train,' Effie suggests. 'If they're ascending, we'll know they've just left Copperwell and we can follow their trajectory. If they're descending, we'll know they're landing in Copperwell, and we can make sure to go in the opposite direction.'

'You'll put the world straight one day, Effie Hart,' Teddy says, smiling slightly and starting, finally, to look like himself. 'Queen of the Britannic Isles.'

'Queen Euphemia Hart the first,' Effie intones. 'Plenty of room here…' she makes a circling motion above her head with a pointed finger '…for a crown.'

'Would Her Highness prefer diamonds or rubies?' Betsy raises her eyebrows.

'I think… peridots.'

'That would be different.'

'*I* would be different,' Effie replies. 'King Glennister has done nothing of any note. I'm sure a queen would do better next time.'

'How long has it been since there was a woman on the throne, Ef?' Betsy asks.

'One hundred and…' She does a quick calculation. 'Eighty-five years. Queen Karolina.'

'Hmm. Queen Euphemia sounds better. What about Teddy and me? Will we be your servants?'

Effie laughs, her cheeks bunching in that funny way they have, so that they are round and appley. 'My advisors, of course. What other position could there possibly be for Theodore James and Elizabeth Blue?'

Overhead, the hickory bird calls to its mate. After a few second, its mate answers, closer this time. Were it not for their calls, Betsy, Teddy and Effie would never know they were there. What else, then, might be hiding in these trees that they cannot see? Something bigger? Something hungry?

Betsy looks upwards, picturing the two enormous hot-air balloons which will be tethered together to keep the air-train carriage afloat. The silks, she thinks, will be stripes of cream and dusty blue. From the throat of the balloons will hang not a wicker basket, but thick brown leather straps, which will loop through slots built specially into the body of the rectangular carriage suspended below. The carriages are always painted to match one of the balloon-silks' colours. Betsy has never ridden an air-train – they are reserved for Copperwell's wealthy – but she imagines them to be impossibly grand inside, with sumptuous seats and a waiting staff and soothing orchestral music playing from a gramophone.

She is, she realises, hoping one into existence. She, like the hickory bird, has been lost before, and there is a mounting flutter of panic at her middle at the thought of being lost again. She does not mention it to Effie or Teddy. That she grew up among the poppy-seed drinkers in Copperwell's dankest alleyways is one part of the secret she keeps from them. Hiding behind that secret is another, less defined memory, which she feels she must protect: of wandering alone amongst the poppy-seed drinkers for the first time, cold and confused; and before that, of being somewhere else, somewhere she cannot recognise, and of running, her arms thrown wide, to the chimes of laughter. A woman's laughter. If she ever finds that place again, she thinks, she will feel at home there straight away.

As the day blooms, they continue to walk through their exhaustion. The forest light turns from black to grey to a faint seashell pink, and finally they are stepping across shadows cast by the midday sun, which gradually dries their sodden clothes, and snow is glinting on the branches and at the toes of their boots, and cold air rushes into their noses and mouths and cleans out their minds just as their bodies start to thaw. The relief is enormous and they pause in a clearing to kick snow at each other and skip and climb nearby trees, until they fall, drained, to the ground and listen to their stomachs growling. It feels as though they haven't eaten in days.

'We could make a fire now,' Effie suggests. 'No one will spot it now that it's light. We could…'

'Cook on it,' Betsy snorts. 'What would we cook? A passing mouse? We'll never catch anything, Ef.'

'No, I suppose not.' Effie slumps over her crossed legs. 'We could easily starve out here.'

'We're not going to starve,' Teddy insists, though he cannot disguise the shudder the thought sends through him. Perhaps hundreds of people have tried to escape Copperwell before them. Perhaps they all got lost amongst the trees. Perhaps these woods are filled with their ghosts.

For the first time in over a year, they do not think about their own shadows, revealed, grey and definite, against the frosty ground, as they sink into their own worries. It is when Effie's head nods towards sleep and she shoots awake again that she glances at Teddy's shadow and, realising her mistake, snaps her head around to hide her blush. The abruptness of her movement draws his attention.

'It's all right,' Teddy says. 'There's nothing to be ashamed of. You can look.'

Effie remains still, her head turned away.

‘Ef,’ Teddy continues. ‘You know me… We’re only embarrassed because the Unified Government and their Shadow Order have made us paranoid. We never even thought about our shadows before—’

‘They didn’t *show* anything, before,’ Effie replies quietly.

‘Course they did! They showed us ourselves as the world saw us.’

‘And now they show the world us as we see ourselves.’

‘Perhaps.’ Teddy shrugs, not overly troubled by the idea. ‘But when they first shifted, do you remember? Everyone was shocked, frightened for a little while, and then people started to accept it, embrace it … until The Order.’

‘He’s right,’ Betsy interjects. ‘We shouldn’t be afraid to look. I’m not afraid.’

‘On three, then,’ Teddy suggests.

‘On three.’

Ignoring Effie’s sigh of resignation, Betsy counts them quickly in. Effie is slower to look down than are Betsy and Teddy, but reluctantly she obliges, and there, on the ground before them, are three completely different shadows. Teddy’s is broader in the back and thicker in the arm than the boy himself, but stands less proudly and sags around itself a little, as though self-conscious of its size. Betsy’s shade is restless, bouncing on the balls of its feet, shaking out its arms as though preparing itself for flight. It is somehow more compact than Betsy – as though having been doomed to echo her shape exactly for so long has caused it to shrink. Effie's shadow shows perhaps the closest resemblance to its owner. Largely, it holds her curved and stocky shape. It shares her muscled calves and impeccably straight shoulders. It has her same controlled grace.

'You're holding everything inside yourself, aren't you,' Betsy says slowly. She has just realised that this is what Effie does, what she always has done. She does not shout. She does not cry. She does not lash out. She is as intricately folded into herself as a paper swan, and Betsy thinks that that is as admirable and beautiful as it is sad. She has just left Copperwell, without knowing whether she will ever see her parents again, and she hasn't so much as grumbled. 'You can let yourself out, you know. It's us! We'd still love you, even if your shadow looked like … Old Man Hatch.'

'Bets!'

'What?'

'Hatch is a good man.'

'I never said he wasn't… You wouldn't want to *look* like him, though, would you?'

Teddy cannot help but smirk at the way Betsy pops her eyes when she says this.

'Go on, Ef,' he says. 'Try it.'

Effie's arm cross over her chest. 'I don't know how.'

'Yes, you do. You wouldn't be able to play your jazz otherwise.'

'But without my double bass, and I'm not unpacking that here, when—'

'You still have a voice, don't you?' Betsy insists.

Effie tightens her arms and angles her head away from them haughtily. 'I'm not singing.'

'Why not? This whole forest is singing. Listen.'

At intervals, the hickory bird and its mate pass their lonely messages back and forth, searching each other out in this strange, cold, new world. They are accompanied by the D sharp sway of high branches, the rasp of autumnal leaves shivering out of season in the gentle wind and the crunch of those which have fallen under Teddy and Betsy's heavy boots, the almost inaudible patter of falling snow. Somewhere, further away, a high-pitched wail echoes among the trees: a mating fox, Betsy supposes; or perhaps an owl, confused about the time of day.

'All right,' Effie says. 'I'll sing – if you sing with me.'

She chooses one of The Quartet's slower songs, a syncopated lament on a broken friendship. Betsy and Ted, having been to almost as many of Effie's shows as she has played, know it perfectly and join in within a couple of bars, their voices less practised than Effie's but not unpleasant. Teddy finds the melody an octave lower than the girls, and as they harmonise, Effie smiles and begins to relax. Soon, her shadow is loosening at its edges, then getting bigger. It retains the same shape, but it grows and grows until it fills the clearing, and finally, though Effie does not move, it throws its arms out wide and tips back its head like a person basking in sunlight or long-awaited rain.

'That's how it feels when I look at the stars!' Betsy says, pointing. 'That's freedom, isn't it?'

Effie stops singing and her shadow gradually shrinks back in on itself until it matches her size almost exactly again.

'That's amazing,' Teddy gasps.

Since The Order was introduced, everyone in Copperwell has been so concerned with hiding their shadows that they have hardly had chance to study them. It seems to Teddy that this might be an opportunity to learn something more about the way they work, to push them to their limits, to test out whether they might be able to control their movement. He considers what his freedom is.

'Watch,' Betsy urges, and she closes her eyes and thinks hard about the round brilliance of the wolf moon, and how beautiful it was. When she hears Effie laugh, she opens her eyes again to see that, while her shadow does not look quite like Effie's did, it is definitely bigger and bolder. It is charcoal grey now, rather than misty, and it is whirling around and around on the spot in the manner of a spinning top.

'Do yours, Ted.'

'I don't know…'

'What?'

'I don't know what my freedom is.' He lowers his head; he can't put his finger on why this embarrasses him exactly, but it does.

'Course you do!' Betsy says. 'It's the horses. Your freedom is sitting on the back of a galloping horse.'

And the moment she says it, and the picture of Jim paints itself across Teddy's mind, so his shadow swells and leaks outwards across the snowy ground and throws out its arms, looking for all the four continents as though it is being carried fleetly across a distant mountain or along a sandy shore on the back of a powerful horse.

'That's it!' Betsy cries. 'That's you.'

'Yes,' Teddy replies quietly. 'I suppose it is.'

They walk until the sun is a glaring peach-white orb above them, and as the sky pinks and fades, and as flat blue dusk slants through the forest, and they see nothing but trees and icy streams, narrow tracks and little clearings. They climb away from Copperwell, moving steadily upwards until they find themselves looking down into wooded ravines. Already, the world feels too big, and the feeling is increasingly difficult to ignore. On the rooftops and in the ginnels of the city, they had been surefooted. Here, every stick or stone seems determined to send them stumbling into the unknown.

At intervals, Betsy removes her hat, lifts Puck free of her hair, and sets him down on a nearby branch for a while. Each time, Puck flies back to Betsy and settles amongst her curls, as though he feels the bigness of this place, too.

'I think he's too cold,' she says.

Effie opens her mouth to speak, then closes it again abruptly and lifts a finger to her lips. When she has both Betsy and Teddy's attention, she points skyward. 'Listen,' she whispers. Sure enough, without the crunch of their boots through the snow and the echo of their voices, they can hear something. Something distant but travelling closer. Something that moves in stealthy silence for minutes at a time before releasing a roaring sort of hiss.

'Air-train!' Betsy breathes, her eyes widening. The hiss is the gas being shot into the balloon.

'Just what we need!' Teddy says, at a normal volume, which seems amplified a hundred times between the looming trees. The girls shush him. 'What?' he replies, quieter now. 'You said…'

Effie flaps a hand at him. 'I know, I know. But what if it's looking for us?'

For a heartbeat, they stand frozen. Then Betsy shrieks, 'Hide!' and without a moment's hesitation, they take off, scuffing out of the clearing and racing between tree trunks which whip their faces and tangle in their hair and sting their legs. They do not slow though. They run until they tumble, one after another, down a sudden slope and manage to halt just short of plunging into a rushing river. They lie panting on the bank, their hands gripping exposed and frozen roots, looking back up the slope to the place where the orrery sits, waiting for their return.

'Do you think we'll be visible here?' Teddy stammers.

'No,' Effie replies. 'No.'

'Can you see it?'

They peer up through the branches overhead into the just-darkening sky. They wait. And perhaps five minutes later, they catch a glimpse of a spectacular air-train: the silks of its balloons are emerald and olive green, and the carriage itself is polished gold from nose to rear; both the balloons and the carriage are trimmed with thick red ribbon, which trails in the wind as it floats – upwards – into the dusk.

'It's ascending!' Effie says. They are moving away from Copperwell. Though whether or not that means they are moving towards Coalbrook is hard to say.

'But … that's not an ordinary air-train,' Betsy says. Even the most sumptuous ones don't have those colours or decoration. 'It has to belong to the Unified Government, doesn't it?'

'Or the king.'

'But where would King Glennister be going?'

None of them answers, though they all hear their suspicions as though the words really have been spoken aloud. They are all thinking the same thing. He's going away from Copperwell because the city is in chaos. He's seeking out somewhere safer. He's running away.

'What a coward,' Teddy says, and for a moment, the statement makes him feel braver.

When night falls, they have still seen no indication of a place they might be able to rest. They had hoped to happen across a woodman's dwelling at least, where they might beg shelter and perhaps something to drink, since their tongues have turned to tree bark. They had thought to find some signs of civilisation. But there is nothing except the trees and all the different sounds they make – the snaps and moans, the hisses and creaks – and Teddy is growing increasingly frightened. Not of the dark – they are used to that – but of the unfamiliar. Shapes hide in the gaps between the trunks: black shapes, which might be men or might be beasts or might be anything at all. Teddy grinds his teeth, to keep them from chattering, but he cannot disguise that his whole body has started to shudder. He stays behind the girls as they slog along a single track, offers to drag the cumbersome orrery for longer than his turn, and remains quiet while Betsy and Effie exchange ideas about the Unified Government and what exactly they hoped to achieve by altering the rotations of the orrery. He is not sure when or how they found out that the government had altered the orrery's rotation, or whether it is this orrery alone which has such incredible power, but he does not wish to ask. Those discoveries took place when he was gone, and if Betsy or Effie mentions his time in the gaol or asks him what it was like, and he allows those remembrances back into his mind, he fears he might collapse under the weight of them. His throat contracts and his heart quickens at the prospect.

When he hears the familiar tick of clockwork, therefore, he supposes that it is coming from his memory. That perhaps his mind is replaying the sound of Erwin's cart and the relief he felt as he was driven away in it, to calm itself. He opens his mouth to check with the girls, then closes it again: he'd feel idiotic if they couldn't hear it. But he soon notices Betsy looking from left to right, tilting her head in search of the direction of a sound. And Effie's pace starting to slow. And he knows then that he is not imagining things. They can hear the clockwork too. It is not accompanied by any music, so it cannot be the workings of some hidden weather pipes. He does not, therefore, allow the hope that there is a building nearby. But that unmistakable click and grind is getting louder, coming closer. And quickly, too. The trees shake, loosing their snow as the ground starts to tremble. Betsy, Teddy and Effie stop and surround the orrery, backs to the crate.

'We can't let anyone take it,' Betsy says.

'We won't,' Effie assures her.

Reaching over the slatted wood, they clasp their icy hands together. The ground quakes as something weighty and determined pounds over it. Teddy finds himself counting the four-beat of footsteps over the frozen ground. He would recognise the gait of a horse in gallop anywhere, and this is the same rhythm, but a horse would never make so much noise. And if not a horse, then certainly not a dog, though they share the gait. But if not a dog… The word leaves his mouth just as a colossal glinting snout edges into view amongst the trees, moving slower now.

'Wolf!'

For a breath, only the snout is visible. It is easily the size of a horse's head. A moment later, the snout is followed by slanted black eyes. Then enormous, peaked ears. A solid metal mane, shaped to stand up in a bristle. A pair of rangy front legs which roll into a stalk. Scythe-like claws which shine even in the dull dark of the forest.

'We have to run,' Betsy says. The words are flattened by her clenched jaw.

'We'll never outrun it,' Effie shoots back, gripping her hand tighter. 'Stay still.'

'And what? Hope it goes away?'

'It might not be looking for us.'

'What else would it be doing?' Teddy whispers.

'I don't know. We don't even know what it is,' Effie replies.

'A wolf,' Betsy says, her eyes darting. 'It's a wolf.'

'It's *shaped* like a wolf,' Effie corrects her gently. 'But it's *made*. The same as the weather pipes. The same as the clockwork carts. I've never seen anything like it. Have you?'

The clockwork wolf takes another stride forward, swinging its brassy head from side to side. It is hunting, Teddy thinks, whatever Effie imagines to the contrary.

'I think…' Effie says, cocking her head as she considers the creature. 'I think it's a guard. A perimeter guard. Didn't Erwin say that no one had left Copperwell in the longest time? Perhaps this is why the Constabulary didn't follow us across the canal. Perhaps the Unified Government built this to patrol the city.'

'If that's the case,' Betsy replies, 'then it's definitely coming for us.'

'*They're* definitely coming for us,' Teddy insists. He uses his eyes to indicate a point in the trees, where another shining snout is nosing steadily towards them.

'We won't outrun them,' Effie reiterates, 'however much we might want to try.'

'Then we just ... stand here...?' As Betsy's voice pitches higher, so the first wolf's right ear flicks in their direction.

'We stand *still*!' Effie hisses. 'They're not real. They can't smell us. If we stay still enough, they might pass us by.'

'Might!' Betsy squeals, and as she does, so the wolves rise up on their haunches and, in a frantic flurrying of snow and grinding of cogs, launch themselves into a terrifying gallop, straight towards Betsy, Teddy and Effie.

CHAPTER SIXTEEN

Vagabonds

Twenty-five miles north of Copperwell, in a dense belt of forest undisturbed by any inhabitant of any city in the Britannic Isles, the land scoops into a natural hollow. This hollow, edged as it is by ancient wych elms, is well protected from wind and rain and sleet. At its deepest point, the ground levels into a plain, perhaps half a mile wide. At the exact central point of this plain a huge fire blazes day and night, its crackles echoing into the surrounding woodland with the insistence of a drum beat, its flames turning the nearby snow to honey.

Arranged around the fire in concentric circles are rows of wooden yurts, their pointed roofs draped with tan, pine green, ochre, plum and deep cherry canvases. Smoke drifts from holes at the peaks of the roofs in thick, white plumes.

People, dressed in leathers and wools in all the colours of autumn, mill quietly around, or sit over cooking pots, or wring out clothes over steaming barrels and hang them from ropes suspended between yurts to drip into the snow below. A hum of activity warms the little community and soothes the beasts they have penned between and behind the yurts. The animals are at once calm and magnificent. They move slowly around their enclosures, pausing here and there to crop up mouthfuls of grass. As they chew, they glance about themselves, their soft triangular ears twitching this way and that, their every movement elegant despite their hulking size. The bucks' antlers cast long, branch-like shadows.

Effie would know immediately that they are red deer, and name them as such, if she could see them. But neither she, nor Betsy, nor Teddy can see anything of this place yet. They lie, deeply asleep, inside one of the yurts, blanketed and comfortable and rendered completely unaware of their surroundings by the soporific effect of the valerian garlands looped around their necks. As they sleep, they dream vivid dreams: Betsy, of being carried through trees on the back of an enormous clockwork wolf, her hair and clothes whipping about her, the seamless rhythm of her galloping mount persuading her that she is safe; Effie, of rushing through the unlit rooms and hallways of number eight, Berliner's Square, pursued at every turn by a faceless figure she cannot identify; and Teddy, of those evenings he spent with his father, brushing down the cab horses, and holding apple cores out on his flattened palm for Jim, and listening to stories of the Aur hastening over the empty plains of the world for the sheer joy of it.

'I will look at it,' Edward had insisted, 'and I will see it. And then I will return home and never tell a single soul about it.'

When Teddy gasps into waking, he does so with those words weighty on his tongue. He struggles to push up into a sitting position, grappling with a thick wool blanket, and glances about, attempting to orientate himself. A spray of wooden ceiling beams; a smattering of small gas lamps set out on the floor; brown and white animal skins thrown around a central fire pit; a sort of harp, leant against the wall, with a pillar made of bone and strings fashioned from twined hair. Above the fire pit, suspended in the rising smoke by its bound back trotters and spinning slowly, is the dark body of a stinking, bristly hog.

Teddy waits, dread prickling around his neck, for the hog's face to be revealed. In his drowsy state, he fears it might still be alive… That it is being cooked alive… That he and the girls might be next. He manages not to cry out at the thought as the hog rotates and Teddy sees, in profile, a single pale tusk, a thick snout, one glassy eye. Dead, thank goodness. Teddy's heart rate slows, and he is better able to concentrate. He notices that the hog's flesh and organs have already been scooped out. What hangs above the fire is the skin, the head, and the feet. They are connected by an intact, but completely clean, skeleton. Teddy marvels at the ship's hull of bones visible through the split-open abdomen.

'Ah.' A voice, from nowhere and yet nearby, startles him. Still in a seated position, he shuffles backwards, so that he is closer to Betsy and Effie's sleeping bodies. How he means to protect them, he does not know, but he is ready to give his life trying. In a way, they have already done as much for him. 'So…' The voice is quiet, measured. It is a voice that could captivate with a good story. 'The Wellian is awake at last.'

Teddy locates the owner of the voice, seated on the opposite side of the fire. It wears a hooded garment and sits cross-legged, its head bent over its hands, which are busy in its lap. Teddy cannot discern with what. He cannot decide, either, whether the voice belongs to a man or a woman. It is deep but soft, unhurried yet confident.

'Wellian?' Teddy repeats. His throat is dry and the word sticks.

'You are Wellians, aren't you?' replies the voice.

Teddy pauses. 'We are from Copperwell, if that's what you mean.'

The hooded head nods. 'Aye. From Copperwell. Wellians, then. We haven't seen Wellians pass through the forests in the longest time, you know. Decades, I'd say. Except for that one, o'course. A special one, that girl. But none other, before nor since, for such a lengthy while. And she never came back, that one. Had to return to Copperwell, she said. Had to find out the answer to a question. Had to try to put matters right.'

Teddy straightens up, trying to see past the smoke and the spinning hog and into the hands of the woman – an old woman, he thinks, now that he has listened to her speak for a longer spell. If she is holding a weapon, he feels certain he could overpower her. She is half his size.

'Do you have a name, son?' she asks, without lifting her eyes to him.

'Theodore James,' he replies, without even considering lying. 'Teddy.'

'Hmm. And your friends?'

'Euphemia Hart and Elizabeth Blue.'

Teddy cannot seem to stop telling the truth. It is the result, he supposes, of his sleepiness. Or the smoke. He feels he has moved out of one dream and into another.

'And what are you doing so far from home, Teddy?'

It is only then that it occurs to him to wonder where the orrery might be. His eyes dart around the gloomy interior of the yurt: black cooking ladles hang on the walls; barrels, perhaps for washing clothes or bodies in, are stacked into a tower; small tables are dotted around, with crudely made dishes and tankards atop them. But he can see no crate.

'Your belongings are safe, Teddy,' says the woman. 'We would not take what belongs to another.'

'How can I possibly know I can trust you?'

'You have come to no harm, have you?' says the woman. 'Euphemia nor Elizabeth, neither.'

'It's Effie and Betsy,' Teddy corrects her. He glances back at them, unwilling to take his eyes off the woman for long. They are swaddled in thick blankets. They breathe slowly and evenly.

'They'll wake soon enough,' the woman assures him, her head still bent over her fidgeting hands. 'It works like a sleeping draught, the valerian.' She nods towards the garland about his neck. Teddy snatches it up. A flurry of the tiny white flowers falls loose and dusts the ground like snow.

'This?' His voice cracks across the yurt, too loud, and he bites down on his lip.

'Harmless.'

'You're certain?'

'I am.' The hood gives a steady nod. 'We use it oftentimes here. You will feel no lasting effect.'

'But… Why did you drug us?'

'To calm you, of course.'

'You sent *wolves* after us!'

'Wrong, Teddy. The wolves simply gathered you from harm and brought you to safety.'

Teddy rises onto his knees. 'We weren't in harm's way.'

'Were you not? Certain about that, are you?' From under the hood, a gentle chuckle issues. 'You don't know these lands, Teddy. That much is evident. The wolves knew it, too. They recognise need and they respond to it. It mightn't be what they were manufactured for, but their temper was readily changed. Seems to me they didn't like the violence they were originally intended for any more than we did.'

Effie must have been right, about the wolves once being perimeter guards. Or something similar at least.

'But … they're clockwork,' Teddy insists. 'They're just like the carts or the weather pipes. They don't have tempers.'

'Everything has a temper, Teddy. Don't you think? Don't you think this here dwelling has a temper, or the river that runs towards Copperwell, or the sky? Don't you feel the difference between those things?'

'Of course,' Teddy replies. 'There's a difference, yes, but...'

'But...'

'That doesn't mean those wolves can think for themselves. They're made of cogs and springs and metal and—'

'Energy,' the woman interjects. 'Haven't you learnt anything from all this shadow play? Don't you see that the shadows themselves have a temper?'

Teddy opens his mouth to respond, then closes it again. She's right. That was what they had observed in the clearing – the tempers of their shadows. Their shadows, like the wolves, do not think for themselves. Nor does this yurt. And yet, they have a character about them, a mood, which sets them apart each from each. Even the two clockwork wolves, when they had appeared between the trees, had been discernible as individuals: one was bolder than the other; it held its head higher. And hadn't Betsy been talking about the orrery having a strange feeling about it, as they'd walked through the forest? A personality, she'd said. Perhaps, then, it was the orrery's temper the Unified Government was controlling.

'Ah,' says the woman finally. 'Now you have it.'

'Perhaps,' Teddy replies, dismissing the thought. He

hasn't time for distractions. He needs to get them out of here. 'But what do you mean to do with us?'

'*Do* with you?' The hoods tips sideways; the head hidden beneath it has been cocked.

'Yes. Do you mean to keep us captive, as slaves? Or sell us onto the ships?' His mind is whirring with ideas which are both unfounded and unexpected. What ships is he referring to? He hasn't the first clue what the coast looks or feels like, let alone any knowledge of the ships which must set sail from it. His words are nothing more than repetitions of rumours whispered amongst Copperwell's children. Stories to scare each other with. There is something tight and fluttering in his throat. It puts him in mind of a little kingfisher perhaps. Or a butterfly, emerging from its chrysalis. Or … Puck! Teddy stomach flips when he sees that Betsy's hat is gone, and with it, the little orchid mantis they have carried all this way. He swallows his dread and continues. 'You might be cannibals! Is that it? Will you cook us and eat us?'

'Teddy,' the woman says gently. With a groan, she begins the struggle of unfolding herself into a standing position. It takes a whole minute for her to reach her full height, though she stands barely any taller than Teddy is on his haunches. When she has clicked and cracked her every joint, she lifts her head and throws back her hood. The woman beneath has the face of a bird – a dove hawk, or a kestrel. Her eyes are large and bright, with glimmering pale green irises. Her nose is slightly hooked. Her cheek and jaw bones are strongly defined. She has silver hair, laced into three thick plaits which travel away from her forehead like spines. 'We mean no harm to you or anyone else. We've always been happy neighbours to the Wellians.'

She loops a string of flowers – different from the valerian, palest blue in colour – around her neck. Teddy realises she must have been binding them together as she sat beside the fire.

'I've never heard the term,' Teddy counters.

The woman's head tilts a few degrees sideways. Despite her obvious age, and the stiffness of her body, her head moves with an alertness Teddy has only ever seen in a hunting animal. She seems, though he would not believe it, to be growing younger as the minutes pass. He wonders if it is the effect of the flowers. 'You haven't?'

Teddy shakes his head. 'Never. But if I am to be a Wellian, can I ask what you might be called?'

The woman raises her hands to her sides, as though she is about to summon some spirit out of the very ground, then rotates her body slightly to indicate the entirety of the yurt. 'As a people, we have been given many names: gypsies; nomads; wayfarers; and, most recently, vagabonds. But I have been given one, and that is Talon.'

'Talon?' Teddy asks. 'A talon is like a claw.'

'It is that.'

Colouring at his own rudeness, Teddy continues. 'I mean, I've never heard it used as a name.'

Talon shrugs, unoffended. 'We live under the stars,

Teddy,' she explains. 'We are often named for the skies or the elements, the animals or the seasons. They are our inspiration. I am the name-giver here now, being eldest, and they are my inspiration.'

'I don't know what inspires Wellians,' he muses quietly. With every observation exchanged, his fear is lessening. This woman, so calm and contemplative, has shown him nothing but kindness thus far.

'What inspires you?' Talon asks.

Teddy thinks of what Betsy had said in the clearing. *It's the horses. Your freedom is sitting on the back of a galloping horse*. And as he recalls her words, so that picture paints itself across his mind again, the colours deepening as he envisages himself flying at full gallop through the forest, his head tucked low into the dancing copper mane of Jim when he was young and powerful, his legs cupped tight around the horse's ribcage, his heart hammering so loudly against his chest that it echoes in his ears.

'Then perhaps, if you were a Vagabond, you might be called Cob or Steed or… Ginger.'

Teddy's laugh escapes him before he has chance to stop it. Is she reading his mind? The idea is too ridiculous to be true, but deep down he doesn't know whether he laughed because he is amused or frightened.

'Ginger?' Talon's eyes glint; she is teasing.

'Or perhaps,' she adds gently, 'Teddy of the Stallions.'

At his back, Teddy hears Betsy or Effie's breathing transform into a snuffle. One of them must be waking. The muscles in his back clench and he drops his smile. Talon's gaze does not falter.

'Don't fret, Teddy,' she says, and her voice is incantation-like and soothing. 'Effie and Betsy are safe here. The creature, too.'

'The creature?'

'The mantis,' Talon replies. And then, with a smile, she turns and strides, surprisingly lithely, towards the yurt's canvas door. There, she pauses. 'You'll see,' she says, and then she ducks away through the rippling canvas and is gone.

CHAPTER SEVENTEEN

A Glow of Mantises

'We're going to have to go out there,' Betsy whispers, nodding towards the yurt's door, which comprises two flags of heavy canvas, hung side by side. A slip of lavender light is visible between them. Betsy and Effie are still groggy, though the valerian garlands have been unhooked from around their necks and flung into the fire. The air inside the yurt is blackened and smoky. Teddy is certain he can smell the hog's bristles burning.

'Not yet,' Teddy replies.

'Why not?' Betsy counters.

Though he had rushed to rouse them the moment Talon had stepped out of the yurt, long minutes have passed since the woman disappeared, and Betsy and Effie are just managing to sit up independently.

'You can't even stand.'

'I can!' Betsy blusters. 'You watch.'

And Teddy does, while she trembles to her feet in the faltering manner of a newborn foal. As soon as she is close to upright, she fixes him with her most obstinate stare.

'Puck, Teddy! We don't know where he is. What if they've—'

‘I don’t think they would hurt him,’ Teddy answers.

‘Nor do I,’ Effie says, rising tentatively onto her knees and resting her body on her broad calves. ‘They could have hurt any of us while we were sleeping, and they didn’t.’

‘They kidnapped us!’ Betsy wails.

It is coming back to each of them in flashes. The bursting snow; the booming approach of the clockwork wolves; the first sight of the figures on their backs, hidden under layers of furs and leathers; the sudden scattering of white blossoms over their heads; the immediate, unstoppable fatigue. Teddy keeps trying to grasp at a slippery memory of looking up and seeing a face entirely covered except for its eyes, but the picture leaks away again and again. Betsy’s solitary recollection is of moving at speed through the trees. And Effie has no sense of movement or image at all; only that of two male voices in urgent conversation.

‘Something must have gone wrong, for them to have escaped the city.’

‘Something’s been going wrong for weeks, months.’

And then being swallowed into the deepest of sleeps.

Escaped, Effie thinks now. Escaped. As if they had been imprisoned there after all.

‘They’ve brought us here for a reason,’ Betsy insists. She has not yet glimpsed a person beyond the yurt walls, but she can hear them: their footsteps crunching through the snow; the lilting voices, calling out greetings or requests; the occasional slosh of water; the hiss and tick of flames. ‘Who are they, anyway?’

Teddy, one eye still on the rotating hog, shrugs. 'Vagabonds, she said.'

'Who said?' Effie asks.

'Talon.'

Betsy scrunches up her nose. 'What kind of a name is Talon?'

'A Vagabond name, I suppose.'

Betsy and Effie share a smile at this. Ted will not be drawn into making fun of the Vagabonds. He has the kindest soul either of them has ever known.

'Honestly, Teddy,' Betsy begins. 'I feel much stronger now. I can go outside. I really do need to find Puck.'

Reluctantly, Teddy agrees – on the condition that they wear one of the skins as a shawl to protect against the cold. The girls allow him to choose a heavy skin for each of them and drape it around their shoulders. Betsy's is dun-coloured and rough haired. Effie's is a deep, glossy brown. Huddling together, they step towards the door, where they pause, unsure of what to do next.

'All right,' Effie says, sidestepping around Betsy and gently shuffling her aside. 'Let me go first.'

Betsy and Teddy stand back as Effie puts her eye to the split between the canvases, then slowly pokes her head through and, with a gasp, stops. 'Oh!' says her muffled voice. 'You have to see this. It's…' She pulls her head back inside the yurt and, with a deep breath, shows them her widest smile. 'Incredible!'

They jostle each other out through the canvas and

gather just in front of the yurt, the heavy skins wrapped close around them, their mouths open in wonder. It is gloaming and black night is running like paint into the fading day. In the centre of the ring of yurts, a large fire burns, distorting the air it licks. And above the flames, in the shimmering heat, a glow of mantises dip and dance.

'Puck!' Betsy breathes. A lump rises in her throat. She won't know him now, amongst so many others.

'He's found his own kind,' says a soft, comfortable voice which is somehow already beside her. She whips around and finds herself looking into the pair of enormous, slightly hooded, pale green eyes. The woman nods. 'It's a good thing, don't you think, Betsy? The little creature belongs with his own.'

'I… Yes,' Betsy stutters. 'He does. I just didn't… I thought…' She would have liked to say goodbye, that is all. 'What are they doing here?' She nods towards the mantises. There are hundreds of them, floating around the fire like light pink ashes.

Talon shrugs. 'They simply arrived,' she replies. 'And we were happy to share our fire with them.'

'It's the heat,' Effie muses. 'It's keeping them alive. You don't ever let the fire go out, do you?' She turns her keen gaze on the old woman. Her eyes are bright as she assesses her new surroundings, taking in every detail and storing it for later exploration. It is what Betsy calls her 'lantern face'. It is what Millie always called 'intelligence'. Effie thinks that it is simply a look of curiosity.

'We don't,' Talon confirms. 'You are correct. We keep it burning always, for the food, for the light, for the water.'

'I bet these are the only ones that survived,' Effie continues, looking from Betsy to Teddy and back again in her excitement. 'They found a constant heat source. And you gave Puck one by stowing him under your hat. It was the closest they could get to the temperature they're used to in the East.'

'Doesn't explain how they came to be here in the first place, though,' Betsy counters at a whisper. 'Them, nor the foxes.'

'And yet you've made the link between the two,' Talon offers, her growing interest obvious. 'What else have you discovered?'

'Just that...' Betsy pauses to flick her eyes over Effie and Teddy, who give tiny nods of approval. 'That certain things are appearing from different parts of the world. The mantises from the Eastern forests. The foxes from Africa. The snow from the Antart. It is as if...' Betsy is threading her thoughts together as she speaks now. 'As if something had caused the world to become ... muddled.' Talon's attention is so focused on Betsy that it feels like a gale is blowing straight into her face. She shifts uncomfortably. 'Do you think we could see the orrery now?' she ventures.

Talon shows them wordlessly to the yurt where the crate containing the orrery has been stowed. There is no fire inside. Along the walls are stacked piles of polished wooden sledges of various sizes, with roped handles and carved feet. Here and there, nails have been driven into the yurt's posts; tattered nets hang from them like grubby wraiths. In the centre of the store is a sturdy hardwood table, on top of which sits an assortment of partly rusted tools, some tankards, a couple of magnifying lenses set into heavy gold cylinders. It is a workshop. For making … weapons?

Effie glances around again. Scythes protrude from a dented umbrella stand, glinting menacingly; small hand axes sit neatly in a chest designed to hold them side by side; clutches of what might be described as spears are bound together and stacked against a far wall. But … why? From what little she has so far seen of them, the Vagabonds don't seem like war-hungry people. Perhaps they mean simply to protect themselves.

'Have you ever been to war?' Effie asks quietly, her back deliberately turned to Talon.

'You are astute,' Talon replies. 'We have not been to war often, Effie. And never by choice. But it doesn't harm to be prepared, o'course. Especially given the disruption in the air.'

A cold shiver runs down Effie's spine at the thought of her parents, trapped in the storm they had created in Copperwell. She can't imagine why the effect was so much more pronounced when *she* sped up the orrery. She hadn't anticipated it, but she should have found a way to get back to her parents, warn them, persuade them to climb into Briny Erwin's cart with her and escape the city. They will be frantic, searching for her. They will believe her injured or dead.

'We caused that disruption, though, didn't we?'

There is a smile in Talon's voice when she replies. 'How do you imagine so?'

'We worked out that the orrery could control the Earth's orbit. That we could speed it up or slow it down. That all it took was music.'

'Music is a powerful tool,' Talon says.

'Powerful enough to make the Earth spin faster?' Teddy's voice rises in disbelief. Effie and Betsy have not yet had the opportunity to fully explain everything that happened while he was in gaol.

'Oh, yes. Powerful enough to link together all the movements of the heavens and the Earth.'

'But why was it different when we did it?' Betsy asks. 'Before, it was hardly noticeable until we saw the effects: the mantises; the snow. But when Effie played that scale, the entire city flew into chaos…'

'A scale played on a double bass can't have caused all that!' Teddy breathes.

Talon shrugs with one small movement of her eyebrows. 'The Earth itself sings, Teddy. As it spins in space, it sends sounds of its own out into the unknown. Don't you think that's beautiful? Don't you think that's admirable – to sing into silence without ever knowing if a song will come back in response?'

Since this is not exactly an answer to Teddy's question,

neither Betsy nor Teddy understand why Talon has mentioned it, but Effie does. Effie knows that what Talon is really talking about is them, and the Vagabonds, and how they're on their own now. They, too, will have to sing into silence and wait to see if anyone or anything sings back. That is what taking the orrery from the Unified Government means. That is what leaving Copperwell has led them to. That is what the woman on Wild Goose Way did the day the Constabulary took her away.

Whatever happens next, Effie thinks, they will soon find themselves singing into silence.

They duly check on the orrery and find that the Vagabonds have not so much as opened the crate.

'We have never been thieves, o'course,' Talon says gently, when Betsy blurts out her shock at finding the canvas Briny Erwin had nailed into each corner still intact. Betsy immediately stumbles over an apology, but Talon waves it away. She is neither embarrassed nor offended. She urges them to eat and rest, so that they might work out what they must do next.

'You have a task at hand, that much is clear,' she says, her eyes glittering. 'I've no need to know what it is, but if I can help you, I shall.'

'But … why?' Betsy blurts. 'You don't even know us.'

Talon smiles gently. 'And yet the world brought you here. Who am I to argue with the world?'

When night finally leaks fully over the forest, every inhabitant of the hollow gathers around the fire and sits below the cloud of dipping and eddying mantises, bowls in hand. A large cauldron sits on an iron tripod positioned over the flames, sending steam into the sky. The mantises revel in it, dancing quicker and shaping more elaborate patterns. The Vagabonds take turns to ladle the simmering soup into their bowls, then sit cross legged on animal-skin mats placed over the snow to drink it. The furs and wools they wear are not brightly coloured, but the Vagabonds have a brightness about them – like the moon, Betsy thinks; like the planets on the orrery. The air swirls with the scents of woodsmoke, deer dung and freshly baked bread. A spiced aroma rises from the soup. The wych elms which stand guard around the hollow creak and sway.

Talon steers Betsy, Teddy and Effie towards three woven mats which must have been laid out especially for them and introduces them to a young man and a young woman, who await them with bowled soup and curious expressions. The woman, Talon says, is called Birch, for the trees, and the man Swallow, for the birds.

Birch is a tall, rangy figure, with hair the colour of a slow sunset, which hangs far below her waist. A cluster of freckles bridges her nose. Her eyes are the colour of amber beads. She smiles and nods as Betsy, Teddy and Effie settle on the mats.

Swallow passes the bowls out, and Betsy studies the definite angles of the man's face, thinking about how every other adult she has known would say something like, 'You must be hungry' or 'Help yourselves, while it's hot' now. But Swallow says nothing. He does not need to. His every movement is mild, measured. Despite the sharp jut of his nose and the thickness of his jaw and the knotted bulge of his knuckles, his presence is calming. Betsy thinks that she would probably trust him with her life.

Effie, meanwhile, is thinking the exact opposite. She might have been tempted into believing so when she first woke, drowsy from the valerian, but they cannot put their trust in these people based on a hot meal and a good feeling. The Vagabonds could be in league with the Unified Government. Or they could just be using Betsy, Teddy and Effie to find out for themselves how the orrery is controlled. They should be quiet, let the Vagabonds do the talking, but she understands why Betsy is so keen to spill their secrets. It is a relief to speak them aloud, and the Vagabonds do have a way of persuading you to… Effie thinks it is a little like magic. Or hypnotism. Something instinctive makes you want to believe they are as gentle and kind as they seem.

Birch and Swallow settle opposite them and, together with Talon, the six make a crescent shape on the snow. Betsy is surprised to find that she is not at all cold. The heat from the fire blares against her cheeks and hands, the only parts of her skin which are exposed, and the soup thaws her insides. As she begins to relax, she glances up and, between the spindly topmost branches of the wych elms, sees the luminous sphere of an enormous wolf moon.

'But that...'

Birch follows her gaze. 'It shouldn't be possible, I know, but—'

'We've already had the wolf moon,' Betsy interjects.

'You know the skies, Betsy.'

'A little.'

'Then you must be Betsy of the Stars,' Talon replies.

Betsy does not respond. She feels a shyness around the Vagabonds that she has never experienced before. In Copperwell, she had known her turf; she had felt sure in her familiarity with every ginnel, every curve of the canal path, every secret spying spot in the shadowy Elm Gardens; she could climb onto the Saltsburg's Laundry rooftop and be able to point out the Serpentine constellation, the Sibyl, the Salubrious, within seconds. She knew the patterns of the sky above Copperwell as well as she knew her own stubborn mind. Now, she wishes she had her cyclopaedia, so that she could map out those stars most visible above the hollow. She should like to show Talon, and Swallow, and Birch that she is not just some worthless girl.

So, she takes a deep breath and explains properly what she and Effie did in their efforts to break Teddy out of gaol; how they sped up the orrery until day and night were flashing past second by second; how she had watched the moon dip and climb as though it were a thrown bandalore.

'We had noticed the changes,' Swallow says, when Betsy finally falters and stops. 'Not only on the date you describe but at other times, too. It was not so dramatic, before, but it was happening now and then. Sometimes three or four times in a lone season.'

'What did you notice?' Effie asks.

'Just the weather, at first,' Birch answers. 'The spring come too soon, or the autumn lasting too long. The trees felt it and grew too quickly, became weak. Then it was the animals. Species which had made the same journeys, the same choices, for centuries, got it wrong. Dove hawks always migrate east for the winter, but last year, they stayed here, struggled against the cold.' She pauses, a thoughtful look clouding her face.

'And there were new species, too,' Swallow continues. 'We've never penned in the deer, but for the first time in as long as we could remember, a bear attacked and took three.'

'A bear?' Teddy's voice is low, but Betsy can hear the panic in it.

Swallow nods. 'A brown bear. He's alone, as far as we can tell. We've laid out food for him since – fruits, some fish.'

'For a bear?'

Talon holds her soup spoon up in front of her. 'Everything needs to eat. He wouldn't have taken the deer otherwise. He must have travelled such a way from the north.'

Betsy glares at Teddy, urging him not to question them any further. She's already decided that she likes it in the hollow, that she admires the way the Vagabonds live, and that she would love to see a real live bear. She might even be able to stay here, after… After what? She's not sure. But there is something they must do: to protect the orrery; to stop the Unified Government's game; to help that poor woman on Wild Goose Way. And when that is all over, she will not be able to go back to Saltsburg's Laundry. Leaning over the steaming vat, draping mucky clothes over the scrubbing board, taking up her hand brush with Mrs S's voice shrilling in her ear and… No. She has just begun to see what the world outside Copperwell has to offer. She does not want to go back.

They talk about the brown bear and the hickory birds, the endless snow and the confused moon, the orchid mantises and the foxes. And then, finally, they talk about the shadows.

It has not escaped any of their attentions that the Vagabonds make no effort to conceal their shadows. The hollow is crowded with the strange shapes of the yurts, the hulking bodies of the milling deer, the towering flames of the vast fire, long wooden sleds trailing rope handles, clay pots stacked in bark-and-rust-coloured columns, pitchforks thrust into the frosted ground, the frequent back and forth of the quietly industrious Vagabonds. Everything is in such close and constant motion that the shadows are hardly noticeable. And besides, they do not seem to be ashamed of their shadows, as the inhabitants of Copperwell are. They have not, Effie thinks, been ordered to feel humiliation.

'You do not try to hide your shadows,' she says.

Talon shakes her head. 'Why should we?'

'We were ordered to, in Copperwell, by law.'

'And if you didn't obey?'

'Then the Constabulary would throw you in gaol,' Betsy answers.

Talon does not gasp. Neither do Birch or Swallow. The Vagabonds, the three friends are learning, are not a people who would do something so unconsidered as gasp. Their shock, however, is evident in their exchanged looks, their weighted pause.

'It seems to me…' Talon begins, and Betsy can see that she is measuring each word before she speaks it, '…that what you three have discovered is a great secret of the government. A great weapon, indeed. Until now, we could none of us fathom why nature had got itself so confused, why the shadows had started playing their tricks. But if this orrery really can manipulate the movement of the planets, speed up the Earth's rotation, then perhaps what the Unified Government's meddling has done is rushed us through our own evolution.'

Talon's conclusion is met by the snapping of the fire, the murmuring of the other Vagabonds as they sit in little clutches to eat and talk, the ghostly *whoo who-whoo* of an owl. It makes perfect sense. They might really have been catapulted towards a time in their evolution they would hardly recognise, where creatures from all the corners of the Earth live together, and people are truthful about who they are. The entire world has changed. Is changing. Perhaps it is even moving towards something better.

'But we haven't aged at all,' Effie considers. 'Why didn't we feel more of the changes?'

'Seems to me,' Talon says, 'that the Unified Government didn't want you to. Look at the weather pipes. What does their music do except drown out the true sounds of nature? For some years now, it seems to me that the government has been determined to remove the Wellians' connection with the rest of the world: its people, its systems, its music. They have a workforce too poor to step outside its routines, and too fearful to imagine what the rest of the world has to offer. Isn't this the first time you have left the city? The last woman to escape told us of it, insisted she had to go back, to try to put things right. We tried to persuade her to delay, that the time wasn't right, but Sika was—'

'Do you think it might be reversed?' Effie asks, just as Betsy opens her mouth to ask more about the woman called Sika.

'Couldn't say,' Talon replies. 'I don't see that it would need to be, o'course. Who are we to meddle? It should, perhaps, merely be allowed to settle. This orrery you have brought all this way with you. Might we consider it?'

Birch and Swallow retire to collect the crate and all six of them gather around it while Effie removes the canvas and she and Teddy lift the orrery free. They set it on top of the upturned crate and, as they take a step back, so the arms twitch into life and begin to swing about in search of their proper rhythms. At the end of each arm, the shining orbs wink and glimmer like eyes: even Saturn, the dullest of them, with its sandy colours, sparks in the glow of the nearby flames. They watch in silence as the planets dip and sweep and finally settle into their rotations. Mars is a blood-red jewel. Neptune is a dusky sky stippled by stars.

'If there's no way to reverse it,' Teddy begins in a hushed voice, 'and it's as you say, Talon, and the Unified Government's meddling has sped things up, then we'll have to live with our shadows stuck like this forever, won't we. Always betraying our secrets. Always revealing our doubts.'

'Are you so afraid of the truth, Teddy?' Talon replies.

Teddy tips his head back and squints up into the dark. 'I don't know if it's fear, but … I don't think I want to know so much about other people. And I certainly don't want other people to know everything about me.'

'Why ever not?' Birch asks and, glancing at her curious expression, Teddy understands that the concept of privacy is not one to which the Vagabonds subscribe. He cannot imagine what kind of place Copperwell might have been, had nothing been kept private. No heavy curtains drawn across windows. No locks on doors and no unexplained noises behind them. No orphan girls secreted in attics and worked to exhaustion. No grieving sons hiding their pain and confusion inside thick cottage walls. No rich girls sneaking through the city at night and using elaborate masks to hide their love of jazz. All the fear people had endured, when the Unified Government confined them to the darkness and ordered them to hide their shadows, would never have been experienced. Privacy, he realises, was promoted at the expense of knowledge in Copperwell. He and Betsy and Effie know nothing real about the world because of it. They would have known nothing of the Vagabonds – who live so close – had they not got lost in these woods.

He does not answer Birch's question. His thoughts have jumped too far forward to return to it.

'Is any of it true, then – what they've taught us about the world?'

'That conversation might take a long while,' Swallow answers. But they cannot resist beginning to pass stories over their soup bowls. Betsy, Effie and Teddy tell of their lessons about the four continents and the four gods associated with them. At the geography, the Vagabonds nod in recognition. To the gods, they do not respond at all; seemingly religion is a concept they are unfamiliar with.

'What of the rest of the Britannic Isles?' Swallow asks, propping his elbows on his knees and resting his chin on his palms when they have relayed all the information they can call to mind about The Antart and Africa and Amerikk. 'You seem to know nothing of that which immediately surrounds you.'

'We were told about how dangerous it was beyond the safely of the canal. About the hunters who swarmed through the woods, and all the creatures we might fall prey to.'

'These woods have always been harmonious,' Swallow confirms. He, Birch, and Talon proceed to describe the various communities who make up the rich and varied country outside of Copperwell: tribes, like their own, huddled under tree canopies as the rain drips or basking under the stars when the clouds clear; towns, dotted along the cliffs and crooks of the coast, peopled by fishermen and sailors and women who pick cockles from the sand and sell them from baskets; families, walking the hills with crooks and dogs and driving herds of cattle and flocks of sheep to new grazing places; metropolises, ten times the size of Copperwell, where clockwork birds fly over the streets, snapping photograms of ordinary people going about their days to make records for the authorities; cities where all steam power has been outlawed, and there are no locomotives, no clockwork carts, no movement beyond that which humans and horses can create for themselves; circuses, packed up into great wagon-trains and hitched from village to town to city, to exhibit woolly mammoths and phoenixes and mermaids.

'But … why wouldn't they want us to know?' Teddy breathes.

Talon cocks her head kindly at him. 'Because, Teddy, those people who have the most knowledge ask the most questions. They are the people who challenge unfair systems, who hold those in authority to account, who bring about the most change. Do you see?'

His head whirls at the people and places the Vagabonds have described. In a world like that, it seems entirely possible that the Aur exists and that he really could go and search out the golden horse of his father's dreams. In a world like that, he might become something more than a canal worker. In a world like that, Octavia and Trudy and Old Man Hatch might be free to live without struggle and hunger and fear. Erwin would have loved it.

'We have to go back,' Teddy blurts. He has barely begun imagining where they might go, what they might see, but his friends' faces are painted across his mind now, and he cannot leave them in Copperwell, believing that there is nothing more for them than scratching a living on the canals and hiding from the Constabulary.

'To Copperwell?' Betsy's eyes bulge in incredulity. 'I ain't never setting foot in that stinking—'

'He's right,' Effie says, placing a calming hand over Betsy's forearm. 'All those people. We can't just leave them trapped there.'

In the firelight, Betsy's slate-grey eyes spark. The girls stare at each other for a while and then, feeling other gazes on their faces, they turn to see Talon, Swallow, and Birch watching them. Talon gives the smallest nod of her head, her lips twitching into a smirk.

'It is what Sika said, too. We should not have let her go alone. We'll accompany you,' she says. 'But first, you must rest.' She opens her mouth to say something more, but she is distracted by a commotion coming from behind the yurts. It resembles a quick drumming sound, but it is softened somehow. Her face falls into a frown. 'The deer,' she breathes.

CHAPTER EIGHTEEN

Shadow Show

When Talon returns – confused and worried but unwilling to reveal why – from calming the frightened deer, it is agreed that Betsy, Teddy and Effie will spend one full day and one full night in the hollow before they begin the journey back to Copperwell. 'You must,' Talon insists. 'You cannot begin your battle in exhaustion.' And she is right. Despite the deep sleep brought on by the valerian, they remain tired. They return to the yurt in which they first woke and sleep until dawn, when a young Vagabond boy by the name of Otter rouses them with tankards of steaming milk.

They sit around the fire now, warming their hands on their tankards and chewing on strips of dried meat. Otter loiters nearby, evidently keen to make friends.

'I could take you to the river,' he offers. 'We take turns to collect the water.'

'Thank you, Otter,' Effie replies. 'I'd like that.' After their race through Copperwell, their plunge into the stinking canal mud, and their walk through the forest, she feels grimy right down to her bones. She can think of nothing more appealing than splashing clean, cold river water over her face.

They traipse down to the river, following Otter's bobbing blond head as he dances between the trees and through the long grass towards the water. They are joined by a Vagabond girl, a year or two older than Otter, who goes by the name of Ermine. She has hair the colour of dropped leaves and flows over the ground as fluidly as the animal she is named for.

At the water's edge, they find three more Vagabonds, splashing barefooted through the shallows. The morning is brilliant and sharp-edged. A light wind scuffs the water, making it ripple. On its surface, the Vagabonds' shadows undulate.

'Astral. Lupine. Thorn,' Otter says, pointing from one to the next. They are a little older than Otter and Ermine. Perhaps a similar age to Betsy, Teddy and Effie. They take turns to throw back their heads, close their eyes, and stand entirely still in the flow of water. The girl Otter identified as Lupine holds her hands out, palms up, as though enjoying a fall of summer rain, and as she does so her shadow slowly morphs and shifts until it takes on the form of a thick-pelted wolf. The wolf shadow flares for a few seconds, before shrinking back into the approximate shape of a girl.

Effie leans close to whisper. 'Lupine. It comes from the Latin, *lupus*. It means wolf.'

Lupine's shadow, even when girl-shaped, retains something of the wolf: the hair is mane-like; the facial features are slightly too long and pointed.

'I don't understand,' Teddy whispers back. 'I thought

the shadows were already showing our true selves. How can she be changing hers even more?'

'Perhaps,' Effie replies, hypothesising, 'the way the Vagabonds view themselves is already more honest than we can imagine. Think about it. The shadow shift didn't matter to them because their given names already revealed some truth of their personalities. Now, maybe they're pushing their shadows to be even bolder, to show more of what really makes them the people they are.'

They're experimenting, Teddy realises. Just like he, Effie and Betsy had done in the clearing. They are simply more practised at it.

'Can *you* do that?' Betsy asks Otter.

Otter nods. 'But only for a heartbeat.' He obliges and, closing his eyes, lowers his head in concentration. His shadow shimmies and slips over the snow and, fleetingly, becomes recognisable as the long slick form of a true otter. He releases his held breath and his shadow returns to the playful, gambolling version of himself that they have followed from the hollow. 'Talon is best at it,' he says. It is clear he feels himself a disappointment.

'You're very good at it, too,' Effie says. 'Do you think you can teach me how to do it?'

Otter's face brightens. 'I can try.'

'Good. Because there's something I want to ask you in return. You and Ermine. Do you think you might be willing to do me a favour?'

Otter nods vigorously.

'Look!' Teddy shoves at Effie and points her attention back towards the three Vagabonds in the water. The girl Otter named as Astral is taking her turn at manipulating her shadow and as she concentrates, so her human form begins to break apart. At first, it seems gruesome, but as her arms and her legs and parts of her torso become independent, so they begin to whirl and wind, like the cogs of the clockwork wolves. No, Effie thinks, it is a looser movement than that. It is less measured. The individual globes of shadow spin and pulse and, on the sun-shone surface of the water, they spark like gemstones.

'It looks like the aurora borealis,' Betsy says. 'It's amazing! Perhaps...' She stops and drops her head. 'Perhaps there's a part of me that looks like that.'

'Betsy of the Stars – that's what Talon called you,' Teddy reminds her. 'I think she was right.'

'I wonder why she hasn't given me a name?' Effie says, a little shyly.

'She'll be making sure to find the right one,' Teddy replies.

'You have a lot of trust in Talon, Ted.'

'I do.' He nods. 'I think I do. Look how perfectly she has named the Vagabonds.' He indicates the shadows on the river. 'She has an instinct for people. Even before she could see their shadows, she could see their souls. You said so yourself, in a different way.'

Effie nods. 'You're right.'

'I know. Now, are we going to try this?' And, grinning

wide, he bends down, drags off his boots, and tiptoes towards the river.

Later, after they have plunged into the river, and attempted to alter the shapes of their shadows more extremely than ever before, run shrieking back through the snow on wet feet, and gathered around the fire in the hollow to warm up, Effie brings out her double bass and starts to play for the first time since she sent Copperwell into chaos. She is careful to avoid the upward tilt of G sharp harmonic minor, for fear of setting the orrery racing again, and sticks instead to flat notes. The result is that the invented tune is melancholy. Or perhaps calming is a better word, Betsy thinks, since the longer Effie plays, the stiller the hollow grows. Children who were scurrying around slow down and come to sit between the crackle of the flames and the vibration of the double bass' thick strings under Effie's horsehair bow. Adults emerge from their yurts and stand, swaying, to listen. The deer cease flinching about their enclosure – as they have been doing increasingly throughout the day – and finally fold down onto their knuckled legs to rest. The dogs who mill about the hollow, sniffing and scratching and tussling, slink onto their masters' laps to sleep. Even the trees seem to swing their branches less briskly when the wind gusts past. The orchid mantises drift around and about each other like blown petals, sometimes landing in people's hair, sometimes dancing over the shimmering heat of the fire.

'So, this is Euphemia's gift,' Talon murmurs, sitting down alongside Teddy and Betsy.

'She's a famous musician in Copperwell,' Betsy replies. 'Though she wears a mask when she plays. Her father wouldn't like it if he knew she was playing jazz, so she hides. They think it's lowly, you see, jazz...'

'That she plays so well is a talent,' Talon says, 'but her gift is that she has the ability to make people listen. That is a special gift, indeed. Too many have forgotten how to listen to the world, just as the Wellians have.'

Betsy wants to agree, but she doesn't quite know how to shape the sentiment. What she does know is that she, Teddy and Effie have all been trying to say *something* for such a long time, but that they haven't been able to find the right words, the best time, the most receptive audience. Betsy lets Talon's words repeat over and over again in her mind. *Too many have forgotten how to listen to the world.* But that, Betsy thinks, is because it has been made so noisy. She has tried to listen! She has sat in her attic room at Saltsburg's Laundry and willed the stars to sound louder than the clanking and chiming of the weather pipes, and the huff of the passing locomotives, and the cawing of the pincher gulls over the canal. And she was so small under all that racket that she could not even make her thoughts heard. That was how she felt. As though even her own thoughts were being silenced.

'I wanted to listen...' she begins. She takes a moment to formulate her sentence. She wants to get it right. 'I just... Everything seemed so much bigger than me.'

Talon gives one of her slow blinks of understanding.

'But even someone seemingly very small can change everything...' she replies, at length, '...if they learn to listen, really listen, and act in response.'

When dusk falls, Effie settles beside Otter and Ermine and rests her double bass against a nearby tree stump. Most of the Vagabonds are asleep, bundled around the fire or inside their yurts. Snores echo through the wych elms. Dogs growl after dreams they are chasing. The orchid mantises dance and dance above the flames, never seeming to grow tired. They must be visible from high above, Effie thinks: a pulsing, pink glow against the darkness, like a heart. She already knows that Betsy has fallen in love with this place and she is afraid that she might want to stay forever. She would understand why. Betsy has never had a true home, never been surrounded by people who think like her. But Effie considers that, despite their disagreements about music and schooling and what she should do next, perhaps she and her parents do think in the same way, regardless of what she might previously have believed. It is just that they have each been so desperate to do what is right for one another, that they have become muddled. They will put everything straight when Effie goes home to Berliner's Square, she thinks. If they ever get home, that is.

'You know how we're going to go back to Copperwell,' she says now to Otter and Ermine, who gaze at her with big, gleaming eyes. In the firelight, they look smaller and younger than they had on the riverside, and she wonders for a moment if they are the right people to entrust with this job.

'I wish you weren't,' Otter replies. 'Or I wish I were coming with you. I've never seen anything of the world except here.' He sighs heavily and, dropping his head, plucks at a budding green leaf which has managed to force its way out of the tree stump he is seated on.

'And I had never seen anything of the world except Copperwell,' Effie replies. 'But I can promise you that you are lucky that this is where you belong. Copperwell has many good things about it—'

'Like what?' Ermine interrupts, before Effie is able to finish her thought.

Effie pauses. 'Well … like wonderful musicians, and schools where you can learn about stories and equations and history. Good friends. Safe homes – for some lucky people. And theatres and universities and an observatory and…' She realises that perhaps Otter and Ermine won't recognise these terms. 'Places where you can study the stars or make believe you are somebody else entirely. But there are aspects of Copperwell that would fill you with horror, too.'

Their eyes grow bigger. 'Like what?'

'Gaols, where you might be locked up in a single, tiny room until you are very old indeed. And people called the Constabulary, who ride around on great horses and who can send you to gaol just for showing others who you truly are. And rules which mean you can never see the sunshine, that you must live your entire life in darkness.'

Otter and Ermine's expressions have changed from those of open wonder to those of tremoring fear.

'It sounds *awful*,' Otter breathes.

'In some ways, it is,' Effie concedes. 'But it's full of good people, and that's why we have to go back – to help them. That doesn't mean it won't be frightening, though. And that's why I need your help.'

'How can we help if we aren't allowed to come with you?' Ermine asks with a frown.

Effie drops her voice to a whisper. 'By protecting the orrery. You've heard us all talking, haven't you? You know how powerful it is?' The pair nod. 'I need someone here to control it while we're gone.'

'We don't know how.'

Effie leans in conspiratorially. 'My double bass,' she says, pointing her eyes towards the instrument. 'Do you have an instrument anything like that here?'

Otter tilts his head. 'We have harps.'

Effie recalls the instrument inside the yurt they first woke up in, with its pillar of bone and animal hair strings. 'Can you play?'

'A little,' Otter answers. 'But not like you. I could never play like Effie of Birdsong!'

'Effie of Birdsong?' Effie repeats.

Otter and Ermine nod eagerly. 'That's what Talon called you. I heard her just tonight. She's decided your name.'

A smile drags at Effie's mouth but she doesn't want the younger children to see how thrilled she is, so she clamps her lips tightly shut. Her shadow will be giving her elation away, she is certain, but the Vagabonds take little notice of the antics of their shadows for the most part, and she resists the urge to look directly at it as it swells like a balloon.

'Bring a harp out here,' she says, 'and I'll teach you both how to play a very special scale. There are a certain set of notes which belong to the orrery, and once you know them, you will be able to control it. Communicate with it almost. These notes unlock it, like a key. And I'll need someone trustworthy to help me with it when I am too far away. Would you—'

'We'll do it!' Otter and Ermine spring up in unison and flow away between the yurts to retrieve their harps.

Effie of Birdsong, Effie thinks, and finally allows her smile to spread wide across her face. Her Vagabond name. Her true name? It might be shortened to Birdsong, to match the other Vagabonds. Birdsong! It makes her feel, despite her nagging doubts, as though she is capable of anything.

And perhaps that is why, when the deer suddenly begin to career dangerously around their enclosure that night, she is the first to race towards them through the dark.

CHAPTER NINETEEN

Spooked

'What is it?' Birch gasps as she rushes up behind Effie. 'Can you tell what's wrong?'

Effie stands at the wooden fence which marks the boundary of the deer's enclosure, her hands clamped around two of the vertical posts. On the opposite side of the fence the deer are galloping around at such a pace that they collide painfully with one another, crash into the wood so that it creaks and splits, lock antlers and shove as though they are fighting for a mate, leap over the slighter deer they find in their paths. Their hooves pound the soft earth so heavily that Effie can feel their weight thundering through her stomach. Their nostrils flare and tremble. Their breath steams on the cold air. It is apparent that they are terrified. It is less obvious why.

'No idea,' Effie replies. 'I can't see anything. Do you think it could be the clockwork wolves?'

The wolves have hunkered on the periphery of the camp, seemingly asleep, since they carried Betsy, Teddy and Effie through the woods to the hollow. Secretly, Effie has stolen around the yurts to take glances at them, to check that they really are unmoving. She has witnessed nothing more than them shifting from their sides onto their backs, like a pair of drowsing dogs, but not enough time has passed yet for her to trust them.

Birch shakes her head. 'The wolves are safe. They have lived alongside the deer for years. Alongside us. They respond to our energy, our spirit.'

On the farthest side of the enclosure, a small deer scatters towards the fence and makes an almighty leap for freedom. She almost clears the fence but, at the last moment, she catches her hind hooves between the posts and tumbles face first into the snow with a deep grunt of pain. Birch takes off immediately, running around the enclosure until she reaches the young hind and, humming gently past her own breathlessness to settle the beast, slowly manipulates the deer's hooves until they slide free. The moment she is released the hind takes flight, bouncing away through the snow and between the shadows of the wych elms with her ears pinned back in terror.

'We have to let them go,' Birch says, breathlessly.

'But what if they don't return?' Effie asks.

'That will be their choice. We cannot make it for them. They'll hurt themselves if this continues.'

Birch is already dragging at a bent fencepost nearby. It has been weakened enough by the slamming of the deer that she is soon able to tear it loose, toss it to the ground, and begin work on a second. Effie understands that it has to be this side of the enclosure that they let the deer escape through. Were they to open the gate on the other side, the herd might scatter directly into the middle of the hollow, destroying everything in their path. She grips the wooden post Birch is struggling with and they drag at it together. The post pops free and they move to the next. They labour in silence but for the heaving of their breath, until they have removed around ten posts. The gap is wide enough for one deer to pass through, and the herd bunches together, growling and shunting in their desperation to be next to flee into the trees.

Soon, more Vagabonds appear from between the yurts and, seeing what Effie and Birch are doing, join them in heaving the fenceposts loose and hurling them aside. When half of the enclosure's northern periphery has been torn down, the Vagabonds stand clear and watch the deer leap through the snow and vanish into the darkness beyond the hollow.

Effie's heart gallops with them. She is panting heavily, as are the fifteen or so Vagabonds who arrived to help. It had felt such a lengthy spell of time, but as more Vagabonds and then Betsy and Teddy arrive to seek out the cause of the commotion, it becomes apparent that mere minutes have passed. Minutes, and the Vagabonds have lost perhaps a hundred and fifty deer. Effie does not know if they are kept for meat or breeding or simply as companion animals, but the loss will surely be devastating.

Soon Talon strides through the gathering crowd in her usual collected manner. The Vagabonds part for her to pass and fall into silence, though she had not spoken or indicated that they should. Her presence is so powerful that they cannot resist the urge to watch her every move. She takes a moment to observe the damage to the fence, the empty enclosure, the deep dents the deer's hooves have left in the snow.

'They were spooked,' she says quietly.

Hums of agreement move through the crowd, but no one ventures an opinion as to what might have so unsettled the deer. They acknowledge that the deer can sense the approach of danger, threat, but the forest surrounding the hollow seems as still as ever. Except…

Betsy appears alongside Effie and grips her hand. 'Do you think it's the Constabulary?' she hisses. 'Do you think they've followed us?'

'They can't have,' Effie replies. 'They're not permitted to cross the canal.'

'Prime Minister Bythesea might have changed the rules.'

Effie shakes her head. Her mind whirs as she thinks through the events which might have taken place since their flight from Copperwell and discards those she thinks unrealistic. Prime Minister Bythesea could not have issued a special order for the Constabulary to pursue them without admitting the enormous importance of what they had taken, and he could not admit to that without arousing suspicion that the Unified Government was losing control. At least, that would be the risk, and she does not believe such a vain and self-important man would endanger his own reputation in such a way. He might, however, have hired someone, desperate Wellians to hunt them down. It needn't be the Constabulary themselves. Given enough of a financial incentive, those poor souls condemned to a life of begging on the towpaths might possibly hand anyone over to the Constabulary. What other choice would they have?

'I don't think...' Effie begins, but she does not have the opportunity to finish before she is distracted by a fast, high-pitched sound. D sharp, Effie thinks automatically. The rushing note is followed by a deeper thud – a B flat – and a groan, and one of the Vagabonds slumps to the ground, gripping the arrow which has penetrated just above his collarbone.

The first arrow is chased by three more. They find their targets with sickening whumps. A nearby Vagabond woman clasps at her thigh; a tall, slim man clutches at his stomach. But they do not cry out. They lower themselves to the ground, where they are surrounded by their friends. It is tactical, Effie realises. They have practised a response strategy should they suffer an attack. It has happened before, then. Perhaps it is not true that they have trailed trouble behind them all the way from Copperwell. Perhaps competing tribes fight for survival in this forest. Perhaps the Vagabonds have enemies. And yet, hadn't Swallow claimed that the forest was harmonious?

The injured Vagabonds hunker down while the others form tight circles around them and, standing shoulder to shoulder, start to rotate. This, Effie concludes, is to cause confusion, since amongst so much contradictory movement, it will be harder for the shooters hidden in the woods to hit a target; they will be less likely to notice, too, when those positioned at the outside of the crowd break away to rush towards the yurts. Moments later, they return to the safety of their numbers and, forming a row between the gathered Vagabonds and the treeline, lift bows of their own, slot in their arrows, draw them back and – *psh, psh, psh* – fire them into the trees.

'What if they hit the deer?' Teddy breathes from somewhere close by.

'The deer are long gone,' an unknown voice replies.

A whistle sounds, long and shrill. With a grinding wheeze, the clockwork wolves spring from their sleep and clatter towards the Vagabonds, where they turn apart from each other and begin a loping revolution around and around the eddying crowd. Movement within movement, Betsy thinks, like the cogs which power the wolves; like the orbits of the orrery's planets; like the inner workings of all those machines she and Effie saw inside the Observatory. Like the solar system itself!

'It's the patterns!' she says, through clenched teeth. She grabs for Effie's arm, then whips around in search of Teddy. She pulls them both close, so that their heads are almost touching. 'It's all about the patterns,' she says. 'Whatever it is that powers the orrery, the machines hidden away in the Observatory, the clockwork which brings the wolves to life. The Vagabonds observe the patterns, the patterns of the planets, and they mimic them. Look! *That's* what the Unified Government has been stamping out all this time. They've separated us from the true music of the weather and the skies. They've made us look away from ourselves. I'm right, aren't I?' She stares deep into Effie's eyes, seeking a flicker of recognition, and though Effie flinches at the rushing sound of more flying arrows passing nearby, Betsy believes she sees a spark of agreement. 'Why?' she asks. 'Why would they do that?'

'Do you know, Ef?' Teddy asks. He is scared and panting.

Effie takes a deep breath. Her eyebrows drop lower over her eyes. She knows, Betsy thinks. She must have worked it all out. All the connections. All the truths. What exactly it is they have become embroiled in. But instead of words of explanation, all Effie offers is a shocked exhalation before she slumps forward into Betsy's arms.

As they crumple together to the ground, Betsy sees the arrow sticking out from between Effie's shoulder blades.

CHAPTER TWENTY

Patience

Betsy and Teddy sit beside the fire in the middle of the hollow and watch the orchid mantises dance. They have not spoken for hours. They listen to the smooth clanking of the clockwork wolves' workings, and the gentle crackle of the fire, and the creaking sway of the wych elms. Seeing the Vagabonds move into formation as they did when they came under attack has set off an endless series of bursting realisations in Betsy's mind, about how the Unified Government has severed the Wellians' connection with nature and instead created a city populated with people so desperate that they would work for a pittance to avoid struggling among the homeless on the towpaths. Hadn't Briny Erwin said something similar when they were at Saltsburg's? She had been too distracted to take it in properly, but what were the words that had drawn her attention? *I think that, for some time now, Copperwell has been dying.* But why? she wonders. Why would a government want to weaken their own people?

From behind them comes a sudden fluttering sound, and Teddy and Betsy whip their heads around nervously to discover a hunter owl swooping through the trees.

Feeling the heat of the fire, she ascends away from it until she becomes nothing more than a shadow. Despite the continued stalking guard of the clockwork wolves, the hollow feels empty and exposed without the deer. Teddy twists his scarf in his fists and turns back to stare into the flames.

'She'll be all right,' he murmurs.

Betsy swallows a swell of anger. She refuses to talk about Effie until she sets eyes on her. She cannot abide platitudes. The Vagabonds, she suspects, would never think to utter such empty words.

Once the Vagabonds had fired enough arrows of their own into the trees to chase off the invisible attackers, at least temporarily, Effie and the others who had been injured had been helped into a large yurt, where the Vagabonds' healers are now cleaning their wounds and packing them with soothing balms.

'They need to be left to their work,' Talon had explained as she'd ushered Betsy and Teddy away from the entrance to the yurt. 'They will call for you when Effie of Birdsong is rested.'

Betsy grinds her teeth. What if she never wakes up from her rest? What will Betsy and Teddy do then? It has been the three of them for such a long time; they function best that way. It has to be the three of them, together.

CHAPTER TWENTY-ONE

Warrior Mother

It takes another day and another night for the Vagabonds' particular blend of plants and herbs to start to close up Effie's wound. Though weak, she is soon well enough to sit up in her hammock bed and talk to Betsy and Teddy, and they can talk of nothing but their return to Copperwell. Effie drifts into sleep now and then, and her friends sit beside her and wait patiently for her to wake again. The Vagabonds come and go, bringing food, checking on those who were hurt in the attack. At hourly intervals, a healer called Zephyr, with eyes and hair so pale that they are almost the colour of clouds, carefully removes the dressing on Effie's back, smears more deep-green balm over the injury, and covers it again.

'You are healing well, Effie of Birdsong,' Zephyr says quietly. 'Wait one more day, though, before you start on these plans.'

'I promise.'

Zephyr inclines her head. 'The deer will all have returned in one more day.'

'The deer?' Teddy asks, frowning.

Zephyr inclines her head a second time. 'They started

to drift back last night. They are coming in threes and fours.'

'I can't believe they came back,' Teddy says.

'Why wouldn't they? It was the fright they were running away from, not us.'

'Then, does that mean whoever attacked us won't return? That they're gone?'

'For now,' Zephyr says. 'Perhaps.'

'Do you know who they were?' Betsy asks at a whisper. Effie and Teddy both hold their breaths, knowing that what Betsy is really asking is, 'Did they come for us or for you?'

Zephyr shrugs. 'We do not know that yet, and so there is little point speculating on who they were, or why they came, or whether they will return. When we find out the answers to those questions, then we will be able to respond.'

'But if they *do* return…' Teddy says.

'Then we will do what we must to protect ourselves.'

'And if you can't?' Effie breathes.

This time, Zephyr does not answer. She bows her head and steps out of the yurt.

The Vagabonds organise a full expedition party to escort Betsy, Teddy and Effie back to Copperwell.

Talon is to lead the party. She insists, and it is obvious that no one dares question her. She is, unquestionably, the Queen of the Vagabonds. When Betsy asks her firstly if that is so, and secondly if she has a crown, she smiles and says quietly, 'Amongst the Vagabonds, it is not Queen but Warrior Mother. And what need would I have of such a thing as a crown?' Betsy thinks of Prime Minister Bythesea and all the rich men of the Unified Government. She thinks of King Glennister and his gilded carriages, his grand ceremonies, his velvet-robed attendants and all their priceless instruments of ritual. *They* seem to have every need of a crown. She has never thought to wonder why, until now.

She considers Talon, as she loops a leather bridle around the slick black nose of the largest deer, her knotted hands moving swiftly, her hooded eyes fixed in concentration, and decides that, in her layered skins and leathers, with her silver-white hair tightened into thick plaits, she appears as majestic as any person possibly could.

Birch, Swallow, and perhaps fifteen other Vagabonds harness a deer of their own, secure their bridles, and swing onto their backs. Each has strapped around them a hog-skin bag, the hair still smoothly attached, in which, Betsy supposes, they will carry food. Or weapons. Though she cannot imagine any one of the Vagabonds possessing a revolver, as some of the Constabulary do, they might carry bows and arrows, and small axes or blades perhaps. Mounted on the barrel-chested red deer, their strong legs hooked about the animals' flinching ribcages, their long hair either plaited and decorated with feathers or concealed beneath rough leather hats, they look both handsome and fearsome. They steer the deer through the hollow, weaving between fire pits and yurts and gathering items they might need as they go. Betsy, Teddy and Effie trail after them, watching as other Vagabonds hand them cylindrical containers of water and small brassy whistles, which they hang around their necks. Otter appears to hand Talon a heavy axe, which she slides into a buckled length of leather and secures across her back. Teddy cannot imagine now how, just three nights before, he had thought her old and weak. She moves slowly, yes, but that is because she considers each action, does not waste an ounce of energy.

'I could come with you,' Otter suggests, his eyes big and pleading, his jaw set in a manner he must believe demonstrates strength. Teddy knows that Talon will not agree. He has already learnt that strength cannot be painted on the outside of a person in the way this boy is attempting.

'Thank you for the offer, Otter, but you are not yet of age.'

'Neither are they,' Otter replies, flicking his eyes towards Betsy, Teddy and Effie.

'No,' Talon agrees. 'But they are going home.'

And already, Betsy thinks, that word – home – sounds wrong.

When they reach the edge of the hollow, Talon reins in her deer and coaxes it around, so that she can address those Vagabonds who are remaining behind. They consist of the old and the young and a group, Effie understands as she watches them shuffling together to listen to Talon's instructions, who are of a similar age to those who sit on their deer waiting to follow Talon to Copperwell, but who have been chosen to stay behind to protect the hollow. It is no accident, Effie thinks, that they live so peaceably and privately here. They have divided themselves into a fighting force and a defensive force, in preparation for threat. They had known, sooner or later, that the cities would sneak far enough into the forests to discover them, to disrupt them. It is not only because Betsy, Teddy, and Effie were brought to her that Talon is helping; she also has to protect her own people.

'We believe,' Talon begins, casting her voice out clearly but not loudly. There is no need to shout; the Vagabonds are always ready to listen to her. 'That the Unified Government of Copperwell has been using that orrery...' She indicates the place where the crated orrery is once again safely stored '...for ill. Protect it. We will ride into Copperwell to demand the freedom of the city's political prisoners, and to ensure that the Unified Government does not possess any other instruments of control. We will ride in by daylight, so that they might see our shadows, and understand that they should not condemn their population to live in darkness. If we do not return in three days, you might not expect to see us again. If that is our fate, do not mourn us, but do hold our memories close.'

Betsy expects that a cheer will go up, but the Vagabonds opt instead to steeple their hands before them and lower their foreheads to their matched thumbs in a kind of bow. Silently, the mounted Vagabonds echo the movement.

Betsy leans into Effie and whispers, 'It's as if we're going to war.'

'Well,' Effie replies, 'I think we are.'

Betsy reaches out to clutch Effie's hand in one of hers and Teddy's in the other.

Talon lifts her head from her bow and, slipping her fingers between her lips, lets out a long whistle. A high C, Effie thinks. The whistle blows through the wych elms and is soon answered by the rush of wings on the air. A flock of birds. A flight of kestrels! They soar into the hollow and swoop and dip overhead, as though awaiting their next order.

'How did you…?' Betsy is breathless. The kestrels' speckled brown feathers and black-tipped fan tails twitch and tilt. They shrill and shriek.

'Remember, there is much to be gained from listening and observing, Betsy,' Talon says. 'Watch.'

She lifts the little brass whistle from around her neck and, putting it to her lips, blows through it two notes: a falling tone. A pause, and then there comes a clicking and a clanking. A grinding. A rhythm that any Wellian would know in an instant. Clockwork.

Despite the reassurance of the wolves' presence over the past two days, ice slips down Betsy's spine. She catches Teddy's attention and bulges her eyes. They are taking the wolves with them.

The clockwork wolves appear from between the trees, prowling and sparking, and Teddy shudders: even after the incident with the deer, this is the closest they have come since they carried him into the hollow. Though Talon has assured him that they are on the side of the Vagabonds, he doesn't see how she can be certain. What if the wolves, when they near Copperwell, revert to their original allegiance? Under the control of the Unified Government, they would be deadly. They must have been deadly when they first patrolled the canal.

'No need to be afeard, Teddy,' Swallow says, appearing beside him. And before Teddy can respond, he approaches the nearest wolf, hooks a toe into the lowest rung of the machine's metal ribcage, and clambers up onto its back. He lays a square of softened leather just behind its withers, in place of a saddle, and settles on it. Then he retrieves a thinner leather rein from his pocket, threads it through a gap in the metal mouldings of the wolf's mane and fashions a handle with which to steady himself. He throws Teddy a wide grin. 'You can take the other.'

'No!' Teddy shakes his head.

'I will!' Betsy says, raising her hand and striding towards the great clockwork beast. Imitating Swallow, she hooks a toe into the wolf's metal ribcage and clambers up onto its back in the swift manner of a marmoset. Climbing onto the Saltsburg's Laundry roof has proven good practice. She swings her leg astride the clockwork back and settles herself proudly. 'Come on,

Teddy. There's plenty of space. Share with me. Effie can go with Swallow.'

With a grin, Effie accepts Swallow's outstretched hand and hoists herself up onto the shyer wolf's back, wincing slightly but not uttering a sound as her wound stretches tight. That the girls are braver than him is no surprise to Teddy. They always have been. But how they can sit so confidently on top of those monstrous machines, he really doesn't know.

'It's just like being on horseback,' Effie insists.

'It is not.'

'All right. Not quite. But if you'd rather try a deer … or walk all the way back to Copperwell…'

Teddy rolls his eyes. 'I don't want to walk,' he admits quietly.

'Then get on with it,' Betsy answers.

With a sigh, Teddy sidles closer to the clockwork animal, his nerves twitching. He is ready to flee, should the wolf swing its head in his direction. But it only stands, entirely still and calm, and waits as Teddy finds a toehold, grips at the metal spine, and drags himself up to sit behind Betsy.

'You are riding Dahlia,' Swallow explains. 'And ours is Idris.' He pats the creature's sculpted neck.

'They have names?' Betsy says.

'Of course,' Swallow replies. 'Every soul deserves a name.'

They nod in silent agreement and, when Ted has finally

shuffled back and forth enough times to settle himself, he leans in close to Betsy and says, past his clenched jaw, 'You can control it.'

'It's not like I'd let you, even if you wanted to,' Betsy returns.

With Teddy finally seated and the Vagabonds mounted on their shining red deer, Talon issues a long swooping whistle, and they begin to walk, then lope, out of the hollow. Strapped securely to a wooden sled is the crate they used to sneak the orrery out of Copperwell. It is weighted down with stones. They cannot risk taking the orrery with them, but if they are being watched, or followed, they have to lead their pursuers away from the hollow. They have to make them believe they are bringing that strange and powerful treasure with them.

Talon takes up the tip of the arrowhead formation. She is followed immediately by the rest of the deer herd, who, as they gather speed, cease their flighty fidgeting and settle into a shared rhythm. The Vagabonds' hair and furs flag behind them. Betsy, Teddy, Effie and Swallow atop the ticking clockwork wolves, stalk in their wake. Teddy gets bumped around a little; he does not know the animal's gait the way he does a horse's. But Betsy seems to have adjusted to it instantly, and she laughs and whoops at the top of her lungs as they begin their trek back towards Copperwell accompanied by the whirling kestrels, a pack of rangy grey lurcher dogs, and their unshakeable belief in what is right.

CHAPTER TWENTY-TWO

Towards the Light

The Vagabonds know hundreds of ways to move stealthily through the forests. After the initial burst of excitement, the expedition party weaves quietly along narrow paths which meander between towering tree trunks, then teeters along the edge of an endless escarpment, then splashes through rivers and edges around great, flat lakes. Effie had not realised the world could open so wide. Keeping her arms locked around Swallow's middle, she commits every valley, every glint of water, every skyline she can see to memory. She would love to live amongst the Vagabonds, as Betsy had suggested, and know these cliffs and gullies as well as she knows the back streets and jazz venues of Copperwell, but she is not convinced that it could ever happen. She is not convinced that they will ever see daylight again if the Constabulary catch up with them – the Constabulary, or whoever is following them – for Talon is certain, and makes it known amongst the party, that they are being trailed at every turn. Consequently they hardly speak as they move towards Copperwell. They do not pause to rest. Betsy, Teddy and Effie endeavour to listen, as Talon has told them they ought.

They each make a list, which they might share later.

The beat of the deer's hooves, Teddy thinks. The huff of their breath. The clank of the wolves' clockwork. The creaking of leather saddles. The crunch of the snow beneath them.

Effie's list is more concerned with those sounds she can most readily attribute a note to: the C sharp *killy-killy*ing of the kestrels above; the A flat moan of tree branches; the F natural flow of a river they cross.

Betsy pushes her listening further. She feels past the immediate noise the party makes as they proceed through the frosted forest and reaches for the rush of the wind. She closes her eyes and follows it as it drops to the ends of her hair then rises to weave between the uppermost branches of the oak trees, and as it climbs further still to race above the forest canopy, and as it brushes the bellies of the clouds. She reckons she can hear it still as it swoops down into the next valley. And on it, she hears but cannot decipher the hushed whispers of those who trail them.

At midday Talon whistles the kestrels out ahead and the party veers into a clearing beside a small pond. When the birds return, Talon declares that they are within five miles of the Copperwell Canal and grants both humans and animals some minutes to rest. The deer and the dogs drink greedily from the pond. Vagabonds and Wellians trudge through the snow to the water's edge, to fill up their tankards and splash their faces, which are raw from the cold wind and the sun. Betsy, Teddy and Effie are so unused to it that their skin is beginning to chap, but they do not complain. They are more determined than ever to move out of the Unified Government's imposed darkness and towards the light.

'Do you really think this will work?' Teddy asks, at a whisper. 'I mean, they will have increased security at the Observatory tenfold since we took the orrery. We'll never get in.'

The plan they have concocted involves Talon leading the Vagabonds through the city towards the Unified Government buildings in Royal Quarter, chanting as they go, to peacefully demand the release of all those prisoners held under the regulations of The Shadow Order, which, she insists, violates basic human rights. Talon is convinced that such a stance, made in broad daylight, will persuade hundreds of Wellians to venture outside and join them in protest, and that by the time they arrive before the government buildings, they will constitute a throng of united citizens. Effie had warned Talon that the Constabulary would not let her get so far, but she had smiled and insisted that she would 'communicate with the Constabulary' when the time came. Meanwhile, it was agreed, Betsy, Teddy and Effie, knowing their way around the Observatory, would return to the orrery room and destroy all those instruments of potential control they had found on their first visit. Though she had said nothing, the thought of it makes Betsy sick to her stomach. All those beautiful instruments. Each, it had seemed to her, with a personality of its very own. She cannot stand to think of the astronomical regulator's golden pendulum ceasing to swing, or the many clockfaces of the gleaming horologium being stilled and silenced. Even those pages covered with the blackened scribbles of so many equations seem to her too glorious to destroy.

'I don't think we should damage anything,' Betsy murmurs now, glancing backwards to make sure Talon and the others cannot hear her. 'I think we should take it all.'

'And do what with it?' Teddy asks.

Betsy gives a shrug. 'Learn how to control it, the way they have. We couldn't do much worse at it. We might even do some good.'

'How?'

'I don't know.' Betsy scuffs at the ground with the toe of her boot. 'I just… I feel like … as if it might need us?'

Effie frowns at her, trying to figure out what it is that Betsy cannot bring herself to say out loud. So often, what leaves Betsy's mouth is entirely different from what she means. She is one of those people who shouts to keep themselves from crying.

'They're just models,' Effie says. 'Clockwork.'

'No.' Betsy shakes her head. 'No. They're more. Hasn't the government proved that? Hasn't Talon? She said that she changed the temper of the wolves.'

'She found a way to alter what they had been designed to do,' Effie insists. 'But… I don't know… Perhaps their temper was nothing more than their purpose. Perhaps it was an accident that I happened to find the sequence of notes which unlocked the orrery. Talon must have found the key to the wolves too, but that doesn't mean they had a temper. They're not alive, and neither is any of the equipment in the orrery room.'

Betsy twists the toe of her boot deeper into the snow. 'Not alive in the same way we are, perhaps. But the Vagabonds have a different way of looking at things, and I think it's clever. I'd like to look at the world and see the potential life in everything, the way everything might be connected, wouldn't you?'

Effie nods. 'Yes. All right. I would like to see the world that way.'

'Then look at it that way!'

Betsy pulls her leg back and kicks at the mound of snow she has been fidgeting with, scattering the flakes outwards like the clocks of a blown dandelion. They hang on the air a moment, glistening, before they drift back to the ground.

'Do you really think it's possible to be a Wellian and just...' He clicks his fingers. '...think like a Vagabond?' Teddy asks.

'Not so easy at that,' Betsy replies. She tips up her chin, indignant. 'But it could be learnt, if a person cared enough to try. And anyway, we aren't Wellians. If we were, we wouldn't have taken the orrery in the first place; we wouldn't have run away into the forest; we wouldn't have broken The Order. We aren't ever going to be Wellians again, are we?'

At this, she expects Teddy and Effie to agree vociferously. Of course they'll never be Wellians again! They've discovered a little pocket of the world so entirely different from their own, that they can surely do nothing but go striding out into the forests, through the cities, along the coasts, across the seas. They might never stop still in one place again, should they choose a wandering existence. Betsy would not admit to it, but she is already harbouring imaginings of the three of them travelling across the four continents, the orrery and the astronomical regulator and the horologium stowed in wagons like spectacles in a circus show, selling tickets to people who will come to listen to them teach the workings of the instruments and reveal how they had overthrown the Unified Government of Copperwell in order to take them back and prevent them from being misused again. It would be a tale of heroism. Audiences would flock from all over. The Wellians – as they would no doubt be known, though the word would mean something different then – would become famous and earn their livings sitting around fires and spellbinding children from Cymru and Eire, Roma and Saigon with the stories they would gather along the way. They would inspire others to venture out and discover the world, to learn to listen to its words and notes, to live *with* it and not simply *in* it.

Teddy and Effie exchange a glance, which causes Betsy to stiffen.

'I think perhaps I'd like to look for the Aur,' Teddy admits, tentatively.

'I thought the Aur was a myth.'

'We thought everything outside Copperwell was a myth until a couple of days ago,' Teddy returns.

'You're right,' Betsy says. 'Course you are. We'll go together. We could help you, couldn't we, Ef?'

Effie opens her mouth to reply, but no words follow. She pauses for two seconds, three – her head is throbbing and her wound is smarting – and then her silence is interrupted by Birch.

'Are you ready?' Birch trots her deer towards them and steers it around them in a tight circle. Betsy can see the animal's nostrils flaring, smell its earthy scent. Along its neck, its skin twitches, causing the hair there to shimmer.

'Yes,' Effie says. She and Teddy begin immediately to follow Birch towards the rest of the Vagabonds and the waiting clockwork wolves. Betsy trails forlornly behind, saying nothing.

CHAPTER TWENTY-THREE

Outside the City

If Mrs S or Briny Erwin or Chief Justice Hart had ever told Betsy that on some future day she would view Copperwell and consider it looked small, she would not have believed them. As the expedition party stands on a hillock just outside the city, however, and looks across the canal, everything seems oddly shrunken. The streets, which before had seemed numberless and intricately intertwined, now appear as modest and obviously patterned as the threads of a spider's web; Betsy hopes they might be as easily broken. The buildings, which she had always thought reminiscent of grand palaces, look both dull and embarrassingly showy. Perhaps it is the light, she thinks. The day is flat and grey, and crowned by colourless cloud. Perhaps she has grown so used to seeing Copperwell by the glow of the moon that it appears strange to her now, exposed like this. Or perhaps it is that her perception has already changed since being among the Vagabonds.

She looks around for Talon, and finds her still sat astride her deer, her head twitching towards the trees, the rushing canal, the rest of the expedition party. Her eyes dart about. Something is wrong – Betsy knows it.

She leans towards Teddy until she is close enough to feel the heat of his breath on the cold air. 'Look at Talon. She's waiting for another attack.'

Teddy considers Talon through a squint. 'Why would they follow us all the way back first?'

Betsy shrugs. 'Maybe they saw that the Vagabonds were too strong, too well organised, and realised they couldn't overwhelm them on their own turf. Now, they're separated, in unfamiliar territory.'

'You're right,' Teddy concedes. 'And look at the position we're in. Forest behind us, canal in front. We've nowhere to go, Bets. They've cornered us.'

'Ef!' Betsy beckons for Effie, who has not yet climbed down off the back of Idris. Effie swings her leg over the enormous beast, slides down its metal ribcage, and gives it a swift pat before joining Betsy and Teddy.

'We think they've followed us back,' Teddy whispers. 'Whoever attacked the hollow.'

She shuffles closer. 'What can we do?'

The Vagabonds are growing busier about them, removing the reins from their deer and letting them mill down towards the canal, throwing scraps to the dogs, who promptly lie down, clamp their treats between their straggly grey paws, and begin to chew. The kestrels hang on the air, their wings rippling, their tails ruddering, their heads entirely still and their black apple-pip eyes fixed on all that is happening beneath. They are poised, Betsy thinks; ready. She is less sure if she is.

‘We have to lead them into Copperwell,’ Teddy says. ‘We know the best routes. We have to get them through the city, the fastest way.’

‘But what if we’re not safer there?’ Betsy asks.

‘We couldn’t be in a worse position than this,’ Effie puts in.

And when, less than a minute later, the first clutch of arrows whirs past them, Effie is proved right. They have two choices: turn into the attack and return fire blindly, without the protection of the forest at their backs; or cross the canal, which has been set raging by the orrery’s disturbances, and, if they make it out of the water, take their chances with the Constabulary. The Vagabonds respond immediately. Pulling their bows from their backs, they slot into a defensive formation, arranging themselves into rotating circles, just as they did in the hollow. At their outermost edge stalk Idris and Dahlia, their heads low and their manes seeming to bristle. Though Betsy had imagined being this close to Copperwell would cause them to revert to their previous allegiance, thankfully the clockwork wolves remain loyal to the Vagabonds, leaping and twisting into the path of as many flying arrows as they can and deflecting them. The arrows clang against their metal bodies and drop to the ground. But they cannot catch them all and a few break through the Vagabonds’ defences to find a human target. Those hit suffer the sharp new pain in silence and continue to fire their own arrows into the trees, towards the just visible faces which appear fleetingly between the trunks before sinking into invisibility again. The faces, Effie thinks, are ashen and timid and … unmistakeably Wellian! The Constabulary really did recruit the most desperate for this terrible job. But there are so many of them, and they are perfectly positioned, and though the Vagabonds continue to fire their arrows, they are shifting backwards all the while towards the black rush of the canal. There is no other way back. The entirety of Copperwell is encircled by this same body of unbridged water.

Teddy slinks between them, whispering, 'Keep going, towards the water. We have to cross. We'll show you the way.' Over and over he repeats the instruction, until every Vagabond has his voice in their ear.

When they reach the canal's edge, they pause in their shooting to swing onto the backs of their deer. Having ridden in on the wolves – who are still patrolling the perimeter of the shifting party – Betsy, Teddy, Effie and Swallow are without mounts. Seeing this, Talon urges the Vagabonds to arrange their deer into two lines, so that they will act as a barrier in the water and keep the others from being swept away. Teddy knows that they cannot mount one of the deer already carrying a Vagabond; the weight of two people and the rushing water would prove too much for the flighty, slim-legged creatures. He catches Talon's eye and gives her a nod and then, with Talon's deer and that of another Vagabond named Howl flanking him, he plunges into the slate-grey water. At the direction of their riders, the faithful deer plunge in alongside him and begin pumping their knuckled legs, snorting in terror at the roiling water, the eyes showing white crescents of fear. Behind them, arrows continue to clang against the impenetrable bodies of the wolves, who wait until all the Vagabonds and their deer are in the canal before striding in after them.

The water is so cold that it clamps around their limbs, making it feel as though they are trying to swim through concrete, but they splash desperately on. They have no choice but to reach the opposite bank and haul themselves ashore in Copperwell, whatever might be waiting for them there. But they are being battered by an onslaught of arrows now, and there is so little they can do to defend themselves. The crate of stones which they are pretending contains the orrery is swallowed by the currents and swirls away.

When they are perhaps halfway across, Teddy paddles around to check that Betsy and Effie are still close behind him. His limbs are trembling and his teeth are clattering together. Betsy looks more composed than he feels, but Effie is paling by the second. Being so recently wounded, she is not strong enough for this.

'Ef!' he gasps, and kicking towards her, he offers her his shoulder to cling to. 'Hold on, come on. We're nearly there.'

They both know that's not true, but they kick on with all their might, surrounded by the rhythmic belly-grunting of the deer, and the steam of their puffed breaths, and the relentless swoosh of the freezing water as it shoves and shoves at them. They kick their legs and punch their arms, and their bodies get colder and more tired, and the opposite bank of the canal appears to grow more distant.

'Come on,' Teddy says, again and again. 'We're nearly there,' he cries, as a Vagabond, pierced by whizzing arrows, crashes off their startled mount into the water.

But they are not nearly there, and they won't make it at all, Betsy realises, unless she takes action. She stops struggling forward and, without a word, turns herself about in the water. Lifting her fingers to her mouth, she whistles for the clockwork wolves as Talon had done and, once she has their attention, signals that they must go back. They must return to the bank – just her, Dahlia and Idris – and fight for her friends.

CHAPTER TWENTY-FOUR

Negotiations

Teddy's voice crackles in her ears as Betsy and the wolves swim back to the bank they have so recently abandoned. He is screaming for her. 'Betsy! What are you doing? Betsy, don't!' He cannot follow her, encumbered as he is by a wilting Effie, and so she looks back and gives him a proud nod. She knows that what she is doing is right. She has to stop the attack. She has to persuade this group of Wellians that they are fighting for the wrong side. If it means saying goodbye to her friends forever, so be it.

Turning away from the canal, she strides up the bank, flanked by Dahlia and Idris. Though she is soaked through, she does not even feel cold anymore. She is too concentrated on what she must do. Her surging adrenalin allows her to put aside the trembling of her bones, the deep ache in her hands and feet. Arrows whine and whir around her, but she does not fear being hit by them. The wolves twist their shoulders and flick their tails and snap their jaws, deflecting each one, and she is grateful. Dahlia and Idris might not be able to defend her when she reaches the attackers – venturing so close will provide every opportunity to strike her down with a quick arrow or a blade – but she needs to see their faces, and for them to see hers, if she is to persuade them that they are on the same side.

Glancing around for the white flit of faces moving in the shadows, she steps among the trees. The wolves stay as close beside her as they are able, but their size makes it difficult, and they have to veer far around trunks and branches which she can easily move between. A single arrow spins past close on her right side and embeds itself in the bark of a towering oak. Betsy flinches but manages not to cry out.

'I need to talk to you,' she begins.

The splashing and shouting of the Vagabonds across the canal is lost behind her, and she does not cast her mind out to seek the sounds. She has to concentrate. Her voice is loud and definite in the quiet between the creaking branches, and she knows, she senses, that someone is listening.

'We're on the same side.'

Nothing but the crush of snow beneath her boots and the occasional snapping twig. Another arrow speeds past her left side – she feels its flight, like wind against her cheek – but she stands firm, and steps steadily forward. The soft click of the wolves' clockwork encourages her. She is not alone.

She senses movement diagonally to her right and realises that she has been walking away from the canal in a straight line when she should have been following the water's flow. Their attackers have not moved deeper into the trees at the approach of the wolves. They have simply shifted sideways. Perhaps they are too frightened to venture into the forest again. Or perhaps they are so desperate to return home that they cannot bear to let Copperwell out of their sights. From those glimpses she has seen of them, they look a sorry lot: weak, hungry, tired. These ideas make her feel powerful and she stands taller.

'The Unified Government has played a terrible trick on you,' she announces. Her voice grows firmer with every word. 'But we have brought help. We can stop them. There's no need for anyone to feel hungry. No need for any of us to live in darkness.'

She pauses, waiting for a response. She closes her eyes and focuses on pushing her listening out, out, as far away from herself as she can manage. And there – yes! She hears them, exchanging breathy whispers.

'And what if she's telling the truth?'

'She's lying.'

'But if she isn't… Everything might go back to how it was before.'

'It'll never be that simple.'

'It might be.'

Betsy clears her throat. 'She's right, you know,' she calls, since it was a woman who last spoke. 'If we try, we might return everything to normal. Copperwell could thrive again. You didn't want to come out here, chasing after people you know nothing about. They forced you, didn't they? The Constabulary?'

Hisses of 'She can hear us' and 'They did' follow.

'What did they promise you? Food? A job? They'll give you nothing. You know that, really.'

Betsy is not sure where these words are coming from, but she knows that she does not sound quite like herself. She sounds like … a more grown-up version of herself, perhaps. Or Effie. Or the woman on Wild Goose Way! Slowly, carefully, she creeps towards the whispers she should not be able to hear. Her attackers have stopped moving now; though one, she can tell, still has an arrow poised in their bow. She can discern their hand trembling, their gritted teeth, the noisy way they swallow in their desperation to make the right decision. Shoot or don't shoot? Kill or don't kill? Betsy is closing in on them. Soon she will be too near to rely on the wolves' protection. Her heart thunders in her chest, pulses along her neck, throbs in her ears.

'It's called an orrery,' she tries. 'The machine they used, to shift the shadows, to alter the weather. To frighten you… But we have it now. They can't do any more harm, as long as we hold on to it.'

She rounds another ancient oak trunk and spots, dragged up into the treeline perhaps thirty feet away, a series of small wooden rafts. They are damaged, tattered together with fraying lengths of rope. They do not look strong enough to hold an adult man or woman, and yet, they must have been used by the Wellians as transport across the canal and into the woods.

'Who would ask you to sail across a swollen canal on a broken raft to hunt down three children? Who would ask you to put yourselves in danger like that? Join us,' she urges, 'and help us put things right again.'

Her request is met with silence, and into that silence flies the one arrow which had, until so recently, been held to a bowstring. Betsy hears its approach – fast, direct, perfect – as clearly as she might hear a huffing stream locomotive or a trundling clockwork cart. She holds her breath, knowing that the attackers can see her now, and waits. Then, at the last possible second, she drops to the snow-cold ground and lets the arrow, which would surely have found her chest had she remained still, speed overhead.

The action is so well-timed, so confidently executed, that it is met with gasps from the hidden Wellians.

'How did she know…?'

'Some sort of magic.'

'I told you.'

'It's a trick.'

Betsy rights herself and brushes the snow from her knees. Her heart is slowing back into its usual rhythm. They have not charged at her, weapons drawn, yet – that's a good start. They have not warned her away. They have not shot more than a single arrow in her direction. She expects the wolves are enough of a threat, even at a distance, to keep them from rushing forward and beating her. Were it not for Dahlia and Idris and their glinting manes and teeth, she might already be bound, gagged, and being transported back into the black heart of the Unified Government to await her punishment. That fate might still be hers if she messes this up. She breathes deep, takes as much time as she dares. She is making it all up as she goes, but she has truth on her side.

'It's no trick,' Betsy insists. 'I have simply learnt how to listen. It's something those people, the Vagabonds, taught us, while we were staying with them. There's so much to learn outside of this city. And it might not be magic, but it's the closest thing to it I've ever seen.'

The Wellians' whisperings have stopped now. There is nothing to hear but the moans of the wind and the gasps of the shivering leaves. To her right, Dahlia cocks her head with a gentle clank.

'Please, come out and speak to me. There's no reason for us to be enemies.'

And, to Betsy's surprise, one of the Wellians does. A girl, perhaps two or three years older than Betsy, steps out from between the trees and stares out through hollow eyes. She is poorly dressed, in grey men's trousers which hang too long and a dark yellow coat with a torn sleeve. Her sandy hair is knotted high on her head. She looks like a sad impression of a soldier.

'What's your name?' Betsy asks. She is unsure why.

'Emmeline.'

'I'm Betsy. Elizabeth Blue.'

Idris swipes his metal tail as another Wellian braves

stepping into view of the wolves. Betsy sees the man eyeing the clockwork creature.

'The wolves won't hurt you,' she calls. 'They're here to protect me. So long as I'm not being threatened, they won't harm anyone.' And she knows now, beyond doubt, that this is true. She is ashamed that she ever suspected them of having bad intentions.

The man – a short, sturdy chap with a dark gaze and a dirty cap – does not dare turn away from the wolf, but he does nod in acknowledgement of Betsy's words.

She waits, offering the occasional encouraging word, as more and more Wellians appear in the forest dark, their faces pale and desperate, and wait for Betsy to say what she has come to say. She senses that some remain hidden, ready to draw their bows, but she has a ragged audience now of around thirty Wellians, and she knows that she, Teddy, Effie and the Vagabonds need them. It is not enough that she has, hopefully, quelled the onslaught of arrows long enough for the others to cross the canal. When they reach the opposite bank, they will be scared and exhausted and they will need every available body to march with them into Copperwell if they are going to overwhelm the government. They will need every last soul. The entire plan, she realises, depends on what she says to these hungry, dispossessed people. She glances up towards the starless sky, wishing it was night-time, so that she could at least feel herself guided through what will come next, and then she opens her mouth to speak.

CHAPTER TWENTY-FIVE

A Life Lost

They drip onto the opposite bank of the canal: the dogs, then the deer, and, strewn amongst them, the exhausted and bone-tired people. Above, the kestrels wheel and panic. Occasionally, they swoop down to perch on the deer's antlers and survey the soaked remains of their expedition party, sprawled pathetically across the canal's icy bank, before rising to keep watch once more.

Effie lies slumped on her side, her eyes closed as if in sleep.

'Effie of Birdsong,' Birch rasps, shaking her. 'Are you all right?'

'Mmm.'

'Can you stand?'

Effie nods and, without opening her eyes, pushes herself to sit up.

'Do your best,' Birch coaxes. 'We need to get off this bank. We're too exposed here.'

'Yes,' Effie mumbles. 'Yes.' The wound between her shoulder blades pulls, as though it will tear open again, but she persists. Birch is right. The arrows seem to have stopped for a moment, but the attack will surely start again soon. She shuffles around onto her knees and reaches out to both sides, expecting to find Betsy and Teddy there, where they always are, but she touches nothing but slushy snow. Her eyes snap open. Before her, Birch sits in a crouch, her both hands pressed to her leg, from which the feathered tail of an arrow protrudes. Her hands run red.

Immediately, Effie reaches out for her, but Birch shakes her head. 'I'll be fine,' she says, though her voice snags in her throat. 'Go and find your friends.'

Effie lurches to her feet. Up and down the canal bank, Vagabonds slump or lie, some clutching at pierced thighs and chests and forearms. Their breath bursts from them in white clouds. The snow has been transformed into a pink and white map.

'Ted!' Though she is unsteady on her feet, she strides along the bank as quickly as she is able. 'Betsy!' she bellows. 'Ted!'

There comes no answer except for the grumbling of the Vagabonds as they check over their spent and frightened deer, straighten their soaked clothes, search what is missing from their bags, check on those friends who have collapsed on the canal's edge. Eventually, she finds Teddy, leaning over a prone body. His tears fall quick and quiet and he does not try to hide them.

'Who?' she asks, stopping some yards away and not daring to look.

Teddy answers without turning in her direction. 'Swallow,' he answers. 'One of the smaller deer got into trouble. He managed to push it out, but he went under… He…'

The image of Briny Erwin being swept away from them haunts Effie, and she shakes the thought from her mind.

'He'll be all right,' she says, though she knows it is not true. He might have drowned anyway helping the deer from the water, but he was no doubt weakened by the three arrows which entered his back and which now protrude from his chest. 'He just needs—'

'I already tried, Ef,' Teddy interrupts. 'I thought if I could pump the water out of his lungs, but…' He stops and shakes his head.

Effie steps closer and cautiously places a hand on his shoulder. They have never touched like this before – in sympathy rather than in jest or mischief. She is surprised by how cold he feels. She peels off the skin the Vagabonds loaned her and drapes it over him. Without taking his eyes off Swallow, Teddy reaches out, catches her hand, and grips it tight. They remain like that for a long time, while around them the Vagabonds slowly recover themselves. The deer cease prancing and begin to settle. The dogs stop whining.

'Betsy?' she ventures, when the need to know the answer to the question outweighs the dread of asking it.

And that, finally, is when he looks at her. His eyes are dark, bloodshot, empty. 'She went back into the forest,' he whispers. 'I…' He chokes on a sob and hangs his head again. It should have been him. He should have gone back to stall the attack. It was cowardly to push on while she went, alone, towards such danger.

'Then we'll go and find her,' Effie insists. 'She won't have given up, and neither will we. Are you listening to me, Teddy?'

But in place of his answer comes the sudden click and grind of clockwork. Spinning around, they see Dahlia and Idris stalking across the canal. The wolves gleam powerfully in the frosted air. They are not carrying a rider, but they are surrounded – Teddy squints at them – by a host of little rafts, which are tethered to the wolves' metal to keep them from being dragged away. On each raft sit one or two shabby people, dressed in tattered clothes and, in some cases, barefoot.

Teddy and Effie rush down the bank, knowing by now that the wolves will not draw danger towards them. They skid to a stop at the water's edge, gripping hands. And that is when they see her, standing proud on one of the rafts and waving wildly – Betsy.

She grins as she steps ashore and throws her arms around Teddy and Effie. Squeezing them tightly, she speaks quietly into their ears. 'Help! They've agreed to help.'

'But who…' Effie begins. She recognises one of the faces who are filing past her onto the bank. It belongs to a long-limbed, small-eyed man; a figure she feels she has not laid eyes on in years – the barman from The Blackened Lantern. 'Wellians!' she breathes.

'A favour for a favour,' the barman mumbles.

'Wellians,' Betsy confirms. 'And they want their lives back, just like we do.'

They ready themselves as hastily as they can – the injured Vagabonds, the exhausted Wellians, the animals both living and clockwork. They wrap those few who have died in animal skins and lay them at the water's edge, ready to be taken back home. They strip off their soaked and bloodied clothes and replace them with dry from the chests they have brought on their sleds and which managed to stay afloat as they crossed the canal. And then they pause in consideration of the waiting city. Betsy, Teddy, and Effie stand side by side.

Betsy listens for a familiar sound, but discerns none.

'Did you ever hear it so quiet?'

Teddy shakes his head. Betsy fancies she can feel his heart thudding against his chest, but perhaps it is only her imagination.

'Nothing,' she continues.

The snow music is a gentle, sustained note, which drifts out across the city like incoming fog.

'This is just how it is by day,' Teddy says. 'You've forgotten.'

'No,' Betsy insists. 'There should be a locomotive huffing, or an air-train passing over, or the Constabulary horses… There's nothing. It's as though the city is empty.'

A shiver ripples down her spine.

'How cold is it?' Effie asks. 'A degree or two maybe, and look…' She indicates the skyline with a pointed finger. 'Not one chimney has any smoke rising from it.'

She's right. Ordinarily, the air above Copperwell is crowded with soft pillars of coalsmoke. Or, more recently, given the coal shortages, woodsmoke. They sweep their eyes across the rooftops. All glisten with cold. On some frosted apexes, ravens hunch, fluffed furiously into their own feathers.

'Suppose everyone is gone,' Betsy says.

'Suppose they're being punished,' Effie returns quietly. 'I'll bet the Unified Government would stop their food, their wood, if they were frightened enough of an uprising. Perhaps they're locked in day *and* night now.'

A weak column of sunshine slants fleetingly across the canal. Teddy glances at his shadow and finds it still knelt on the ground, head hung low. He takes a moment to appreciate that it is able to continue to show its sorrow, then wonders when he last felt the need to check its appearance... Not since they had stood on the riverbank near the hollow and watched Astral, Lupine and Thorn experiment with their shadows' forms. There, he had almost forgotten that he was supposed to be ashamed of it. Now that he is back in Copperwell, he has to try hard to remind himself of the fact that he should not be ashamed of it. That's just another lie.

Effie turns towards Betsy and Teddy. 'Forget the Observatory for now. We can worry about all that later. We shouldn't just march with the Vagabonds; we should lead the way. This is not the Vagabonds' home. It's ours, and theirs.' She indicates the once-threatening Wellians who stand sheepishly behind the Vagabonds. 'And it's our duty to reclaim it.' She pauses, takes a deep breath. 'It should be me who demands they let my father go.'

Betsy's face opens into a smile. 'Yes! I knew you'd think so. Teddy?'

Teddy dips his chin firmly and sets his jaw. 'Yes.'

'Yes!' Betsy says again, and, reaching out to clap Effie and Teddy's shoulders, she whips around on her heel and prepares to stride off in Talon's direction. *We're going to lead the march*, she will say, and her mouth will be full of the arguments she will make when Talon denies them the opportunity to power through the streets of Copperwell, into the Royal Quarter, and stand before the Unified Government building to make their demands. But Talon is unlike every other adult Betsy has ever known, and she will not say no. She will only rearrange her furs more comfortably around herself and, lowering her eyelids, incline her head in that special Vagabond bow which Betsy is already starting to imitate.

'Once the deer are calmed,' she will say, 'we will begin.'

Betsy smiles at the thought. We will begin… It feels like just the right sentiment. For they are about to begin, aren't they, to bring about a better Copperwell? She hesitates for a second, thinking through how she might say this to Teddy and Effie. She opens her mouth, in an effort to shape the idea, but she does not have the chance to speak it, because that is when they hear the gunshot.

CHAPTER TWENTY-SIX

Listening Lessons

The revolver, fired into the air, sends the deer into a frenzy and instantly they scatter along the bank of the canal, slipping on the icy ground and knocking each other into the water then scrambling desperately back out. The shot echoes across the empty city, followed by the unmistakable clatter of hooves over cobbled ground. The dogs stand alert and twitch their ears, searching the direction from which the sound is coming. Instinctively, the Vagabonds and the Wellians gather closer together. The Vagabonds do not attempt to keep the deer from fleeing, but instead concentrate their efforts on retrieving their bows, counting out their remaining arrows, glancing about for a sheltered place where they might form a defence but finding none.

'The Constabulary!' Teddy spits, his eyes bulging.

'They won't hurt us,' Betsy says. 'There won't be enough of them. They're not expecting us, and especially not with their own army added to ours.'

'But they *are* expecting us,' Teddy returns. 'We've just been chased straight towards them!' He throws an arm back in the direction of the forest. 'No wonder the

Wellians kept their distance. No wonder they followed us all this way. It was a trap.'

Betsy really can hear his heart thundering now. He flinches like the deer; he swings his shoulders aimlessly about; he stomps his foot as if gearing himself to run, anywhere, without a thought for what might happen next.

'You're not going back to gaol, Teddy.' Betsy grabs his wrists and shakes him until he looks down into her face. 'I won't let them take you,' she promises, and the expression on her face is so fierce that he actually believes her. Didn't the girls come for him when he was locked away in the dark? They've always looked after each other, Teddy, Betsy and Effie. That's not going to change now.

The Constabulary horses drub closer and closer, and the three friends lean in until they are touching foreheads, so that they can talk over the noise.

'We'll never stop the Constabulary,' Effie says. 'All we can do is run.'

'Where?' Teddy counters. 'We can't go back across the canal, and if we run the length of it, they'll just follow us.'

'We can't run anyway,' Betsy interrupts. 'Not now. We've come this far. There's no way we're showing them fear now.'

'What, then? Stand here and wait to be shot?'

'The Vagabonds will come up with something,' she insists.

'Arrows and frightened deer are no match for bullets and trained horses,' Effie says.

'They'll come up with something,' Betsy says again. 'I trust them… Don't you?'

Effie considers the question for a moment. 'Yes. I think I do. But we've just met them. We can't know everything about them, Bets.'

'Nothing is perfect,' Betsy replies. 'But look how much they've risked for us. Swallow…'

Teddy takes a long, deep breath. 'We have to put our faith in them,' he agrees.

And yet they feel utterly helpless as they stand and hear the Constabulary clatter out of the drab and silent city. The Vagabonds have, once again, arranged themselves in a circular formation and started to rotate about like the cogs of the clockwork wolves. They move in opposing directions, some in large, loose circles, others in small, tight rings. The dogs and the kestrels echo their movements. The newly converted Wellians, too, slowly begin to imitate them, spreading amongst them, becoming them. The impression is of an eddying sea of people, difficult to count and impossible to still, and much more numerous than the Vagabonds' expedition party truly is. It's a clever illusion. And as the Constabulary gallop out of Copperwell and onto the frosted canal bank, it is their first sight of the Vagabonds – a great, shifting mass of people, hulking under their layers of animal skins, their plaited and knotted hair giving the appearance of horns or antlers. Flanked as they are by the snarling lurchers with their bristling grey fur and flashing eyes, and guarded to left and right by the enormous brass wolves whose heads are the size of a man, they appear a fearsome army.

The Constabulary's horses are reined in and skid to a stop on the slippery ground, tossing their heads in fury at having their gallop interrupted. They are all the exact same shade of glossy black. The constables on their backs persuade them, with much muscling and hauling, to line up, side by side. There are eight of them: like the planets in the solar system, Betsy thinks.

One of the constables – a smug, stocky man, with shoulders as wide as Briny Erwin's – straightens an arm out in front of him and they catch the glint of cold, black metal in his hand. The click of his revolver being cocked reverberates across the eerily silent city. A clutch of dove hawks startle off a rooftop and dart away. The other constables mirror him and raise their revolvers one by one.

So, Teddy thinks, they have all been issued with revolvers now. They'll fire indiscriminately at the Vagabonds. They'll kill them all. Bullets will prove quicker than any arrow. He hadn't realised that he had been crouching so low, but he stands suddenly upright now. He realises what he must do.

Before Betsy or Effie can stop him, he pushes through the circling Vagabonds and, when the constables notice him, stops, takes a deep breath, and calls out, 'None of them are Wellians!' He gestures vaguely towards the Vagabonds, hoping the constables will not notice the ragged band now mixed amongst them. 'You can't shoot them without consequences, like you would us. The rest of their people will come. They're protected.'

A moment of indecision follows. The constables consider the milling Vagabonds, who are so calm under the threat of gunfire, the boy who has emerged to defend them, and the creatures, living and clockwork, who are so intent on protecting them. They could shoot into the crowd, but somehow it seems like that course of action would achieve very little. They could try to arrest them all, but it is obvious they would not give up any information about the children and the stolen orrery. The constables glance from Teddy and the Vagabonds, to each other, and back again, unsure of what to do next. The horses, sensing their riders' unease, begin to jostle and jounce.

The gelding belonging to the constable on the furthest right breaks out of formation and sidesteps towards the Vagabonds, whipping its tail frantically. The constable is thin and ashen-faced and his eyes pop wildly as he struggles to regain control of the powerful horse. After some desperate minutes, panic-stricken and embarrassed, he raises his revolver again and, without taking aim, fires it mindlessly into the air. A second later, a lone kestrel thumps onto the ice: a flutter of flightless feathers and bright red blood.

'Stop!' Talon says, and though she does not shout, her voice is somehow made audible to every person on the canal-side. To Teddy's surprise, they all, without question, obey. The Vagabonds cease making their rotations; the dogs stop pacing; the horses grow quiet and calm. Even the constables pause and wait to be told what to do next. It is as though they have been hypnotised. As the kestrels descend, without their murdered friend, back into the forest to find branches to perch on, Teddy looks at Talon, his mouth opening in shock.

'How did you…?' he breathes.

'Come, Teddy of the Stallions,' Talon says, beckoning him. 'Sit here with me.' She looks around. 'Betsy of the Stars,' she says. 'Effie of Birdsong.'

Teddy, Betsy and Effie move automatically towards her. She indicates that they should seat themselves on the ground and they fold down, cross-legged, onto the icy bank. Talon sits down with them, so that they mark the four points of the compass: north, south, east, west.

'You can control people,' Teddy says. 'With your thoughts…'

'No,' Talon answers. 'It is only that I know how to listen, and how, in turn, to ask others to listen to me.'

'That's why the clockwork wolves protect you.'

Talon inclines her head: yes.

'And how you all act together when you're threatened.'

Talon inclines her head again.

'And why you're able to live in the forest without being hurt by bears and things.'

'I imagine so.'

'Until we arrived, that is,' Betsy puts in.

As they talk, all about them is continued stillness. Effie cannot concentrate on the conversation, so worried is she that every person and creature on the bank of the canal will suddenly snap back into life. Surely Talon cannot keep up this sort of influence. Only a hypnotist could manage it. Or a witch. And Talon is neither… Unless… Considering all they have learnt about the world in the last few days, it is not unreasonable to think that witches exist. That magic exists!

Betsy asks a question which Effie does not hear.

'I'll show you,' Talon replies, and Effie understands that they are being offered a lesson in listening, while eight menacing men of the Constabulary and their frighteningly powerful horses stand by and wait. It is unbelievable. What is more unbelievable still, though, is that Talon has possessed this talent all along and she did not use it to keep the deer from spooking, or those Vagabonds who were shot from being hurt, or Swallow from being drowned. Why wait until now to use it?

'You have been practising, haven't you? Good. That will help. Now close your eyes,' Talon instructs. Betsy and Teddy do so immediately, but Effie takes a moment to consider the woman before she complies: her hooded eyes seem deeper than ever, but gentler, too; her skin is tight and wan at the points where her grey hair has been pulled back, and loosely wrinkled everywhere else; her lips form a small but reassuring smile. She is older, so much older, when she is holding everyone's attention like this. It is obvious the act drains her. That must be why she hasn't done it until now; it takes too much from her.

With a sigh of resignation, Effie closes her eyes.

'First,' Talon begins, 'I want you to block out the sounds all around you and listen solely for the beat of your own hearts.'

This, Teddy thinks, is easier here than it might be in any other location. He is terrified, and his heart knows it, and there is no ignoring its relentless throbbing. He has been trying to block out its noise all this time, but now he focuses on it until it fills his ears and it is as though he is underwater and every thump is amplified.

Talon can tell by his changing expression that Teddy has it, and soon thereafter, Betsy does too, but Effie has closed herself off to the idea and will need more persuasion.

'And now listen only for the sound of your own thoughts.'

This is harder, Teddy thinks. While he reaches for the voice his thoughts use to speak – his own voice, but quieter and buried deep inside his mind – he can only grasp at snippets of it. It is as though his thoughts can only show themselves clearly to him when he is not concentrating on them, when they are unexpected. It is reminiscent of the way his shadow shifts, and he wonders how long it would take him to learn to control both.

Effie's thoughts come to her as musical notes more often than anything else, so this instruction she finds easier than listening for the thump of her heart. If she happens to find the answer to a puzzle, it has always chimed to her in a confident C natural. If she is worried, her thoughts tend to play to a downward minor scale. Now, as she attempts to absorb Talon's lesson, she hears inside her mind the notes of the C major arpeggio playing over and over, and knows that she is getting somewhere. Though what has changed she cannot fathom. It must be that Talon is doing something to help them, something they cannot yet begin to understand. If they could have learnt this skill by themselves, they would have done so on the ride here, when they all tried so hard at it.

'And now,' Talon continues, because each of the children has their eyes shut fast and is evidently managing at least a part of what she is asking, 'pack all those sounds away, and move your listening further away from yourself.'

This, Betsy understands immediately. It is like moving through the different invisible layers of the air, or taking flight and observing the world from a greater distance. She shuts off the noise of her own thoughts and expands the space she is concentrating on, so that she hears the rush and tumble of the water along the confused and angry canal behind her, and the huffing of the horses as they catch their breaths, and a low humming, which must be the Vagabonds' way of soothing each other or the animals. She takes another imaginary step outwards, and now she can hear the creaking of the trees across the water, and the shuffling of the kestrels' feathers as they shift to keep their balance against the dip and sway of the branches. With a single thought, she widens the space she is listening to once more, and now she can sense the deer, a way down the canal, crowding together to find the safety of their numbers, their sleek red bodies bumping and bristling. She can hear their ears twitching in search of threats, and their nostrils flaring as they sniff out danger on the air.

'It's amazing,' she whispers. Because it is. Never before has she been able to hear like this. Never before has she been able to isolate the sounds around her, investigate them, cast them aside or amplify them. 'I can hear every move the deer are making.'

How can Talon have taught her to do this with just a few words of encouragement?

'I didn't teach you, Betsy of the Stars,' Talon replies, and Betsy gasps as the question which had sat only inside her mind is responded to. Her eyes spring open and she stares at Talon, whose voice continues to sound in Betsy's ears, though the Warrior Mother of the Vagabonds is not even moving her mouth. 'I simply showed you what you should be listening for. Told you what was possible. The rest you did yourself.'

Betsy reaches out to each side of her and clasps Effie and Teddy's wrists. Their eyes spring open and they turn to check she is all right. 'I can hear into her mind!' she says, as steadily as she is able. She does not take her eyes off Talon. 'I can hear Talon's words without her having to speak them.'

Teddy's frown of concentration deepens into one of confusion. 'I can't even hear the deer,' he says.

'They're miles away already,' Betsy responds offhandedly. So surprised is she by hearing Talon's thoughts, that she hasn't considered that she has heard the sound of the deer's hooves over the ground they have travelled and knows that they have left behind this iciest stretch of the bank, galloped over swept clear warehouse yards, and gathered on softer earth. Which must mean they are near the timber yard, where the ground is forever mounded with sawdust.

Talon's face breaks into a wide smile. 'You have it!' she says. And Betsy's shocked expression transforms into a wild grin. Privately, she thinks that perhaps this is the first time she has possessed a talent.

'I have it!' she says, swinging her attention from Teddy to Effie and back again. 'Did you hear that?'

'It's about all I *can* hear,' Teddy replies. He is not being petulant; he is worried that, if he cannot grasp this talent, too, they will not be able to make their way into Copperwell as planned. They will not be able to demand that the government frees the city. Talon would not have chosen this perilous position to stop and teach them the skill if she did not think it important. Imperative, even.

'It will take practice, Teddy of the Stallions,' Talon replies. 'You and Effie have heard different sounds from Betsy, but you will, in time, learn to hear all that you want. Didn't I tell you once that the Earth itself sings? Haven't you begun, since leaving Copperwell, to discern the music of the world?'

'I suppose,' Teddy says.

'Good,' Talon answers. 'Then you have started to hear what you must hear. And together, the three of you will continue to learn.'

'The three of us?' Effie interjects. She cannot fail to hear the significance of Talon's phrasing. Its echo clangs in a miserable A flat in her mind. 'Without you and the rest of the Vagabonds? But how will we—'

'We can't carry on without you!' Betsy protests. 'We need you!'

'For the moment perhaps,' Talon says, and the words sound like the hush of a lullaby.

'But,' Betsy continues, 'what can the three of us do alone? We're not capable—'

'You are not capable of what? Of escaping the prison of your city? Of outsmarting the Unified Government? Of making your people understand the illusion they have been made to live under? Oh, you are capable of all that, and much more.'

'But we're just…' Teddy begins.

'Just…' Talon answers. 'Just a canal worker? Just a jazz player? Just a laundry worker? Is that what this place' – she tips her head back to indicate the city – 'has made you believe?'

'She's right,' Betsy says, swinging her legs underneath her to sit taller on her haunches. 'We've been listening to the wrong sounds, that's all. And we've been making the wrong sounds ourselves because of it. But now that Talon has showed us how, we can make different choices. It's not just jazz music played in secret or the Royal Academy, Ef. It's not just canal work or your dreams, Ted. We can choose any and all of it. We can invent new options. We've survived gaol and being chased by the Constabulary and drowning. But Briny Erwin didn't and Swallow didn't, and we owe it to them to be better...' She pauses when her voice catches. 'We owe it to them to believe we can be better,' she finishes. She does not lower her head, as she usually would, to hide the fact that her eyes are brimming with tears of grief, and fear, and excitement. She knows it is important that she reveals them, just as she is learning to reveal her shadow. These are the truths of her. And to think that for her entire life she has believed that she needs to hide them! She won't let one more Wellian grow up thinking that way. She'll stop the Unified Government's games, just as the woman on Wild Goose Way urged her to. She and Teddy and Effie will stop them together.

'Will you help us?' she asks Talon. She knows the question does not require further explanation.

'If you need us,' Talon pledges.

'The Constabulary,' Betsy says, rolling her eyes towards the eight men who block their path into the city.

'I can convince them to remain where they are for twenty minutes. Perhaps thirty. We'll have to be quick.'

'There'll be more, though,' Effie warns. 'They didn't

chase us across the canal only to send eight constables after us. They'll have set up ambushes.'

'Danger may await us,' Talon agrees. 'But is that good enough reason not to try?'

Neither Betsy nor Teddy nor Effie responds to this question. There is just one possible answer. They must go.

With a nod, Betsy casts her mind out to listen for the deer again and, once she senses their nervous fidgeting, she thinks, very clearly and using every ounce of her concentration, the words, *You can come back now. It's safe.*

And sure enough, short minutes later, there comes the purposeful pounding of many hooves covering the cold ground.

CHAPTER TWENTY-SEVEN

Revelations

They set out across Swindler's Quarter under a glowering sky. The clouds are sullen and ashy. The streets are snow-silenced. On the rooftops, the ravens and the dove hawks harrumph. The scritch of their claws over the frosted tiles is the only sound apart from the sad note which issues from the weather pipes – which, Effie notices, are quieter now that their bottoms have been swallowed by the snow.

They move in the Vagabonds' usual arrowhead formation. Betsy, Teddy and Effie linger at the arrow's tip, but do not quite dare step ahead of Talon. Not yet. Talon, in her wisdom, does not urge them to greater bravery – they have shown extraordinary amounts of that already – but waits patiently for them to work up to it. Copperwell, after all, is their city. They will lead the way more ably than any. The band of Wellians who have joined their ranks know the canals, yes, but some are poorer even than Betsy. They are beggars. They will not have spent hours exploring rooftops and alleyways with their friends. They are made meek by hunger and shame. They trail quietly along with the Vagabonds, trying to disappear amongst them.

By the time they reach the edge of Factory Quarter,

weak fingers of sunlight are spreading through the cloud with increasing frequency. Their shadows are still blurred shapes, faintly formed. They reveal little, as yet, and Teddy is glad of that. As much as he endeavours to imagine himself straight-shouldered and bold on Jim's wide back, as he had in the forest clearing, he knows that right now his shadow might expose him as a small, cowering thing.

'Poppy, Ness and Celeste first,' Effie says. 'They're close by. They'll join us.' They know they need to amass a significant crowd if they are to stand a chance of reaching the Unified Government building.

To the accompaniment of the deer's proud hooves, and the panting of the dogs, they pass The Stag's Antlers and continue down Inca Street for a while – not pausing to consider the darkened windows of the apothecary or the milliner's shop – and turn into a narrow alleyway. The buildings here are three storeys high, but they are not grand. The stonework is grubbier than on Inca Street. The shops – a butcher, a fishmonger, a bakery – stand empty, their doors locked, their wrought-iron signs too despondent even to swing and creak. Effie stops at the frontage of a haberdasher's and, tipping her head back to stare up at the first storey window, shouts, 'Poppy!' Her voice echoes down the deserted street. The deer toss their heads and flap their ears but do not startle. Their moods are soothed by the riders who sit astride them, calm and confident and imperturbable, despite everything they have already faced and everything they might yet encounter.

They wait… Nothing.

'Poppy!' Effie hollers again. 'Ness?'

For another three or four heartbeats, nothing. And then the wooden frame releases a crack as a window is shoved outwards by a solitary inch. A small face appears in the crack. Poppy takes in the spectacle below with an audible gasp. What must they look like, Effie wonders? The enormous deer, with their inquisitive antlers. The Vagabonds mounted atop them, made broad and intimidating by the layers of skins they wear and their elaborately knotted hair. The rough-haired dogs, as tall as some of Copperwell's cab ponies. The sorry Wellians hiding in their ranks. The silent clockwork wolves, whose glinting metal teeth could reach in through Poppy's window and pluck out a human girl with no trouble at all.

'What in the name of the four gods…' Poppy breathes. Then, louder, 'Effie! What are you…? Who…? We thought the Constabulary had had you!'

Effie allows herself a small smile. 'They should have liked to have. Listen—'

'Get home, Ef!' Celeste's pointed face appears in the wedged gap between window and pane. 'Get home before the Constabulary catch you for real. You know you ain't allowed outside no more.'

'We're marching on Royal Quarter,' Effie insists.

'You're mad,' Poppy replies. 'They'll throw you in gaol soon as look at you.'

But the clatter of hooves over cobblestones does not

follow, and eventually Poppy, Celeste and Ness are coaxed out of the rooms they share to join the expedition party. They are helped up onto the backs of the clockwork wolves and begin to laugh nervously as the great mechanical beasts click and clank them through the streets.

They proceed towards Lawmaker's Quarter, making short detours along the way to visit the dwellings of Teddy's workmates on the canal.

Old Man Hatch is too frail and stooped to be expected to march, but Teddy knocks at his door anyway, thinking to enquire after children or grandchildren who might come with them. They will need every possible body to stand against the Constabulary and the men of the Unified Government who give them their brutal orders. Hatch, with a delighted laugh, declares that his two daughters will readily swell their numbers and that he will come too. When Teddy objects, he refuses to be dissuaded and, with his bow-legged gait, he shuffles alongside them at a surprising pace, directing them to the street where Trudy Birdwhistle lives with her parents and eight siblings, then chattering with each of the Birdwhistle children as they all wind their way towards the towpath tunnel off Dragonfly Way to collect Octavia Bennett.

The Birdwhistles and Hatch finally fall silent as they reach the towpath tunnel and Teddy steps amongst the homeless, the destitute, the forgotten, searching for the only girl he has ever kissed. They sleep under tattered blankets, pressed up against the tunnel walls and huddled into mounds for warmth. Here and there, small fires have been lit in pots or on cobbled-together tripods, and they spark and gutter as Teddy edges around them. The bitter stink of boiling poppy-seed tea swamps his nose. Each body is identical to the next, wrapped up as they are, and none lifts their head. Teddy will never find Octavia like this. He decides instead to address every person who has found themselves in this unfortunate place.

He clears his throat. 'We're marching on Royal Quarter,' he begins, as Effie had back on Inca Street. 'We're going to demand the Unified Government puts an end to The Shadow Order. Look…' He gestures down the dank length of the tunnel, at the end of which, in the circle of light, can be seen just some of the Vagabonds, the canal workers, their former attackers and all those other people who are gathering together to fight for themselves at last. Already, they seem a united tribe. Their numbers must be keeping the Constabulary temporarily at bay, since the time for which Talon had said she could hold them off has passed twice over.

'And why would they listen to you?' comes a voice from beneath a filthy hood.

'Because we have proof that it was them who caused the shadows to shift. We've taken the…' Teddy searches for the appropriate word. 'We've taken their weapon from Copperwell. It is hidden. Safe. If the city stands against them, they will have to back down.'

'And what about the Constabulary? Where are they?

It's the middle of the day. Why haven't they tracked you down? You're making enough noise, all of you.'

At this, Teddy pauses. He has to work out his suspicions before he speaks them if he going to sound convincing. As they've walked from street to street, Old Man Hatch and the others have described the changes the Unified Government has made to The Order over the few days since their escape: the restriction on going outdoors at any time of night or day, the increased violence inflicted on apprehended rule-breakers, the removal of heating fuels and food from Copperwell's poorest inhabitants. And Effie was right – there was no way they'd have sent a mere eight men to intercept them. Teddy's stomach lurches as he realises that they're walking into another trap.

'None of us can move in this city,' says another voice. Teddy cannot determine from beneath which blanket it issues. 'And you're leading a march! They must be letting you. Don't you see?'

'That's as may be,' Teddy replies, collecting himself. He is unsettled, but he will not be deterred now. These people do not know the orrery's secrets. They do not know how powerful an understanding he, Betsy, and Effie have happened across. 'But once we tell them what we know—'

'I will vouch for him,' comes a timid voice. Teddy recognises it as Octavia's – a faded version of the one she spoke with a year ago. She appears from nowhere, a grey blanket shawled over her head. She steps into the middle of the tunnel, where all of the homeless can see and hear her. Even beneath the blanket, it is evident that her bones jut out. 'If Ted says they have something over that selfish, corrupt government,' she goes on, 'then I believe him, and I'll go with him. Whatever the consequences, it cannot be worse than this.'

'Gaol would be worse than this.'

Teddy seizes his opportunity. 'I've been to gaol,' he replies. 'The Constabulary threw me into a basement cell for political prisoners this very week. I know what it's like. But I'd risk going back there, I would, to do what is right.' He waits a moment, to see if anyone will counter his statement. When they do not, he continues. 'We've all given something up for this.' He indicates the place where Betsy stands. 'Betsy has abandoned the only safety she has ever known. And Effie...' He glances around for Effie, then points her out. 'Effie has left behind her entire family...' Effie stares at her own feet: she cannot think of her mother and father yet; she has to see this through first. '...to give everyone in Copperwell back their freedom. Look how many others have already joined us. Don't you see? You could be free of all this. The Unified Government and the Constabulary combined cannot keep the entire city down if everyone acts together.'

Tears rise in Teddy's throat and he stops, hoping he has said enough.

'I'm going with them,' Octavia insists. 'And if you had any sense, you'd all go with them, too.'

'How can they know what's best for us?' says another disembodied voice. 'They've never lived as we do.'

'Actually…' Betsy's voice blares down the tunnel and she repositions herself under the arched stone. She is thinking of the scrap of material she left pressed between her mattress and her bedframe in the attic room of Saltsburg's Laundry, the letter folded inside. 'Actually, *I* have.'

She feels Effie's and Teddy's heads snap in her direction, but she concentrates on sweeping her eyes over the bundled people who inhabit the dirty towpath tunnel. She has not looked at the letter for many months, but she knows the words by heart: *Elizabeth*, it reads. *I'm sorry I have to leave you. I will return the moment I am able, but should something happen to me, should I not be able… I know that the canal community will look after you. They mightn't have much, but they are in possession of as much honour and kindness as any people I have ever met. Don't forget that, Betsy.* It is signed, *Your Mother.* When she was younger, Betsy had poured over those two words, tracing a fingertip over the letters, wondering if the hand that had shaped them was identical to her own.

'I lived here with you for a time,' she says. 'Does none of you remember me?' She waits as a few of the older homeless people nod and mumble. 'So, it's your choice. You can trust the government who left you to starve and freeze, or you can trust the people who are offering to help you. My name is Elizabeth Blue. You might have known my mother.' She does not offer a name, because she does not know it. 'If you believe that the people of Copperwell deserve better, come with us.'

Turning on her heel, she strides away. Teddy lopes to catch up to her, then falls into step at her side.

'We ought to go to Hangman's Alley, too,' he says. 'It's the working people who are most likely to come. Those who've been coldest and hungriest.'

Effie falls into stride at Betsy's other side. 'He's right. And then, Berliner's Square.'

'Do you think the servants will come?'

Effie nods. 'The neighbours, too, when I tell them what has happened to my father. More importantly, though, if my mother is there and involves the Women's Enfranchisement, women will come from all over the city. Hundreds of them. They'll bring their families. We'll far outnumber the Constabulary in no time.'

Over the next two hours, they exhaust every idea, with their eyes and ears always trained on the dark corners, watching for signs of the Constabulary. Some gawp at the Vagabonds. Others take fright at the sight of the clockwork wolves and refuse to go near them. No doubt, everyone is terrified. But a sea of people, moving in determination towards the Royal Quarter proves irresistible, even to the city's meekest inhabitants, and when a bright afternoon sun finally dislodges the early clouds, it shines down on a vast army of Vagabonds and Wellians, united in their quest to right all that the government has done wrong. And at the very front of this makeshift army, striding proud and sure through the streets of the city, are Betsy Blue, Teddy James and Effie Hart. The snow-covered cobbles glitter as though scattered with stars and, silhouetted over the streets, the shadows of the crowd are bold and clear. Each is shaped identically. They stand tall, their shoulders back and their chins high. And on their heads, they each wear an exact shadow replica of King Glennister's crown.

CHAPTER TWENTY-EIGHT

Revolution

Less than an hour later, they sight the Unified Government building. It looms before them, casting its enormous, pointed shadow. Though the day is bright now, there is no way to see inside; the windows are photogramic reflections of the blue and white sky. Perhaps Betsy, Teddy, Effie and the others are being watched from within. It is impossible to tell. The solitary sound, as they stand and consider the fortress-like building, is the occasional shuffling and snorting of the deer.

'What should we do?' Betsy whispers to Talon.

'It's not for me to say,' Talon replies. 'What do you think you ought to do?'

Betsy's huff sounds louder than those of the deer. 'Tell them our demands.'

'And what are they?'

'I know what you're doing,' Betsy replies. 'You're making me decide for myself.'

Talon's lips tweak towards a smile. 'Isn't that how it should be?'

'Yes, but … how do I know if I'll get it right?'

'You won't. The future cannot be predicted, even by

those of us who have long listened to the whisperings of the world, but you cannot let that make you afraid of it. Make a decision, Betsy of the Stars, and if it doesn't feel right afterwards, make another. Now, what is it you want?'

Betsy sighs. 'The opportunity to learn properly about the orrery and all those other instruments they have in the Observatory. The freedom to live under the skies, as you do. The chance to … make a success of myself.'

Betsy bows her head, embarrassed suddenly by her admission. She would never have spoken so plainly before, but something has changed. She has seen Copperwell differently. She has seen herself differently. It matters little whether the secret hope she's been harbouring – that the woman on Wild Goose Way was her lost mother – is a true fact. She doesn't need her to have been. She has, she realises, been waiting for someone's approval – as though that would give her permission to be better. But the only person whose approval she has ever needed is her own. Isn't that what Talon is teaching her? If she is to make her own decisions, then she can permit herself to be the very best version of Betsy Blue she can be. The boldest version. The bravest version. The most generous version. Hasn't she already begun, in marching here, determined to make Copperwell a better place, even though… the thought arrives simultaneously with the realisation … even though she has no intention of staying, whether Teddy and Effie leave with her or not.

She needs to return to the forest. If it turns out that the

one Wellian who had lived amongst them, the one Talon had mentioned to Teddy, really was the same woman they'd seen on Wild Goose Way, and if that woman was indeed her mother – well, that would be perfect. She would be returning to her own people. But she needs to do it anyway, because whether they started off as such or not, the Vagabonds have become her people now. She has to go with them, be at Swallow's funeral – if they even have funerals. She has to practise the skill Talon has just begun to teach her. She cannot go back to Saltsburg's Laundry and shut her mind into that tiny space again. She has never been so certain of anything. She had suspected she wanted it when they were at the hollow, but now she knows it.

'Prime Minister Bythesea!' she bellows suddenly.

All heads swing in her direction. Teddy is at her side in a blink. 'Bets! What are you doing?'

'What we agreed to do,' she replies. She inhales as deeply as she can and shouts again. 'Prime Minister. We have come to request that The Shadow Order be abolished, and that the people of Copperwell be allowed outside during daylight once more.' Her voice catches and she glances at Teddy and Effie, seeking reassurance. Though Teddy seems to be struggling to swallow, they both nod eagerly, their eyes big and bright. She looks to Talon, to make certain she has the timing right. Talon blinks her approval.

'We know what you did with the orrery,' she continues. 'We know how it works.' She stops and they wait, breath held, for something to happen: the Vagabonds, the canal workers, the homeless, the W.E. led by Effie's mother – who had, until she had heard news of her returned daughter, been trapped inside number eight Berliner's Square by her heartbreak – and dozens more besides.

And soon, just as they have come to dread as they proceeded unhindered through the city, they hear the thunder of hooves. The Constabulary emerge from everywhere and nowhere to surround them. They are atrocious in their black masks and full-body suits. The horses barge and rear, tossing their eyes and manes and gnashing their teeth against their bits. White strings of sweat fly free and splatter those people nearest to them, who, to their credit, do not react. The swollen expedition party stands calm and firm as the horses march closer.

'They'll be trampled,' Birch says, arriving beside Betsy, Teddy and Effie. 'Won't they? Those horses will crush people…'

'They will if they're forced to,' Effie answers.

'The deer will prove no match for them,' Birch warns.

'No. But hold steady. We won't have to hold them off for long.'

'What's your plan?' Teddy asks.

'You'll see,' Effie replies. 'Soon.'

Teddy grumbles. 'It had better be good.'

The Constabulary, numbering perhaps two-hundred men and two-hundred beasts besides, are advancing inch by inch. They have formed a ring around the gathered crowd and are forcing them closer together. Teddy begins to feel breathless as people are pushed tighter against him. The noise the Constabulary makes is hideous. They bang their truncheons on the strengthened shoulders of their uniforms so that it sounds as though they are drumming on shields. The enormous horses bray furiously; they are frightened and fearsome in equal measure. They must weigh ten times that of any person. Teddy looks down at Betsy, who has her eyes closed in concentration, and understands that she is doing what Talon has shown them: picking out the sounds she needs; discarding those she does not; making her voice heard. Perhaps the Constabulary are advancing as slowly as they are because the Vagabonds are sending sounds of doubt into their minds. That must be it. Why would they not simply stampede through the crowd otherwise? And why would Talon be standing silently by, unless her whole consciousness was concentrated on some other task? Teddy cannot think on any of it for long. He is suffocating. His ribs are sure to crack. He stretches his neck long and searches the air above the heads of those people who are crushed now all around him.

'Ef,' Teddy gasps. The sleek brown shine of her hair is within touching distance, but his arms are pinioned to his sides. 'How much longer?'

'Not long,' she shouts back. But he catches the flash of her eyes and understands that what she really means is *I don't know*.

The drumming of the Constabulary's truncheon beating builds in speed and volume as they urge the horses closer and closer. Some screams go up from the crowd, but largely they remain quiet and Teddy marvels at their courage. How downtrodden they all must have felt, to be willing to stand up to the Unified Government like this. How hopeless. And still they have found the mettle to battle for their futures. Straining to see across the crowd, he spots a limp body being passed overhead: a girl, perhaps sixteen years old. Many hands support her as she flops away from the constables who have evidently injured, perhaps even killed, her. Teddy struggles against a bout of nausea. How many more people will the Constabulary kill on the Unified Government's orders?

'Ef!' he cries again. And this time, when he finds her eye, he sees that her expression has changed to one of confidence.

'Listen!' she mouths, and tips her head back to look into the sky.

Teddy mirrors her just as a sudden wind gathers itself up, charges down Wild Goose Way, and whips onto Grand Oak Street. White clouds roll frantically across the sky, chased by larger, charcoal-coloured versions, then furious black ones. The protestors brace themselves against the new gale as their shadows are swallowed by sudden darkness. Effie smiles – Otter and Ermine must have got it right. Far away in the hollow, the orrery is spinning faster and faster, and dragging time with it. The sky lightens and darkens; a new moon rises and, a second later, whirls away; the sun flares in its place. It is as though they are trapped at the point of a spinning top, watching all the colours of existence pass chaotically by. The kestrels are tossed grievously around and hurl themselves downwards, seeking shelter. The dogs snap at the air, thinking it filled with demons perhaps. The deer are terrified, naturally, but they are hemmed in by so many bodies that they can do nothing more than shuffle around in panic – unlike the Constabulary's horses which, with nothing at their tails to stop them, buck and spin and launch into their escape. Some manage to throw off their riders, others do not, but all, without fail, gallop as fast and as far as they are able in a futile effort to outrun the skies.

It is then that the heavy double doors of the Unified Government building creak open and Prime Minister Bythesea is finally heralded out by four of his staff, who about-turn and stand, arms clamped to their sides, to form a sort of human corridor for him to pass through. It has been many months since anyone saw Prime Minister Bythesea in public. It has been speculated that his shadow must be unpleasant indeed. Teddy holds his breath, waiting to see if the rumours are true, but the Prime Minister's shadow is disguised by the gloomy cast of the mighty building. He lifts a neat brass speaking-trumpet to his lips, so that he need not project his voice. For all his supposed power, he hasn't any of Talon's skill.

'Citizens,' he says. 'Return to your homes and the Constabulary will not escalate this matter. Your lawlessness will be excused this once.'

Against the power of the wheeling sky, his voice is small and whining. His threat – for it is certainly intended as a threat – feels desperate, given that at this very moment the majority of the Constabulary are frantically attempting to rein in their careering horses as they flee. There will be more constables, of course, but their numbers have been severely depleted. And when the Unified Government was in possession of the orrery, one last chance was never offered. Look at the woman on Wild Goose Way. Look at Teddy. Look at Jeremiah Hart. So why now?

'They're frightened,' Teddy says, realising it just as Betsy does. 'Whatever else their plans consisted of, they must still need the orrery...'

'But what for?' Betsy wonders. 'They've already caused the shadows to shift, and that didn't seem to have any purpose other than being an excuse to impose more laws. They've made the most of that, so what else...'

'I think I've worked it out,' Effie says, sidling closer to Betsy and Teddy in the crush so that she might confide her thoughts privately.

'I thought you were quiet,' Betsy retorts, as she and Teddy lean in.

'It was a mistake,' Effie continues. 'They never meant to shift the shadows.'

'Then ... what?'

'They figured out the same thing we've figured out – that in controlling the orrery, they could push time quicker. Meaning, they must have thought, that they could sort of...' She pauses, to make certain she is getting the words right. They are amongst the most important she has ever spoken. 'Look into the future.'

Teddy is puzzled. 'But what for?'

'Money. Power.' As the crowd, no longer trapped by the horses, begins to loosen around them, Effie casts about for an example. 'Think of the coal.'

Teddy frowns. 'The coal?' He's familiar enough with the coal; it's just one of the wares he unloads from the barges. Or used to. It was one of the heaviest and muckiest of the cargoes imported into Copperwell. He was glad when they started to take increasing deliveries of chopped wood and bamboo bee nests and dandelion tea in its place.

Effie speaks in an enormous rush. 'You've noticed that it's started to run short, Ted. So, what if the Unified Government thought that they could look forward through time and find other fuel? If they were the only ones with knowledge like that, they could use it, keep it for themselves, sell it, trade with it. Copperwell would grow rich. But the people, the workers – they wouldn't. They wouldn't know what was happening. We noticed the smallest changes at first, didn't we? We were at the eye of the storm. But we don't know what damage has been done to the rest of the country, or the world, even. I mean, why would the mantises come here? Why would the foxes? Unless they were gravitating towards the calm at the centre of the chaos.'

'But ... all that,' Betsy says, incredulous. 'To hold on to their wealth?'

'Not to hold on to it,' Effie says.

'To increase it,' Teddy finishes.

'Massively. Erwin knew it. Do you remember, Bets, in the attic, he said, You can't drain silver from the poorest without risking revolution? And Copperwell could have become the richest city in the world. Think of everything they could have learnt before the rest of humanity: new fuels, new technologies, new medicines. But they risked a revolution, and now they're getting one!'

On the steps of the Unified Government building, Prime Minister Bythesea's voice is droning on and on. The words are lost to them.

'And the shadows shifting was just an accident…' Betsy says, nodding her understanding.

'It must have been,' Effie says. 'An unexpected by-product of their experiments. They simply tried to turn it to their advantage, to use it to exert more control. The intention while they were building their own power was to make everyone else so poor that they became … imprisoned almost. What better way to ensure that the wealth they planned to gain was never distributed equally? That's their game. That's what the woman on Wild Goose Way was warning us about – they're playing a game where the winners end up all-powerful, and the losers entirely powerless.'

'And in total secret, too, so we couldn't even try to win.'

'But … we can now.'

'What's the signal?' Teddy asks then, his gaze fixed on Effie. 'You must have set up a signal, to have the orrery sped up and slowed down. What is it?'

'The kestrels,' she replies. 'Their return is the signal for Ermine to slow it.'

Teddy spins around to search out Talon. She is some feet away but, as the crowd continues to loosen, he manages to stride towards her, pulling Betsy and Effie along with him.

'The kestrels,' he says, breathless. 'Can you send them back to the hollow, all at once.'

'I can, Teddy of the Stallions.'

'On my say so?'

'I can.'

'Ted, what are you—?' Effie begins, but Teddy raises a hand to silence her.

'Trust me.'

'I just…'

'I'll say when,' Teddy says to Talon, who responds with her usual stately nod. 'Bets – we have to tell them we know it all. Not just the orrery. Everything. We have to make them believe we can undo their entire plan.'

'How?'

'Tell him we don't even need the orrery to do what they have done.'

'But—'

'Just tell him, Bets. Use your voice. He's already showed that he's listening to it. Tell him and leave the rest to me. Trust me.'

Betsy sets her jaw. 'I do!'

She turns back to Prime Minister Bythesea, who continues to intone through his speaking-trumpet and, realising that she will not get his attention against the din of his words, and the storm, and the mounting murmurings of the relieved crowd, she steps forwards and walks up the wide front steps of the Unified Government building.

'Arrest her,' Prime Minister Bythesea calls offhandedly to his attendants.

Though her face is burning and her pulse is cantering, Betsy takes a deep breath and steels herself. She is ready to fight if they grab for her. But none of them moves, so she chances speaking.

'We don't need the orrery.'

At that, Teddy mouths 'Now' to Talon and, on her whistled command, the kestrels launch themselves skywards with a chorus of piercing caws. Everyone on Grand Oak Street throws back their heads to watch them go. Prime Minister Bythesea flinches then tries to hide it under a cough.

'She's just a girl!' Betsy hears one of the attendants say. The Constabulary hadn't worried about Teddy being 'just a boy', but then she supposes he is tall and stronger looking than her. He is beginning to change into a man, whereas Betsy is still short and bird-small and these burly guards must be afraid of hurting her in public. She can use that to her advantage. She continues to climb up the stairs. She doesn't know what else Teddy wants her to say, so she says the first words that enter her mind. ‘There’s a whole world outside Copperwell, and it’s *nothing* to be frightened of. It’s filled with wonder. People who live under the stars, and gentle bears, and forests filled with foxes and birds and creatures you couldn’t even imagine. And kindness, too. And excitement. And all the things *you*,’ she points an accusing finger at Prime Minister Bythesea, ‘tried to ban from Copperwell.’

‘We’ve tried to ban nothing,’ the Prime Minister blusters. ‘We’ve tried to protect you.’

The sun hoists itself higher overhead and Prime Minister Bythesea sneaks a look upwards, calculating how close to the edge of the building it is, how much longer he has before its shine reaches his hiding place.

‘From what?’ Betsy replies. ‘From living freely?’ She emphasises the last word and the Prime Minister’s head whips back towards her. His eyes flicker, then harden into slits.

‘You can’t possibly know anything, child.’

Betsy can feel Teddy and Effie now, moving up the steps behind her, and extends her neck to make herself as tall as possible.

‘I know that plenty of people live without the rules and restrictions you have imposed on the people of Copperwell. And I know that there’s no reason the Wellians couldn’t, too, if you didn’t keep them cornered and scared in their allocated Quarters. It’s not danger that lies beyond the canal. It’s knowledge!’

'Nonsense,' Prime Minister Bythesea replies. 'These are suppositions, accusations. You are not dealing in truth.'

'Then prove me a liar,' Betsy replies, quick as a blink. 'If what you're saying is true, show us your shadow as you speak those words.'

'I—'

'Step away from the building and show us your shadow,' Betsy insists.

Day and night whir by moment on moment, lighting Betsy, Teddy and Effie's shadows large over the wide stone steps. *Flash, flash, flash.* They appear and disappear, as rhythmic as a heartbeat, as vital. And they are prouder and more definite than ever.

'It's not your place, girl—'

'My name is Elizabeth Blue,' Betsy says, speaking calmly over him, gradually projecting her voice as Talon can, over the man, over the storm. 'Betsy of the Stars. I am an orphan, and a laundry maid, and a Wellian, and a Vagabond, and I know everything there is to know about the skies above me, but I know nothing of the world beneath my feet. And I mean to change that, Prime Minister. I mean to change that for me and for every other inhabitant of Copperwell. And there's nothing you can do to stop me.'

'Arrest her!' Prime Minister Bythesea orders and, as he flails his hand to get his attendants' attention, so he releases the speaking-trumpet and sends it arcing through the air. It lands with a clatter, then clanks down, down,

down, and rolls to a stop at Teddy's feet. Teddy grabs for it and, in one circular movement, throws it to Betsy. Betsy leaps a little to catch it and, when she has a firm hold on it, hesitates. Who is she to speak to or for all these people?

'The people need to hear you,' Birch calls, nodding encouragement as she and Talon mount the steps.

Betsy lifts the brass instrument to her mouth and turns to the crowd below. From here, they look impressive indeed. They are formed up like a battalion, their faces upturned and rapt. The Vagabonds still sit astride their deer like the warriors in the greatest stories Effie can call to mind: of Queen Hildegarde, who exchanged her crown for armour and led her men into bloody battle; or Julia Morrow, who threw herself from the safety of her ship and swam seven miles through rough seas to return to those of her people still stranded onshore. Of Millicent Shaw – Millie the kitchen girl – who fought three brutes twice her size with the ferocity of a lioness to give Betsy, Teddy and Effie the chance to escape.

The Wellians have made flags from their scarves and hold them aloft now, to snap and ripple in the wind. Time pulses by – a day for each clock tick – and each switch from dark to light sees the gathered people moving closer. From Butter Street and Filament Road, Sleuth Street and Hangman's Alley, they are joined by groups of children, canal workers, chimney sweeps, factory workers, service maids, cab drivers, grooms, street sellers, gentlemen, noblewomen, scholars, newspapermen, lawmakers. More and more Wellians fill the square and surge towards the Unified Government building as purposeful and unstoppable as waves towards the shore.

'They're like a defending force,' Effie breathes. 'The Order of the Orrery.'

She clutches Betsy's hand and smiles wide.

'People of Copperwell,' Betsy begins, and then she lowers the speaking trumpet to her side, because she realises that she does not need it. Her words ring out just as clearly as she says, 'I have challenged Prime Minister Bythesea to step out and show us his shadow.' Though she has turned her back to him now, she can sense Prime Minister Bythesea flustering behind her. 'You have all been brave enough to reveal your innermost selves. Don't you think your Prime Minister should be willing to do the same?'

In flashes of startling daylight, she sees hundreds of heads nodding in time with Birch and Talon and Teddy and Effie.

'Prime Minister, please…' she says, stepping aside and positioning herself alongside the attendants. Teddy and Effie do likewise. Surprisingly, the attendants do nothing to admonish them. Perhaps they are too scared to act without the might of the Constabulary there, ready to provide reinforcements. Or perhaps, deep down beneath their need to earn a living and their worries, they think this man cowardly and unbefitting of his title. Perhaps they, too, want change.

Eyes bulging, Prime Minister Bythesea snaps his head

from left to right in search of assistance. No one moves. Teddy half expects the Constabulary to come galloping back into the gathering, smashing people aside with their truncheons, crushing children and dogs beneath the hooves of their thundering black horses. But there is no movement except for the slow forward inching of the crowd and, suddenly, the slowing of the storm. The kestrels must have reached the hollow. Soon, time will settle back into its usual rhythms.

'See,' Betsy says, turning back towards the Prime Minister for a moment. 'Didn't I tell you we don't need the orrery to do what you have done?' She lifts her hands to indicate the calming sky.

With a growl, Prime Minister Bythesea turns and flees into the building. As one, the crowd begins to surge up the steps. They do not move in anger. They do not rush. The Vagabonds, dismounted now, lead the way, their strides perfectly matched, while the deer drift away to await their riders in the gardens. They set an even pace for all those Wellians who follow behind. The left-right of their feet sounds like the beat of a battle drum, louder and more even than that of the Constabulary's truncheons. The attendants, glancing around to check they might go unnoticed, melt into the approaching swell.

'Go carefully,' Betsy says. If so many people begin to move too excitedly, they might cause another crush. 'Nobody else needs to get hurt today. Please, take your time.' Her voice ricochets between the enormous buildings, and though a thousand eyes are fixed on her, and Prime Minister Bythesea is still shrieking somewhere just inside the building, and the Constabulary might appear at any moment, she does not feel nervous at all. Betsy of the Stars, Talon had named her, and for the first time she feels as though the name fits. She is shining with confidence. She is still and certain. She is brighter than she ever has been before.

She waves her arm as she speaks, ushering old friends and new friends and strangers up the steps and through the doors. They move in silence, but for the even pound of their footsteps, falling in perfect synchronicity. They will put an end to the Unified Government, Betsy has decided, not by force but with peace. They will move from room to room, inviting every man and woman they encounter to join them, to choose to live truthfully and kindly, to help Copperwell find its rightful place in the world again. Now that Prime Minister Bythesea has proved himself a coward, and his staff seem to have stopped doing what he says and stand aside as people of every shape and size and belief and background file calmly past, even the employees of the Unified Government will be able to respond to reason. Deep down, they must know that The Shift, The Order, and all the oppression of the past year was wrong. They must. By the end of the day, every soul in Copperwell will be free to reveal their true selves to whoever they might choose.

And what greater freedom could there be than that, Betsy wonders.

CHAPTER TWENTY-NINE

The Monarchs of Copperwell

As they move through the grand hallways of the Unified Government building, watched by oil portraits hung in gilt frames and statues shaped in flawless marble, Effie finally allows herself to think about her father. He must have walked through these hallways a hundred times, for meetings with the Prime Minister or Chief Constable Pridmore; perhaps even with King Glennister, since nobody, not even those in such high positions as Chief Justice, is ever invited into the King's private residence. But where is Jeremiah Hart now? Thrown into the basement of the Gaol for Political Prisoners and left to rot there in the dripping dark? Effie shivers at the thought. But it won't be forever. She will break him out. She promises herself.

'We'll get my father out, won't we?' she whispers to Teddy. 'You'll help me.'

Teddy takes hold of her arm and gives it a gentle squeeze. 'Course we will,' he replies. 'We won't leave anyone behind.'

Except Briny Erwin, thinks Teddy, and Swallow. Except Millie, thinks Effie.

They swallow their sadness and proceed from hallway

to hallway, from grand chamber to grand chamber, until they reach the heart of the building, which is a vast, circular, debating chamber. Wooden benches curve around an empty platform and lectern, rising up and up towards the ceiling rafters. The room smells heavily of beeswax and stale tobacco smoke. The highest benches are lost to gloom. Betsy, Teddy and Effie file along one of them and sit together in the shadows.

'What next?' Betsy asks. 'I can't speak again. I've got nothing left to say.'

Effie manages a small laugh. 'I don't believe that.'

'All right, well, I have … but they'll be tired of listening to me. And besides, we want to make sure *everyone* was heard.'

'That's it, then,' Effie replies. They are conversing in murmurs. 'This must be the debating chamber. Let's offer everyone a chance to speak. They can take turns, for five minutes each perhaps, and tell everyone else how they think Copperwell should be run.'

Effie's eyes spark as her mind begins to race ahead with the idea.

'Look,' Betsy says, shoving at Ted with her shoulder. 'It's her lantern face.'

They share a smile, but Effie does not notice; she continues without pause. 'Each Quarter could elect their own leader; and each leader would have equal say in decision making and passing laws. If Lawmakers' Quarter, Factory Quarter, and Swindlers' Quarter were all treated equally, they could work together to make sure everyone has a say.'

She focuses on Betsy and Teddy finally.

'That's it, isn't it?' she asks. 'That's what we're here to do?'

'Why are you asking us?' Teddy says. 'It's you who'll be the next Chief Justice.'

'There's never been a female Chief Justice,' Effie replies.

Betsy rolls her eyes. Isn't it obvious? 'Then you'll be the first! Go on.' She indicates the empty platform, and Effie, flaring her eyes and giving a nervous grimace, trots down the steps between the benches and takes up her place behind the waiting lectern. Her hands grip the edge of the wooden desk, turning the tips of her fingers white, but she is composed as she clears her throat and addresses the people who file into the debating chamber.

'Please,' she says. 'Find a seat. There is something I would like to propose…'

For the next nine hours, people from every corner of Copperwell walk shyly up to the lectern, grab its oak edges for support, and plead their case. Some do so at a mumble, their heads low. Others begin hesitantly before finding their rhythm and launching into passionate speeches. Most trip and stagger through their arguments, unused to formulating their ideas for an audience. The people of Swindlers' Quarter, the chamber learns, have been without sufficient food for months. In Factory Quarter, men and women must go out to work for twelve or fourteen hours a day, leaving their children to fend for themselves, because they cannot afford to have them cared for. The complaints from Lawmakers' Quarter range from being left without proper housing after the storm damage to seeing their businesses ruined as the rest of the city grew poorer. Effie ushers the speakers expertly through their allocated minutes. She is sympathetic when required, stern very occasionally. Though she is younger than almost everyone in the chamber, it soon becomes apparent that people tend to defer to her. She is as natural a listener as she is a musician. The two skills go hand in hand.

'Does anyone else wish to speak?' she asks, finally. The hours have been fascinating but long.

The last man to speak is a worker at one of the grain factories – Mr Roddy Meek. He twists his cap in his hands as he describes, his ears and neck flushing crimson, the difficulty of raising a family of eight in just two damp rented rooms.

'It's a problem for many,' Effie says gently. If she has learnt nothing else over the past hours, she has learnt that.

'Thank you, Miss,' Roddy replies, turning to meet her eye for the first time since he stood. He is rough-edged, with an unshaven jaw and wide, tired shoulders. He wears a faded green overcoat and a bewildered expression. He reminds her of Briny Erwin. A lump tightens in her throat as she remembers the last time she laid eyes on Erwin, the black drag of the canal water, the quiet. She swallows the lump. She knows Erwin is gone, but there are people she can still help, in his honour. She will do what she can.

'No – thank *you*, Sir. You've helped many people today, I'm certain.' She is the perfect echo of her father.

'I've done nothing very much, Miss,' Roddy replies. 'But you and your friends – I've seen what you've done. You've returned light to the city. You've brought us hope. Mark me, you'll be the Monarchs of Copperwell.'

Effie turns to the place where Teddy and Betsy are sitting, in the first bench. Teddy's eyes are gleaming, just as she imagines her own are. Betsy's, however, are dull and distant. Already, she is somewhere else. There is still something she is worried about, and Effie means to find out what – but not now, because she has just spotted, low amongst the rows of people filed behind Teddy and Betsy, a familiar face.

It is small and slight and ashen. It is purpled on one side by an enormous bruise and a split lip. It is beautiful and friendly and smiling and smiling and smiling. It belongs to Millicent Shaw!

CHAPTER THIRTY

Stars, Stallions, and Birdsong

Less than a week later, Betsy, Teddy and Effie stand on the Observatory roof and look out over Copperwell. Calm pink light spreads over the roof tiles, the chimney stacks, the treetops. The canal water is the colour of rose petals. The weather pipes which adorn the walls of every house, every shop, every factory along the canal's edge, gleam like newly polished gold. Copperwell shines in a way they had half forgotten. Crisp white snow still pales the streets, though there hasn't been a fresh fall since the Vagabonds helped them bring the orrery back to the city and return it to the Observatory, and what remains has not stopped the street sellers from dragging out their wares.

In every square, on every corner, stalls piled high with fruits and flowers, painted pots and figurines, polished clockwork toys and stuffed teddy bears, are crowded by grinning adults and gabbling children. Some are so small that they hardly remember a time when they could stand outside and feel sunshine warm their skin. They will burn their ears and noses today, every one of them, but their parents cannot think to send them back inside, not even for a moment. Today is the brightest since Betsy, Teddy and Effie emerged from the Unified Government building and declared the city a democratic one to the roar of the gathered crowd.

They couldn't be sure, then, that Prime Minister Bythesea would flee Copperwell, taking those most loyal members of the government with him. They couldn't be certain that those constables who managed to ride or limp back into Copperwell really would refuse to do the dirty work of those corrupt people who had grasped power any longer. But they had decided to announce it, to speak it into truth, and armed with the belief of the city they knew they could make it happen.

Far below them, a snowball fight erupts. Musicians bring violins and saxophones and accordions out onto the pavements and improvise jazz tunes, which passers-by dance to, grasping hands and whirling each other around until they grow giddy. Cab drivers loose their horses' reins and let them plod or trot as the fancy takes them. The air steams and crackles with the scents of cooking meat and bubbling soups. It feels as though the passing fairs that Betsy and Teddy can recall in their earliest memories – as whirs of glorious colour and the constant beat of music – have returned to the city now that the Unified Government's stolen wealth has been restored to its rightful owners.

'Look!' Ted says, tapping at Effie's shoulder. On Wild

Goose Way, two black foxes gambol between the tree trunks. So fluidly do they move together that they look like an individual and its shadow. And it would not matter if they were; nobody has judged anyone else's shadow since it was confirmed that Prime Minister Bythesea and a clutch of his cronies had escaped the city by air-train under cover of darkness. There is nothing to be ashamed of anymore. 'Do you think they'll try to find their way to Africa?'

'I hope not,' Effie answers. 'It's a long way, and they'll be safe here now.'

King Glennister, having been petitioned by Chief Justice Hart within an hour of his being released from gaol, had agreed to almost all of Effie and her father's demands, and the orrery is safely shut away in the Observatory, which will now be owned and run by the scholars at the university, and open every day to visitors. The orrery will not be hidden but displayed in a glass case for all to see and admire, and none to interfere with. It will serve as a lesson, to warn against the greed and secrecy which led to the passing of The Shadow Order. The other instruments will be studied by the scholars, to discover what they are capable of, and perhaps, Betsy thinks, it might be proven that they really do have tempers of their own. One day, she might even know enough to study them herself.

'Everyone will be safe,' Betsy says, nodding definitively.

'I hope so,' Effie replies. 'There'll be so much to do, though. Buildings to repair after all that storm damage.

And more food must be sourced. And fuel, to replace the depleted coal. Wood will do for our fires for now, but we can't cut down every tree surrounding the city – that would devastate the balance of nature, strip too many animals of their homes. There has to be a better way…' She pauses. She does not have the answer to that problem just yet. 'And Prime Minister Bythesea might try to come back.'

'He couldn't,' Teddy insists.

'He could,' Effie says. 'I don't think he will. But King Glennister couldn't stop him last time, and it's a possibility we need to be ready for.'

'You will be,' Betsy says. 'You always think of everything, Ef.'

'We'll do it together,' Effie replies. 'We'll help each other.'

'Actually…' The instant Betsy attempts to start the sentence, her head begins to thump, but she knows she has to make her admission now, before she gets entangled in Effie's clever, generous plans.

She and Effie lock eyes, and she can see that Effie already knows. Perhaps she simply hadn't wanted to admit it. Betsy hardly wants to herself. She cannot imagine being apart from Teddy or Effie for a single day. They are the only family she's ever known. She swallows hard.

'I'm not saying I'll never come back,' she mutters. 'It's just—'

'You need to know what's out there.'

Betsy nods.

'And find out what happened to your mother?'

'I'm not sure,' Betsy answers. She would like to find out where her mother went and why she was forced to leave Betsy behind, to get to know the woman who left that mysterious note, but she knows now that the answers to those questions won't change who she is. 'I think it's more important that I find out about me.'

'I understand,' Effie replies, grabbing Betsy's hand in her own and holding it tight.

'You could come with me…' Without the interference of the orrery, the canal has regained its calm and it has been easy enough to set up daily crossings by boat. They can come and go as they please.

Effie looks down the length of Wild Goose Way, not realising that she is sighing heavily. The city is as beautiful today as it was the first time they climbed up onto the Observatory roof. No: it is more beautiful, now that is has been opened up by possibility. They have a chance – a once in a lifetime chance, perhaps – to shape its future, to make it better than it was before, and that is such an opportunity! Effie is not sure she is capable of leaving that behind just yet.

'I don't know that I can,' she says. 'There's so much to do here, so much to fix…'

'You're right. You're going to make Copperwell special, Ef. It's like you were meant to do it.'

Teddy wraps his long arms around both girls and pulls them close to him.

'What are *you* meant to do, though, Bets?' he asks.

Betsy smiles a sad smile. 'I don't know yet, but I'll find out… What about you?'

There follows a spell of quiet on the Observatory rooftop. Below, the people of Copperwell dance and sing, and the weather pipes chime their mellow notes. Above, dove hawks swirl with mockingbirds and ravens and hickory birds; they are learning each other, acclimatising to the presence of strange new species amongst the old. Everything – person and weather and animal – falls into tune.

'I thought,' Teddy ventures finally, 'that I really might go and look for the Aur.'

The Aur – the golden horse of Edward James' invention.

'So you *do* think it really exists,' Betsy says.

'I don't know,' Teddy replies. He doesn't mention that he has spent entire nights at the library this last week, searching for any mention of the creature, and that already he has found the names of three adventurers who claim to have seen it. 'But that shouldn't stop me looking for it, should it? Imagine what I might discover along the way.' Plus, he thinks to himself, he has already given Octavia his home. It is time he found another.

Betsy nestles deeper into Teddy's chest, and it is such a safe, warm, comfortable place that she wonders why they have never touched like this before. Silently, she hopes that he won't let her go for a long while yet. She promises herself, too, that this will not be the last time she wraps her arms around Teddy James.

‘Why did your father tell you all these stories, though, if they might not be true?’

‘I think perhaps he was teaching me to be brave. He knew he was dying, Bets – I’m sure of that now, looking back.’

She turns her head so that she can look straight up at him. His heartbeat thuds against her ear. He looks different today, she thinks: taller; older.

‘Do you feel brave?’

‘Right now,’ Teddy smiles, ‘I do.’

And it’s true that since the moment they left the Unified Government building, Teddy has been braver than ever he has before. It was he who led the way to the Gaol for Political Prisoners and demanded to speak to Chief Justice Jeremiah Hart; he who approached those constables still guarding the Observatory and explained to them that the government was running scared and would no longer order them to do what was wrong; he who gathered food from the stores at the canal and walked every street of Copperwell, distributing it to those most in need and talking to each and every one of them, asking them what they required and how he might help.

‘You might really find the Aur,’ Effie adds. Her voice is muffled by Teddy’s old green scarf, which she rests her cheek against. ‘Think of all we’ve seen lately that we wouldn’t have believed before.’

‘What will you do if you do find it?’ Betsy asks.

Teddy takes a deep breath and repeats his father’s

words, almost verbatim. 'I will look at it. And I will see it. And I will never tell a single soul about it.'

For a moment, they simply stand there, clutching each other, watching the people on the streets below going about their business without once scurrying up close to a wall or dodging away from a slant of sunshine. Their shadows – as variously independent and timid and bold and coy and wilful as the people themselves – are largely ignored. As they should be. They have come to learn that, more often than not, they are a reflection of that person's feelings at a particular time. A person's depths and intricacies can never be known at a single glance. There is so much more to an individual than that.

'I don't want to be without either of you,' Effie admits. Her voice is tight with unshed tears. Betsy swallows and swallows, trying to force her own welling emotions down into the pit of her belly. Effie hardly ever cries, and if she starts now, Betsy doesn't think she can bear to witness it. Not when her own mind is clogged with the thought that they will never again sneak into the attic at Saltsburg's Laundry to sit on her bed and look up at the stars; they will never again share tankards of drinking cocoa in the shelter at the end of Hangman's Alley and whisper their hopes and plans into the steam from the passing locomotives; they will never again sip pints of apple ale in The Blackened Lantern or The Laughing Judge while Effie prepares to play with The Quartet. They *might*, Betsy corrects herself. They *might* never. It's not as if she will never see her friends again. It's just that everything is different now. They are not quite the same people they were last winter. They are not the same people they will be next winter, either. There are a thousand adventures ahead of them.

'Neither do I,' she agrees.

'Me neither,' says Ted.

'But we can't live each other's lives just to stay together…'

They all know this to be true, but it doesn't make it any less sad.

'Let's make a promise,' Betsy begins. 'Let's agree to come here, on this same date, every year. Even when you're Chief Justice of Copperwell, Ef.'

'I'm not going to be Chief Justice,' Effie replies.

'Just because there's never been a female—' Teddy says.

'No,' Effie interjects. 'What I mean is … I was thinking Prime Minister would be more suitable.'

'There's never been a female Prime Minister,' Betsy teases, echoing Effie's words.

Effie smirks. 'Then I'll be the first.'

'All right. Well, when you're Prime Minister, and Teddy is an explorer travelling the world in search of the Aur, can we promise to meet back at the Elm Gardens, and come here, and look out at the city together.'

'Would the Warrior Mother of the Vagabonds have the time?' Effie quips.

Betsy feels her cheeks colouring, her ears burning. She isn't sure if that's what she wants for herself, exactly, or whether the Vagabonds would even allow it, so how does Effie… She glances from Effie to Teddy and back again. They are both fixing her with that knowing, amused expression.

'Lantern faces,' she mutters.

'You fit there, Bets. Betsy of the Stars. Talon saw it straight away.'

It is fair to say that when the Vagabonds had deposited the orrery, rested a while, then readied themselves to return once more to the hollow, Betsy had imagined herself galloping along with them, her hair dragged by the wind and her legs tight around a red deer's broad ribcage. As she had watched them go, she could practically spot herself amongst them. It had felt a bit like grief. But she hadn't felt able to leave just yet.

'Perhaps it is where you came from,' Teddy offers. 'Perhaps it isn't. But it's definitely where you're going.'

They tighten into a hug again but release each other more quickly this time.

'Where I'm going,' Betsy says, cocking her head in that self-important way of hers and taking a step away from her friends, 'is down there…' She points down towards the square, where the street sellers are flipping sugared griddle cakes and tossing seafood in an enormous hissing pan. 'I want a tankard of cocoa and a bag of roasted chestnuts. Do you know, I even saw Mrs S there earlier munching on a toffee apple!'

Teddy and Effie exchange a glance. They know that

Betsy is trying to distract them from their upset, and they're happy to go along with it.

Effie bites down her tears and stands straighter. She can hardly believe how cumbersome and awkward she once felt compared to her friends. What she feels now is sure and strong and ready to confront all the injustices of this glinting city.

Teddy, seeing the change in Effie's stance, mirrors it. These two girls have taught him everything he knows about being courageous, and he means to keep on emulating their endless daring. It is the best way, he thinks, to approach life.

As Betsy waits, she allows herself to picture a future moment, when she will arrive at the hollow and step between the wych elms and ask the Vagabonds to accept her as one of their own. Betsy of the Stars, she thinks. Teddy of the Stallions. Effie of Birdsong. That's right. That's them.

They each look over the crenelated edge of the rooftop and down at the glorious chaos of so many people, laughing and loving and living together: the pirouetting dancers; the smiling street sellers; the scampering children; the jesting friends; the jigging musicians. Somewhere in the crowd are all their friends and family. They are safe, guarded by the two enormous clockwork wolves the Unified Government had once used to trap the inhabitants of Copperwell inside the circular boundary of the canal and which the Vagabonds have gifted back to the city. Betsy, Teddy and Effie will join them, for a while. They will forget their sadness, their impending loss, and they will eat roasted chestnuts and dance till the sky darkens. And then they will take up their separate paths, and stride off into the world, and find out what it has to offer them.

'So,' Betsy says finally. 'Are you coming?'

Acknowledgements

I must sincerely thank…

The Firefly team – and most especially Penny Thomas and Janet Thomas – for all they do for books and Wales, and for their belief in my stories.

My dogs, Betsy, Teddy, and Effie (2011-2021) who inspired the characters in this book with their love and funny ways, and who will now stay together forever in fiction.

My parents, Keith and Louise, for persuading all their friends to buy my books before they've read them themselves.

My boyfriend, Matthew, who continues to pretend to listen when I talk about books, and sometimes remembers some of the titles.

Those friends, too numerous to name but always appreciated, who champion my pursuit of this mad career.

My agents, Jenny and Rukhsana, who believe I have something to say.

The Books Council of Wales, for generously supporting this book.

And lastly, and most importantly, the biggest thank you goes to my son, Phinneas, who is teaching me what it means to be a mother and being ever patient while I learn.